The Starlight Princess

Paperback ISBN: 9798999745804

eBook ISBN: 9798999745811

LCCN: The Starlight Princess, 2025921064

Cover Design: AC Designs

Map/Cartography: Created by Milo Keronen of Stardust Book Services

Editing: Kriti Tripathi of StoryArk Editing

Book Formatting: Adegoke Bolu of PublishWithBolu

Inner Page Graphics: Laney Jaye of JSaga Designs

Character Art: WANTED by Melxartz

MAP OF ELEMI

The Nightshade Mountains
Training grounds
Brackenhold
Sunsport
Night Spire
The Netherfields
The Dark Geyser
Gravemire
The Red Wastes
The Scarlet
The Wicked Swamp
The City of Embers
The Burning
Dustfall
Firerock
THE FERVER OCEAN
FIRE PASS
ELEMI

Sinburn Sea
Shattleervold
Stormbend Forest
Willowwood
The Temple of Gaia
Sunhollow
Gaia's Keep
Everwillow
New Farmstead
The Wild Swamps
Lands
Gaia's Gulf
Volantis
The Oasis Peninsula

THE ELEMENTALS SERIES: BOOK ONE

THE STARLIGHT PRINCESS

AMANDA CIRILLI

DEDICATION

This book is dedicated to all the dreamers who wish

on a star...

Enjoy, little Starling.

TRIGGER WARNINGS

Please be advised that this book is recommended for
ages 18+ due to the following content:

Language, animal hunting, drug and alcohol use, loss
of parents, violence, death, and explicit sexual content
READER DISCRETION IS ADVISED.

Contents

Prologue

Grass tickled my cheeks as I lay on the ground on an unusually sunny spring day. The bright blue sky stretched above me, filled with puffed white clouds drifting past. My mama and papa lay on either side of me as I pointed at a cloud overhead.

I smiled. "That one looks like a flower." It seemed to dance before me.

Mama raised her hand next pointing to a different one. "That one looks like a cat."

After a moment of quiet, Papa spoke finally.

"All I see are big white puffs," he grumbled before laughing, making both Mama and me laugh too. It was the perfect day. Mama wasn't working at the sewing shop in the village, and Papa wasn't at his butcher stall in the square. I sighed with contentment as we savored the rare joy of simply being together.

A sudden tremor in the ground shattered the peace. A chill swept through the meadow, jolting us upright. The sky, once vibrant blue, darkened to ominous shades of

gray. We glanced at each other in confusion. Papa's hazel eyes flickered with concern as we

got to our feet.

Tendrils of darkness burst from the trees. My father's eyes widened as the dark magic hurtled toward us. "Run!" he yelled, already snatching my hand.

We turned and took off into the woods, dodging hanging branches. The trees, once alive and green, withered and blackened as the darkness chased us. Green leaves turned to ashes before they hit the ground.

"Faster!" Papa screamed, squeezing my hand tighter.

I clung harder to Mama's hand. Papa dragged us forward, his pace nearly impossible

to match. Mama's grip slipped from my sweaty palm. The tendrils wrapped around her

ankles, pulling her into the abyss. I screamed. Her face twisted in terror as her large brown eyes locked into mine. She clawed her fingers into the ground trying to resist the pull.

"Go! Go!" Papa ran, dragging me even harder.

"Mama!" I cried as I looked back. I forced my eyes shut, hoping that the horror wasn't real. Screams filled the air. My heart sank to my stomach. Bile rose in my throat.

"She's gone, Myalis. Keep moving!" Papa's grip was ripped from mine. I froze. His hand, gone. Tendrils encircled him just as I turned.

"No!" I screamed, racing back toward him, my vision blurred by tears.

"Keep running!" That was all he said before the darkness swallowed him. My heart

shattered, but I ran. The darkness pursued me. I tripped on a root and crashed onto the ground.

Tendrils slithered over me like snakes, tightening around my throat. I couldn't breathe. Couldn't think.

"You belong to me," it whispered—a voice of shadows and dread—just before it consumed me.

WANTED
BY DECREE OF
KING VORAS
Myalis Lucernas
REWARD
5,000 gold for any true information
10,000 for her capture & return

Chapter 1

Myalis

I jolt awake, my heart racing from the nightmare that haunted my past. My breath comes in shallow gasps, sweat beading on my brows. Looking around, I realize I'm in the safety of my meager hollowed-out hole. Lying on a bed of furs, I'm covered by a blanket I'd bought from a local stall in Stormsbend Forest when I first arrived.

It's been a year since I found refuge in Gaia's Keep after spending ten years running from the Dark King. Running ever since my magic awakened. These powers were unfamiliar—not ones that conformed to normal Forsaken Elementals, the name for people who received magic passed down from the ancient Elementals. They're the creators of all life as we know it: Gaia, Prometheus, Hydros, and Tazra. My magic, however, is different.

The magic of earth, water, fire, and darkness once ran rampant upon the continent of Elemi. But now, thousands of years later, the powers of the offspring of the Elementals—the Forsaken Elementals—had dwindled, especially under the rule of the Dark King. The Dark King, Tazra's heir, has ruled Elemi for centuries. It's all we've ever known. Each territory within Elemi must bow down to his power, and no other rulers may rise unless they wish to be obliterated by the King himself.

When I turned thirteen these powers manifested within me. I remember not knowing what they were, and honestly, I still don't know how to control the magic within me. Every time I'm tempted to use it, the memory of my parents' faces being taken away by the darkness haunts me. I was naïve then, but now as an adult, I think they knew what having this magic would cost us.

It only took a few days after my thirteenth birthday for the Dark Knights to come and collect me for the Dark King himself. How he even found out about my magic still eludes me. They just showed up at our door. When Papa refused to hand me over, they returned when we least expected it, killing both Mama and Papa, and shattering my world as I'd known it. My survival instincts kicked in and I ran. Ran as fast as I could—just as Papa had commanded. I fled my poverty-stricken village of Dustfall and hid.

Eleven years later, and I'm still on the run. However, I've been safe for a year here within Gaia's Keep. It's the earthbound kingdom where the Forsaken Elementals of Gaia, along with thousands of others, live and thrive. Though the Dark King rules over all of Elemi, he doesn't hunt every being with magic. Only me it seems.

I slipped past his Dark Knights the last time they found me. I've since found refuge here in Stormsbend Forest. The eternal spring foliage here has made it easy to hide.

When I first arrived, I wandered the woods until I found exactly what I needed—a massive tree root system that sank into the ground. It took a couple of days, but I hollowed it out and made myself an underground burrow. I now call it home. Whenever I leave, I cover the entrance with bushes and leaves to blend it in with the surrounding forest.

It's not much. Just enough space for my bed of furs and the supplies that I often carry—a hunting knife, a dagger, a bow, and some arrows and a quiver. I own a few sets of clothing and a solid pair of boots. On chilly nights, I layer up and pile on whatever furs I can. It's not that bad. I've survived so far.

The nightmares of being captured by the Dark King and his men push me forward. The recurring memory of my parents being ripped away by the darkness still haunts me. It's been over a year since I've seen the King's soldiers. I can't help but hope that his pursuit has ended—that I might be able to live the rest of my life in peace.

Over the years, I've learned to make do on my own. I hunt for my food, and when I need coin, I hunt extra and sell my kills to the cart vendors scattered across the local villages. For a day like today—my twenty-fourth birthday— I plan to hunt extra, and celebrate with a drink at the local tavern, The Dirty Fox.

The tavern straddles a narrow stream. Its two halves are joined by a wooden overpass. The usual patrons are wanderers, travelers, and Gaia's Keep's folks down on their luck. It's lively, and to mark my birthday and another year of survival, I want to let loose.

I climb out of bed, and trade my nightshirt for a worn green tunic and a pair of tight, brown, suede leather pants. I throw on my mid-calf black boots and cinch the laces tight. Raking my fingers through my hair, I find my leather string and tie it back into a ponytail, pulling the long waves away from my face—easier to manage this way. It's so long, I sometimes wake up strangled by the strands in the middle of the night. At times, I think about cutting it all off.

I grab my small rucksack, bow, and quiver, slinging them over opposite shoulders and climb up the makeshift ladder carved from the thick, anchored roots. I peek outside through the foliage to make sure no one sees me.

I surely look ridiculous crawling out of the ground, like a deranged squirrel. Rolling my eyes, I quickly shrug off the thought and step out into the open. I cover the entrance with fallen branches, so it's hidden again.

Not far from my tree is a beautiful stream where I get fresh water to drink and to wash myself. I usually bathe after sunset—less chance of anyone stumbling upon a naked woman in the woods. I remind myself I'm trying to keep a low profile, so, no need to bring unnecessary attention.

The river water is cool and refreshing as I bend to the bank and dip my fingers in. Just as I touch it, ripples flutter through the quiet water. I frown. There's no fish. It's an unnatural ripple. I squint at the water but see nothing.

Shrugging it off, I fill my water canteen and plan for the day. If I hunt enough today, I can sell the extras to the butcher for coin. Maybe I could afford myself a little birthday present; a new tunic or a robe. I scoff. Such a frivolous item, a robe. I never had one, not even as a child, but I sometimes dream of it now.

Who am I kidding? I live in a fucking Ficus root buried in the ground. My possessions are few—only what I need to survive, or to run.

Once I wash and relieve myself, I head into the woods to check my snares and traps. A rabbit is caught in one of my contraptions. As sad as it is, it's them or me. I try not to think about it as I break its neck. The sound of bones crunching still makes me flinch, but I always whisper a prayer for the creature and thank it for helping me survive another day.

When I hunt or whittle, I remember Papa. He taught me how to hold a knife, and how to kill and skin an animal. It's nasty business, but I never shied away from it— much to Papa and Mama's surprise. Mama worked as a seamstress in our village dressmaker's shop and wanted me to learn her trade. My heart strayed to Papa's job though. He was Dustfall's main butcher—the place where I was born and raised—and his work involved catching and selling whatever he hunted.

Dustfall is a poor village within the Netherfields, the territory of Tazra, and home to the Dark King. No Man's Land is mostly a barren area except for a few pockets of life, like Dustfall at the Netherfields' southern tip. My village was half a day's walk from the ocean, and though Netherfields is the land of eternal winter, warm days sometimes shined upon us. Those rare days drew people to the beach to soak up the fleeting warmth.

We never had much. The village was nothing but little wooden huts with thatched roofs, and people with carts of goods hoping to make coin. My parents made it work, and we felt blessed for our meager possessions. We had a roof, a bed, and usually food in our bellies. More than that, we had each other, and that was all that truly mattered.

Papa always stressed the importance of being self-sufficient. I wonder if he was preparing me for this life. He taught me to whittle, to kill mercifully for food, and to make fires and shelter. Everything I know about surviving I learned from him. Sometimes, when I do these sit outs, waiting for my next kill, my mind wanders to him and to simpler times. It's as if I can still hear his voice, clear as day, guiding me through the hunt.

But Papa is gone. It's been eleven years since I heard his voice. Eleven years since the Dark King's soldiers killed my parents and began searching for me. I shake off my thoughts and focus on today's task: the hunt.

Chapter 2

Myalis

The day proves fruitful. I leave the butcher's shop, having sold him three rabbits and a big-eyed doe that I'd been lucky enough to cross paths with.

She was a beauty. Even the butcher mused how he might have it taxidermized rather than butchered. Whatever he does with them isn't my concern. All I care about are the thirty-two pieces of copper he gives me in exchange. Enough not just for one drink, but five. I could even gamble a round or two of cards. A perfect birthday celebration if you ask me.

With coins jingling in my pouch, I happily make my way through the woods to The Dirty Fox. The wooden structure stands alone just outside the village. As I approach, I hear raucous music blaring from inside. Beautiful, green-leafed trees frame the sprawling building, which dominates a glittering stream. The amber glow inside the vine-covered tavern pours through its many windows as the sun sets. Dusk's beauty overtakes the landscape, vibrant oranges melting into purples and blues before my eyes.

I haven't bothered to clean or bathe since leaving the butcher's stall. Instead, I headed straight here. The clientele at The Dirty Fox didn't give a shit. Hence, the name. The tiny village of Sunhollow is tucked deep within Stormsbend Forest. It doesn't have much to it: a butcher's shop, a clothing trader, a blacksmith, and then the village market, where farmers sell their daily bounty. On its outskirts, merely steps away, stands The Dirty Fox. My hidden dwelling lies on the opposite side. I don't feel like traipsing all the way back just to scrub off some dried blood and dirt from my hands. It's my birthday, and after a long day of hunting, I'm just ready for my drink.

Once-white plastered and dark-wood walls are now covered in boughs of ivy. Fallen leaves from surrounding trees carpet the red-shingled roof, greened with mold. The place has been here for gods know how long—but it's built to last.

I throw open the pine-and-iron front door, and a wave of sounds explodes in my ears. From the corner stage, the musicians pound a lively jig, while raucous laughter erupts across the bustling room. The space is packed with Gaian folk. Mostly large, burly men slamming their fists on gaming tables as lovely, busty ladies circle them, offering good luck and a drink. My gaze lands instantly on Badger, the barkeep, as he fills and slides pints down the bar. A large smile cascades across his face as he chats with the patrons lined along the counter, taking their orders.

Badger is a middle-aged Gaian Forsaken who works with nature of his own free will. He's the long-term owner of The Dirty Fox. He grows his own hops and brews special concoctions he's immensely proud of. It's his passion—the thing he enjoys using his magic for. Badger dominates the bar with an easy, commanding presence. His boisterous personality makes him the kind of barkeep who always draws me back here for more.

In appearance, though, he's a bit on the gruff side. His black hair falls to his chin, streaked with white at his temples—something that makes him resemble his namesake. Working long hours like he does leaves him a bit greasy. He sports a short beard and mustache, black but peppered with gray. Standing around six feet tall, he's well-built, though his baggy, thick linen clothes mostly hide his physique. With his sleeves rolled up and an apron tied around his waist, he stands ready to tend to his customers.

I weave my way through the maze of occupied wooden chairs and tables. Luckily, I find an empty seat at the bar. With my bow, quiver, and knapsack still strapped to my back, I ungracefully plop onto the wooden barstool and let out a slow, decompressing breath, feeling the tension in my shoulders slink away. Badger's narrow green eyes meet mine, and a crooked smile tugs at his thin lips.

"Ey, Mya! How's it going?" He fills a pint with something, sliding it in front of me before I can protest.

"Good, Badg. Tired, but good," I reply, wrapping my hand around the wooden mug and bringing it to my lips. Froth tickles my upper lip as I take a swig. The pale amber leaves a lingering taste of orange, lavender, and honey in my mouth. I nod in delight. "This is great, Badg. Is it new?"

"It is. Just finished fermenting this mornin'. Figured I'd give you the first try. On the house."

Badger winks. "You just let me know when you finish that one, and I'll get you your next." His attention shifts to the burly, hairy man three seats down, and he turns away from his call.

"Heya! How's come da broad gets a free pint, but I can't even get tha one I ordered ten mins ago?" the large, muscled man with an ugly underbite whines as Badger approaches him. I study the sweaty, hairy brute as he eyes me up and down, a look of disgust twisting his face. Badger grabs a half-gallon mug and pours the amber liquid into it.

"Because, Erug, she's a lady. A rather lovely one who deserves it—unlike you, you drunken swine." Badger sets the overflowing brew before him, then spits in it, shooting me another wink. The bar goes silent for a beat— then erupts in laughter. Erug, apparently—the burly man whose drink just got spit in—huffs out a laugh that sounds like rocks grinding together before downing it in one go. Utterly unbothered by the spit.

Liquid spills down the sides of his mouth as he chugs, and I look away before I gag at the sight. His brow is too prominent, and his nose is too crooked for me to fancy another glance. I tune out the rest of the chatter and sip my drink at a leisurely pace.

The tavern is warm tonight, especially with all the bodies packed inside. Overhead, iron chandeliers hold blazing waxed candles, each one enclosed in a glass jar. The musicians keep up their jovial tune, prompting a few brave souls to dance. Gaming and dining tables are full. Badger's wenches roam between tables serving the men, and I realize I'm one of only six women here who isn't working.

I watch one of the women flirt desperately with a man for a few moments. I know it all too well. More than once, I've come to a tavern just for a lay. A woman has needs—and it's the only way to meet someone even if it's just for the night. I turn back to the bar, and a lone patron at the far end catches my attention. A hooded figure sits almost motionless. Only a firm jaw protrudes from his cloak—a five o'clock shadow creeping along his jaw. A drink sits before him but he's smoking a small wooden pipe. A plume of smoke curls from his full lips.

My brows knit as I discreetly study the stranger. I've never seen him here before. My stomach flutters and a fleeting thought sends a chill down my spine—what if he's a Dark Knight in disguise? Have they finally tracked me down after all this time? My heart races as I beckon Badger over. He heads my way the moment his eyes meet mine.

"Who's that?" I nod toward the stranger in the dark-green, hooded cloak. Badger's upturned nose shifts in the mystery man's direction.

"Ah. That." He sighs. "Yeah, just a deadbeat. No use wastin' your time on the likes of him."

"Does he come here often?" The question escapes before I can stop it. A wry smile creeps across Badger's toothy grin, gaps peppering his imperfect teeth. Leaning on the counter, he comes close.

"Often enough," he admits. "You interested in him?"

I arch an incredulous brow at him. "No," I reply, flatly. "Why? Should I be?"

Badger's thin lips pull into a deep sarcastic frown. "I dunno. Maybe you're looking for a little entertainment." I glare at him catching the amusement gleaming in his eyes.

"Even if it's my birthday, I'm not in the mood for that tonight. I just want to drink myself into oblivion," I explain.

"Shit, it's your fucking birthday?" Badger announces, far louder than I'd wished for. Suddenly, more eyes are on me than I care to acknowledge.

"Why didn't you say so, Mya? Drinks on the house!" He spins to the giant oak barrels and pours another liquid into a mug and places it before me. "Happy Birthday, little lady."

Heat rushes to my cheeks. "Thanks," I mumble, sinking further into the unyielding bar chair. I down the rest of my first brew and then immediately the second one feeling the dizziness of alcohol.

"Another of your new brew," I slur, placing a couple of coppers on the counter for Badger. My eyes drift back to the stranger at the end of the bar while another cloud of smoke looms around him.

My curiosity piqued; the mysterious aura surrounding him is enough to drive someone mad. Almost no one hides their face here at The Dirty Fox. No one cares. Yet something about those sumptuous lips call to me. I glance down at my hands on the wet, sticky bar—and find my next drink waiting. Grabbing it, I push myself off the bar stool and take a lap around the busy room, trying to distract myself.

I wander past different tables, catching snippets of random chatter as I head toward the game tables. The sticky wooden floor clings to my boots, irritation pickling at me. Each step makes a squelching noise. Damn floor. Damn drunks and their spilled drinks. The smell of mead and beer wafts through the air, and as I pass the tables, the heavy stink of male sweat makes me want to gag.

All the gaming tables are full, so I fight my way over to the dartboard—but that's taken too. I finish my third drink, then snag one off a tray from the buxom beer maid as she passes by. I flip her a copper in return. Before long, I finish my fourth, faster than I meant to. The room spins, and I quickly realize that I need to relieve myself. I make my way to the back of the tavern, to the door leading to the outhouse. A grotesque thing, but I'm desperate—those brews went straight to my bladder.

Thankfully, there's no wait, I do my business quickly and stumble back out. It's fully dark now as I amble my way back to the tavern door. But as I reach for the knob, I bump into some sort of wall. I blink, focusing my gaze and realize the hooded figure is standing there, blocking my path. When I look up, gleaming eyes peer at me from beneath the cloak.

"'Scuse me, sir." My slur is worse now.

"No." His voice is deep, the word rippling sluggishly in my head. I try to reach around him, but he shifts and blocks my path again. I step right. He follows. A step back to left. He's there. My frustration burns hotter.

"'Slee move," I command, not fully realizing what I just slurred out.

"I'm good." His tone is teasing, like he's toying with me. I grit my teeth, my hand sliding to the dagger at my waist.

"Look… gedda fuck outta my way and lemme back in." I barely string the sentence together. "Is my birfday and I'd like ano'er drank."

"Okay." Still, the hooded figure doesn't budge. Silence grows between us, broken only by crickets and frogs singing from the nearby stream. Through the door, the band plays and laughter roars, and all I want is another fucking drink.

"Wha tha fuck is yur problem?" I yell, reaching for the handle behind him. He finally steps aside, and the door swings open. "Stay tha fuck away from—me." I slur, stepping back inside and heading to the bar. Mind still spinning, I spot an open seat at the end of the bar and drop myself into it.

"Badg," I call. "One more." I slam a few coppers on the bar—a little too hard maybe.

Badger's laugh rumbles in my ears. When I turn, I find the hooded stranger in the seat beside me. I roll my eyes as Badger sets another pint in front of me. I reach for it, missing the first time, seeing two pints instead of one.

My head lulls as I let out an exasperated breath. I try again, this time managing to pick it up and bring it to my mouth. I take a long swig, and it dribbles from the corner of my mouth.

"Why're you followin' me?" I murmur to the hooded stranger. He pulls out his pipe and lights the remnants inside, taking a long, slow inhale.

"I'm not." His voice is calm, sensual—and fucking irritating and alluring all at once.

"You are... firs' you follow me to tha outhouse an' block my way inside... now yur sittin' here nest to me..." I take another sip, not caring that my words were getting sloppier or how unladylike I'm behaving.

"Perhaps I too had to take a piss." His comment is irritatingly nonchalant.

"Ha, ha," I roll my eyes as he takes another drag from his pipe. The smoke curls into my senses, and I realize it's some kind of scented hallucinogenic—only worsening my already blurry head. I sway in my seat, my head pounding. I hurry to finish my drink and slide off the chair. My legs are jelly, and I feel myself falter. I grip the bar for balance.

"Thanks, Badg, fer the lovely evenin'," I call, louder than I should. He gives me a weary nod, and it takes everything in me not to collapse on the sticky tavern floor as I make my way to the front door.

When I finally reach it and slip out of the chaos, the fresh night air fills my lungs. I pray for it to sober me up, but it doesn't. My head spins and a wave of nausea rolls in my gut. I try to gather myself but the darkness swirls around me. Panic claws at me, as if I'm under attack. All my fears spring to life before my drunken eyes, and I find myself backed up against the tavern wall, hyperventilating. I squeeze my eyes shut, hoping the world will stop spinning. My fingers grip the ivy clinging to the tavern wall as my chest heaves. The darkness begins to strangle, taking hold of me.

I hear the door open and shut, and suddenly a warm body is in front of me. I dare to open my eyes. The hooded figure looms over me, his hood now down. I stare up at the man who'd hidden himself beneath that hood the entire night—attractive as sin. His stormy eyes gaze at me studying, searching for what? I can't tell.

"Are you alright?" he leans in, our lips barely inches apart. Panic, anxiety, lust—everything floods through me at once. My drunken senses can't make heads or tails of any of it. My blurred mind craves something to ground me and before I realize, I slam my lips onto his, catching that sensuous mouth between my teeth. He reciprocates, pressing his body to mine, thrusting my back into the wall. Our mouths latch, our tongues dancing, like we want to devour each other alive.

His body against mine feels so right it makes me throb with desire. One of his hands tangles in my hair while the other grips my ass, yanking me tighter against him. A moan slips free—but am unsure if it's his or mine as my fingers claw through his silken, wavy hair. I press my lips harder to his, our tongues tangling, savoring his taste. Gasping for breath, I tear away—just before everything goes black.

Chapter 3

Myalis

I wake up with an excruciating headache, a wave of nausea rolling over me as I turn in a warm, comfortable bed. My head sinks into a soft pillow, and I keep my eyes shut to avoid my stomach from lurching. Sunlight glimmers against my eyelids, and my brows furrow in frustration being woken by it. I roll over, settling deeper in my self-made cocoon—until a startling realization hits me.

My eyes bolt open, sobriety slamming into me, as I take in my surroundings. This is not my underground home. Instead, I'm in a tiny hut, sprawled in an unfamiliar bed. I fight back the surge of fear, tossing the knitted blanket aside. I'm *naked*.

"Gaia above," I breathe, mortified. What have I done? I clutch the blanket again, unsure where my clothes are, and jump out of bed. I can't remember a thing from last night, and when I scan the bed, there's no sign of the stranger. I pace around frantically, searching for my clothes, but they're nowhere to be found.

"Oh, gods," I whisper over and over, trying to piece together scraps of last night. The Dirty Fox—I was at The Dirty Fox. I had a drink or two... or maybe like four or five. Shit, I lost count. I'm not sure if I gambled. I vaguely remember walking around the tavern, snooping at the tables. I groan in disgust, trying to fill in the missing pieces. I wanted to celebrate my birthday—not this hard, though.

Heavy footsteps thud outside the door, and I grasp the blanket tighter against my body, suddenly realizing just how vulnerable I am. My chest tightens as the knob rattles—and when the door swings open, I gasp. Memories flood back in a rush, as anger takes over me.

"You!" I snarl, pointing a finger at him. The tall, muscular man steps into the room, minus the mysterious cloak from last night. In daylight, I see him far more clearly than I did last night. My heart skips a beat. He wears a casual gray tunic and black leather pants with heavy boots. A silver chain and pendant hangs around his neck, dangling over a flash of bare chest revealed by his tunic's undone top button.

He's taller than I recall, at least six-two, towering over my five-foot-six stature. Broad shoulders taper to a lean, narrow waist. I study his face—his deep stormy, blue eyes scan my naked body that I'm desperately trying to keep hidden beneath the knitted blanket. A smirk curves across his sumptuous lips.

"What are you doing here?" I demand, noticing the small tray in his hands. It carries a cup of something hot and a few slices of toasted bread with jam.

"Good morning to you too," His voice purrs as he heads toward the bed I'm standing beside. He moves with more grace than I'd expect from a man his size. When he bends to put the tray on the bed, my eyes drift to his behind. I shake my head to snap myself out of it.

"What are you doing here?" I repeat, shielding the blanket tighter around me.

"Well, this is my home, so technically, I could ask you the same." His blue eyes flicker with amusement as they sweep down my body again.

"Gaia above! You brought me to your house!" I snap, not entirely sure why I'm so angry.

"Yeah, well, I couldn't leave you at The Dirty Fox. Gaia only knows what would've happened there. I didn't know where you lived. When you blacked out, this was the only reasonable place I could think of." His tone is casual, light, like this has happened to him before. His voice is pleasing—too much—but I shrug it off and try to stay focused.

"I blacked out?" I ask, incredulous. A crooked smile spreads on his face, revealing large, white teeth I hadn't expected. His heart-shaped face sharpens his masculine features: his chin, his nose, those high cheekbones. Gods above... why is he so damn handsome?

"Yes, you did. In my arms, as a matter of fact."

Heat floods my cheeks. "Gaia above, did we... did you...?" My voice trails off, but he gets what I'm asking.

"No. Nothing like that. I promise I don't take advantage of drunk-ass women who strip naked and crawl into my bed."

Appalled, I arch a brow before glaring at him.

"I swear it," he says again. "You passed out from Badger's ale. He brews it strong."

He sits gingerly on the bed, hands raised in surrender, showing he means no harm. He doesn't break eye contact. His eyes are stormy seas, swirling blue and gray. I'm captivated.

"I brought this for you," he says. "It's medicinal honeysuckle juice and bread to help with the hangover you're probably suffering from." A coy grin tugs at his lips. He thinks he's clever, insightful. I resist rolling my eyes, remaining silent and vigilant.

I take in the room, but with the two of us in it, it feels small—almost suffocating. There's a small wooden bed, a nightstand, and a tiny dresser. A couple of daggers and knives hang on the wall. They're simple in design, but pretty. No other personal effects. The room looks hardly used. My gaze lingers on the weapons, and something clicks. Where are my weapons—the ones I brought to the tavern?

"Shit!" I start searching again, more frantically this time. "My weapons." Panic consumes me as the gravity of my situation hits. I'm naked, in a stranger's home, after blacking out from a night of drinking. I storm around the room, frustration boiling under my skin. "Where are my clothes?"

"You threw up on them. I took them to the stream to wash since you'd already taken them off voluntarily. They're drying now."

I stare at him in disbelief. He laundered my clothes?

Heat creeps into my cheeks. *I threw up in this stranger's house. Gaia above, what the fuck did I do last night?*

Frozen, I stare at this too handsome man—naked and wrapped in a blanket—straining to remember everything.

"Your weapons are downstairs in my living room." His voice snaps me out of my stupor.

I can only imagine the puzzled look on my face. I shake my head in disbelief, "You have a downstairs?"

He chuckles. "I live in a treehouse. Rooms all through the branches, different floors."

"How the—"

"I built it myself," he cuts me off before I can ask how in the hells he managed it. He gestures toward the tray on the bed. "Come, rehydrate, eat. I promise I didn't poison it."

"Well, that's not suspicious," I mumble, shrugging at the tray. Awkwardly, I grab the cup keeping the blanket tight around me and sip the honeysuckle juice. It's delicious—tangy with a hint of citrus—and as it bubbles down my throat, I start to feel better. Not that I'll admit it to him.

"It's not often I have guests," he confesses. I stand close to the tray. He sits beside it so I'm automatically close to him. His five o'clock shadow is darker than last night, and his black, wavy hair is partially tied back in a small ponytail atop his head. His gray-blue eyes lift up at me, studying me as if searching my soul.

I break the gaze and scoff, hissing through my teeth. "I can see why. Given your suspicious behavior at The Dirty Fox last night," I counter.

He inhales sharply. "It wasn't suspicious." His gaze meets mine again. "And I certainly don't regret it." His handsome face twists into a mischievous look—more playful than deadly. He's flirting with me.

My face flushes again before I remember the predicament I'm in. I force myself not to fall for his charm he's trying to tempt me with, recalling his weird behavior from last night. "You practically stalked me into your bed."

"I did no such thing." His tone is teasing, confident. He shifts on the bed with his arms braced at his sides as he props himself up. "You're the one who drank herself into a stupor. At any rate, you intrigued me."

"Why?" My response is short, curt.

"I don't know. When you walked into the tavern, your bright coppery eyes were sparkling like stars, and something drew me to you."

Sparkling like stars? Did he know about me? About my power? Truth is, I don't even know who the hell this guy is. Maybe he's a rogue Dark Knight? I need to get away from him. My chest tightens as I feel trapped. I can't let anyone find out what I am. Especially not him. He knows enough.

"Thanks for keeping an eye on me, and for not taking advantage last night, but I must leave." I grab a piece of the bread and dash toward the door. When I open it, my heart drops at the sight. We are *very* high in the tree. My vision tunnels as I glance at the ground far below.

"Holy shit," I whisper, my heartbeat climbing into my throat. The nausea that had been fading surges back, and my stomach churns. The tree is an elaborate network of huts, rope bridges, and ladders. It would be enchanting—only if I weren't terrified of heights. There's a reason why I live underground.

Mouth agape, I freeze in the doorway. The sound of his boots scuff from behind, and his large frame looms over my back. "Do you need help getting down?" he asks, voice laced with jest. His lips brush my ear, sending a shiver down my spine.

My stomach knots, twisting my face. "It would seem so," I grit out. Without warning, he grips my waist and chucks me over his shoulder. I cry out in protest, but he just chuckles.

"Hold on," is all he says before he starts down the ladders, crossing tiny rope bridges I'm sure will snap under our weight. I hold my breath and squeeze my eyes shut, too afraid to struggle against his grasp. When he sets me down on the grassy forest floor, I let out an enormous sigh of relief. I glance up at where we came from and shiver. Still, seeing what this man has built is incredible. The oak tree is vibrant and healthy, but ancient. It's weathered many years, maybe even seen Gaia herself.

I don't know how long it took him to make this his home, but it's clear he built it to last and withstand anything. I gawk at its towering height. Its massive trunk hoists before me. If I want to wrap my arms around it, they won't even reach the sides.

I spot my clothes hanging from one of the low branches, and I stalk over, grabbing them as fast as I can. He watches me. I'm not used to being around one person this long, and he already knows too much—he's seen me at my most vulnerable. Claiming he saw the "stars" in me. I can't risk exposing myself any further.

I notice an array of bushes thick enough to hide behind and change, and I rush over. Dropping the blanket, I quickly pull on my semi-damp tunic and leggings. I ignore him, hoping he'll just forget me and leave me be. Once I'm dressed, I see my boots under the tree—clean, polished even—as I pick them up and study them.

"You also threw up on those." He crosses his arms, cocking his head to the side. I give him a wary look. Another dashing smile spreads across his chiseled face. "They're worn out. Might I suggest getting yourself a new pair?"

I glare at him, but still feel obliged to apologize for him cleaning up my drunken mess. "Sorry for the inconvenience... and thank you for cleaning my stuff."

As soon as I slip the shoes on, he turns as if to show me back inside his elaborate treehouse—but I rise, pivot on my heel, and dash into the woods.

I run as far and as fast as I can determined he won't
follow me. I tread carefully, leaving as little trail as
possible. My head pounds, and my stomach still churns,
but I force the illness down and stay focused. I don't need
to get further tangled with a strange, handsome,
irritatingly cocky man. Gaia above... why did he have to be
so sexy? I don't need complications. I need to remain
hidden—and alone—if I want to stay safe.

When I'm sure I'm far enough away from him, I
stop to catch my breath, listening for any sounds of
pursuit. When I'm sure I'm safe, I begin the trek home.

Stormsbend forest is vast, but I'm good with
directions. I know how to track them. I've been living here
a while now. I made sure to acquaint myself with
Sunhollow village and the surrounding forest early on. I'd
never been to the stranger's treehouse before, but all I need
to do is to find the village and then cut back to my burrow.

It doesn't take me long to reach my sacred fig tree. I
clear away the branches from my hidden entrance and
descend the carved root ladder. Relief fills me as I lay on
my familiar bed furs, ready to sleep off the hangover. My
stomach still churns, killing my appetite, and my eyes
droop the moment I lie down.

I'll hunt again tomorrow, I tell myself. And then, it hits me—I forgot my fucking weapons at that creep's treehouse. "Fuck!"

My bow, arrows, and knives are my lifeline. I have to get them back—but I'm too proud to go crawling to that treehouse now. Guess I'll have to buy new ones. I've got a few coppers left from yesterday, and maybe, if I find game in my snares, the butcher will give me enough coin to replace them, and I won't have to face that man again.

I groan, furious with myself for running without my weapons. I want to smack myself, but I'm too tired. Instead, I roll my eyes. I can't think about it. Right now, I just want to rest. I take a deep breath, and sleep claims me.

Chapter 4

Myalis

Lucky for me, I have an extra knife. Later in the day, after I've slept off my hangover, I check my snare traps scattered throughout the woods. At least I have them to help me catch prey. Unfortunately, my luck's run out since yesterday's fine catch. I tell myself it must've been a birthday present from the Elementals, and sigh as I reset them.

I'll go hungry today unless I spend some of my remaining coppers from yesterday. I could get something from the baker, or head back to The Dirty Fox for a brew and whatever the daily special is. Either would be fine, but I know I should probably save it for a new bow set—or boots. But when my stomach growls and refuses to settle, I decide to spend a couple coppers at the tavern.

As the sun sets, I approach the familiar clearing from the night before. The grand tavern sits gracefully above the rippling stream. One side houses the bar and the kitchen; the other side of the stream lies the inn. The scene is picturesque as I notice the sun sinking behind the sprawling building. I can hear the muffled sound of the band playing.

I approach the door and when I open it, everything springs to life around me. Travelers drink and gamble. Laughter fills the packed space. The stink of horrid body odor and spilled ale fills my nostrils. Oddly, it's comforting.

As I traipse across the sticky floor to the bar, Badger, as usual, is entertaining the patrons: teasing, serving, and laughing with them. He's such a slick salesman, I sometimes wonder why he hasn't aspired to greater things.

"Well, well," Badger sings as he slides behind the bar and stops in front of me. I perch on the barstool as he quirks a dark brow at me. "Look what the cat dragged in. How's it going, Mya? Have a memorable birthday?" He chuckles, leaning an elbow on the bar, eager for my response.

"You could say that." I mutter with an eye roll. His mouth curls to one side as he clicks his tongue, like he wants more detail, but he restrains himself and rolls his shoulders instead.

"What can I do for you?"

"What's your special?" I ask without hesitation.

"Chowder," he replies.

"Sounds good. I'll have that, and if you have any of your special brew from last night, I'll take a pint," I state. "If you don't mind, I'm going to snag a table over there," I nod toward a small table at the corner with two empty chairs. No one sits there, and from that corner, I can blend into my surroundings with ease. Sitting at the bar draws attention—not what I want today, considering who I ended up with last night.

Badger bows, gesturing as if tipping a hat at me. "You got it, little lady." He moves down the line to help his other customers. I watch him turn on his barkeep charm as I slither from my seat and stalk to the secluded table out of everyone's view. I meander between the tables of gamblers and drinkers, eavesdropping on bits of conversations here and there. Most burly men swap tales of old glory days or myths about the Elementals. I stifle a laugh, linger just long enough to hear, then move on. I reach the corner unnoticed, and slink into the wooden chair, staring out into the tavern.

The Dirty Fox is a dimly lit dump—yet somehow cozy. I soak in the familiarity of it as I make my way through the tavern. Smoke from patrons' pipes hangs in the air, causing a mild haze scented with everything from fruity to earthy. That, mixed with booze and body odor, makes this place a real gem of Sunhollow.

Fast-paced music fills the air, and my foot taps lightly to the beat. The fiddler plays with such energy that sweat drips from his brow, plastering his long blonde hair to his broad forehead. I watch the band, enjoying their music, and tell myself I made the right choice coming to The Dirty Fox tonight.

The thud of the wooden pint and bowl on the table pulls me from my thoughts, and when I look up at the server, I groan.

"You again?" I whine, my face twisting in displeasure. It's the handsome stranger from last night. He sets down my ale and food, and plops himself into the empty seat across me.

"Indeed," he replies, a smirk forming on his heart-shaped face. "You left so quickly I didn't even get to ask your name." His deep blue eyes glow in the amber light as he gazes at me, waiting.

"I have no intention of giving you my name." I say, sipping my ale before tasting my chowder. The hot food fills my belly, and I groan in delight. But, with his eyes on me, I refuse to give him the satisfaction.

"Well, I'm River," he announces, extending his hand across the table. His hand is calloused with veins standing out along the muscles in his arms. River's arms look strong and fit, likely from years of laborious work. I stare at him, unmoving, fighting the urge to gaze for too long. When he sees I'm not taking his hand, he inches it closer and raises a dark brow.

"You could at least show me the decency of a handshake. After all, I did take care of you last night." He gives me a seductive wink, and I scowl, tossing my spoon into my bowl before thrusting my hand into his for a shake.

As our hands touch, the warmth of his skin sends a jolt down my spine. My body hums with unexpected desire as his fingers grip and caress the back of my hand. My heart races, but I keep a straight face as his eyes lock on mine. It's an intense gaze that I can't escape. It only fuels my lust for him. I stop breathing for a moment before I realize our handshake has become a handhold. I pull free from his seductive grasp, ignoring whatever that feeling was.

His lip curls as if he knows I'm flustered. I wonder what kind of power this man holds to pull that kind of reaction of me. He has to be a Forsaken.

"Thank you." He tilts his head, and I go back to my chowder.

"Anyway, you don't need to tell me your name. I already know it." My stomach drops, and my eyes widen in horror.

I inhale, my voice barely a whisper. "How?"

"I asked Badger. In return, I told him I'd deliver your food." River grins, making my heart flutter. Gods above, this man is too gorgeous for his own good—and he knows it. Angry and mildly betrayed, I lean forward to meet Badger's gaze—he's apparently been watching us with interest. I glare, and even from across the room, I see that snake chuckling and giving me a coy wave.

"With the tavern being busy and his barmaids running circles, it took little coaxing to get it out of him. Your name in exchange for free food delivery to the table."

"What do you want?" I turn my attention back to the smug ass. His glossy black hair is pulled into a small bun on top of his head, but the shorter strands fall just above his shoulders.

"I just want to get to know you, that's all." He holds his hands up in mock innocence.

"Bullshit." I reply, shoving a spoonful of chowder in my mouth. The word catches River off-guard. He props an elbow on the table and rests his chin in his hand.

"Well, truth is, I figured you'd want your weapons back. But maybe you're right. Maybe there's something else about you that I find intriguing."

I quirk a brow at him, waiting for more.

"There's nothing interesting about me, River." I spit his name with disdain. "I'm a simple woman just trying to survive. And I prefer to do it alone."

"Why?"

I shrug. This guy just won't take a hint, will he?

"Because that's how it's been for most of my life. I don't need anyone. Especially not some horny forest hand who's fast becoming the biggest pain in my fucking side."

I flash him a sarcastic smile, chug my ale, and push to my feet. His eyes track me as I leave him sitting there. I stalk toward the tavern's entrance, avoiding the gross, hairy, reeking men and the buxom women tending them. I think I'll have to find a new tavern if this River guy keeps stalking me.

I slam the door behind me, and the world goes quiet. The smells of The Dirty Fox fade, replaced by the soothing scent of nightfall. I stride into the woods, heading home. River having my weapons pisses me off, but I can get new ones. I don't want his company. I don't need his companionship. Even if his touch does elicit feelings I haven't felt before.

No. I shake my head. This man won't cloud my mind. I can't let anyone get close. I can't risk it. What if he's a Dark Knight? What if he's trying to manipulate me? I fear what will happen now that he knows my name—something I'll never forgive Badger for.

I trail off into the darkness. Night critters fill the air with their sounds. Crickets and frogs sing their songs as I make haste. A mist surrounds me, my heart racing as I quicken my pace. I've been terrified of the dark—ever since it killed my parents. The Dark King hunts me; he and his soldiers dwell within the darkness. It's kept me on edge for the past eleven years.

Perhaps I've gotten too comfortable in my cozy banyan tree dwelling. Maybe I've overstayed my welcome in Sunhollow. The Dark King will find me again, eventually. He and his Dark Knights always do. It's a blessing from Gaia he hasn't found me yet. After all, it's been a year.

A twig snaps behind me, and I spin on my heel. I draw my tiny knife, ready for whatever might come at me. Nothing but silence surrounds me. I hesitate before turning and moving on. My pace hastens, matching my panic.

"Starling," the whisper rides the wind. A barely audible, chilling call stops me dead. "Come to me."

My lip quivers as the woods darken around me. Is it real or are my eyes playing a trick? My chest heaves as I circle, scanning for where the whisper had come from. Smoky tendrils curl around me, freezing me in place.

A hand clamps around my wrist, yanking me from my daze.

"Move!" It's a command. River drags me from the darkness, and we dart through the woods. His grip on my wrist keeps me tethered, and we run with matching strides. I don't know where we're running to—only that I have to keep moving.

"This way!" River weaves us through the thick bush and soaring trees. He's more agile than he looks. He's light on his feet as he bolts through the dark woods, like he knows every inch of them. Perhaps, he does.

I follow, breathless, my legs burning from the pace as River refuses to let go of my wrist. My mind flashes back to eleven years ago, when Papa and I ran like this. I fight not to freeze at the thought. River's firm grip keeps me in the present.

We burst from the tree line into a sprawling field, and River finally lets go of his grip. I stop, bend over with my hands braced on my knees, catching my breath. Sweat-damped strands of my wavy hair hang in my face. When I look up, River's eyes are scanning the clearing, distant and distracted.

Dark Knights emerge from the trees—dressed in black leather armor and hooded cloaks. A scene straight from my nightmares. I straighten, glancing around as they circle us, at least twenty strong. Two against twenty are odds I don't like, especially with only a small knife. River sizes each soldier, before his eyes meet mine.

In the darkness, River's eyes begin to change, clouding over. I have never seen anything like it. He shifts into a defensive stance and waits. The soldiers close in, and for a split second, all I hear is my own breath. Time stands still, a calm before the storm.

A soldier attacks, rushing toward me from behind. I'm about to stab him when River lifts a hand to the sky. Lightning cracks overhead, electrifying the clearing. I stare at him in awe. He wields the lightning as a weapon, hurling it at every Dark Knight around us. They all drop at once. Wide-eyed, I watch River blink—his eyes clearing back to normal. Those stormy blue eyes clear again. He glances around the circle of fallen Dark Knights and smirks. He fucking smirks!

"You're a Forsaken," I stutter, taking a step back.

"I am," his tone is proud. "I guess now I know why you're terrified of the dark. What does the Dark King want with you?" He folds his arms against his broad chest. My gaze stays on the still bodies around us. All of them dead.

"What did you do to them?" My voice is even, but inside I'm a whirlwind. I try to keep my body from shaking as the raw power River wields sinks in. I've never seen anything like it, and the longer I stand motionless in front of him, the more afraid I become of what he could do to me.

"I gave them a shock of electricity. Enough to stop their hearts." River approaches, stopping in front of me. His gaze burns into the top of my head. I keep my eyes on my boots until River places a finger beneath my chin, forcing my gaze to meet his. Moonlight spills over him, bathing him in an ethereal glow. The storm in his eyes has calmed as he searches my face. Understanding flickers on his face.

"I have no intention of hurting you, Mya." My breath hitches at the sound of my name on his lips for the first time. Damn Badger for telling him. "I'm only trying to protect you."

I step back from his touch, anger flaring in me. "Why do you even care? Who are you?"

River shifts his weight, as if he wants to close the gap but hesitates. He peeks around the clearing again before looking back at me.

"It's not safe out here. Come back to my home, we can speak more freely there."

"I'm not going anywhere with you."

"Mya, the Dark Knights just came for you. More will follow once the Dark King learns what happened here. We should go to the Temple of Gaia and seek sanctuary." His expression is almost desperate.

"The Temple of Gaia? What are you? A priest or something? I see your temple pendant." I nod toward the spiral pendant hanging around his neck. Noticing it earlier, I wondered why he's wearing it. Why does he want to take me to the Temple of Gaia? Why does he think I need sanctuary?

River chuckles. "No, I'm not a priest. Do I look like a fucking Gaian priest?"

He gestures down his body, and I can't help but gawk at his bulky, muscular figure, dressed in plain clothes that hang tightly on him.

"I don't know. It's not like I've ever seen one in person," I mutter, and it's true. In all my time in Gaia's Keep, I've never ventured into Everwillow, where the Temple of Gaia lies. The sacred temple sits so deep in Gaia's Keep, that I've always feared I'd get lost within the woods and never make it out.

"Well, trust me, they don't look like me. At the Temple of Gaia, they're all priestesses. Please, Mya, let me escort you there."

I sigh, exasperated, throwing my hands in the air. "Why? What's going there going to do for me? No matter where I go, no matter where I hide, eventually the Dark King finds me. I've just been lucky this past year, he hasn't."

River quirks a brow. "You sure about that? They seemed to know exactly where you were and exactly how to strike. What does the Dark King want with you anyway?"

Again, River repeats the question I don't want to answer. I'm growing tired of his questions, and his stalking, and the insinuation of his words makes me wary of him.

"It's none of your business." I storm past him, heading toward my tree.

Whether he follows or not, I don't care. I just want to go home. After a beat of silence, I think maybe River's finally let it drop. Maybe he's going to leave me alone. But then footsteps close in from behind me, and I silently roll my eyes.

"What if it is my business, hm? What if it's the whole world's business?" He moves ahead, cutting me off mid-stride.

I scoff. "That's a bit dramatic, don't you think?"

"Don't you want to know why the King hunts you?"

"I know why he hunts me," I growl trying to walk past him, but this time, he grabs my arm.

"Why?" River's nostrils flare, his mouth tightening, jaw tense as his gaze burns into me.

I hold his gaze stubbornly, matching his stare. We stand in silence. When I realize he's not letting go, my shoulders slacken. As if the weight of my eleven year fight is finally lifting.

"Because of my power." I admit. It's the first time I've said it aloud to anyone. River leans in, and a scent of freshly burned campfire with an undertone of honeysuckle envelops me. Pulling me toward him, he grazes his lip on my ear.

"And what power is that?" River whispers the words, as if wanting to steal my secrets. I shake my head.

"I don't know what it's called," I confess, stepping back from him. He still holds my arm. Our eyes locked, he stays silent for a long moment before speaking again.

"Do you know how to use your magic?" His voice is low, sensual.

I shake my head. "Not really, no. No one's ever been able to teach me anything about it. My magic is unstable, which is why I don't use it."

River lets go of my arm but stays close. My pulse jumps with his presence. He draws a deep breath before speaking again.

"What if I told you that the priestesses at the temple could help you figure out and learn whatever power you have?" His eyes are eager. I'm hesitant.

"Why would I want to learn about my powers when I have no desire to use them?"

"Because the Dark King is hunting you. That means, he sees something in your powers that he considers a threat. I think you'd like to know how to wield your magic."

He pauses while I stare at him. When I don't respond, he shrugs. "Wouldn't it be nice to stop running? To stand and fight for yourself?"

This man is exhausting. As his words sink in, my posture relaxes. Honestly, it isn't something I've ever really thought about.

When I first went on the run, I tried—discreetly—to find information about my magic, but there was nothing.

No mention of what I could do. I had to be careful who I spoke to. Sometimes I wondered if I was a mistake within the universe—one the King simply wishes to erase.

The more I think about it, the more I like the idea of not having to run. I could settle somewhere permanent—not some random hole in the ground beneath a tree. I could buy a small plot of land, build a little shack, keep warm, and not worry about going hungry. Maybe find work. Maybe even meet a man to settle down with. Can those dreams really come true for me?

It all flashes within my mind for a moment—the thought of a fruitful future. One where I'm not afraid—where I'm truly free. Maybe River has a point. If I knew how to use my powers and defend myself, I might never have to worry about the Dark King again. Perhaps if I go to the priestesses at the Temple of Gaia, they'd tell me my powers came from some twisted Prometheus line. Maybe it's a weird fire gift?

I stare at River, and he gives me a steady look. I don't know this man. I'm not even sure if I want to know him. But what I do know is that within the past twenty-four hours, River's taken better care of me than anyone has since my parents died.

As much as I hate to admit it, I'm starting to trust this Forsaken Elemental. And if what he says about the priestesses is true... I owe it to myself to learn what my gift really is.

"Fine," I relent. "I will go with you to the Temple of Gaia."

Chapter 5

River

Gods, this woman is stubborn! My tension eases when she finally agrees to let me take her to the Temple. Thank Gaia. I know she's not safe. I suspected it the moment I saw her, but after seeing this attack, I know my hunch is right. Could she really be the Lastborn?

For years I've studied the legend of the Lastborn, the last heir of Myrea, prophesied to rise from the ashes like a phoenix. Yet, no such being ever surfaced. I've traveled far and wide in search of the one thing that could weaken and even destroy Finis Voras, the Dark King. I've made countless visits to libraries and temples in search of any way to end the Dark King's reign for good. It's taken so long, and I've journeyed so far, only to hit obstacle after obstacle.

When I finally stumbled into the Scarlet Lands—the kingdom of the ancient Elemental Prometheus—I found a hidden library buried in the sweltering dunes. There, I discovered an ancient scroll which opened my eyes and shook me to my core. That ancient text mentioned *five* Elementals, instead of four. Thousands of years have passed since the rule of the Elementals, and before they ascended from Elemi, the Elemental of Order, Myrea, had been obliterated. No mention of her exists, and none of her people survived. But how? And why? Then, I read the prophecy of the Lastborn—said to be Myrea reincarnated—destined to bring peace, balance, and guidance to our world.

From that moment, it's been my mission to find this prophecy. Together we could finally end the Dark King's vicious reign. Days turned to weeks. Weeks to months. Years later, I'd lost faith in it. I started to believe it was just a myth. After running into dead end after dead end, I gave up. I returned home and drank the world away.

Until Mya walked into The Dirty Fox, with a sparkle in her stunning copper eyes that drew me to her. Even now, studying her beautiful heart-shaped face, wide eyes, and full lips set in a rebellious pout—something about her just feels right. Like this is my path. She's my destiny.

I follow her to the tiny hole she calls home, tucked beneath the expansive surface roots of a giant, old sacred fig tree, where she quietly packs her belongings. I can't get through the narrow entrance she uses to slip in and out from beneath the ground, and I can't help my amusement as I watch her. She scowls, and I force myself to keep an air of impartiality.

Mya doesn't trust me. That's fine. I understand why. I can only imagine how I've come off to her. A stranger stalking her, pressing for information. Her fear is obvious. I don't know what she's endured, but whatever it is, it still haunts her. Mya's chasing demons... or more accurately, running from them. She's wary of everyone new. And after she saw me wield Gaia's magic, her fear only grew.

I understand that too. I remember when my powers first manifested. I was only eight, early for most Forsaken Elementals. But with my parents being strong wielders themselves, thinking back, I guess I shouldn't have been surprised. I remember stunning the priestesses at the Temple of Gaia when I first began bending the weather around me. Head Priestess Elera rushed me into the stone room so I wouldn't hurt anyone.

I learned the ability to wield the weather element there. I also discovered just how dangerous my power could be. They began training me, mostly in meditation, so I could control my powers rather than unleash them. Over the years, I taught myself, occasionally helped by Nani, one of the bolder priestesses, who agreed to train me in secret. Nani also wielded weather, and I think she sympathized with a young boy whose parents were murdered for their powers and standing in Gaia's Keep.

The Dark King saw my parents as a threat to his reign. He killed them in cold blood. I was orphaned at four and forced into the care of the Temple of Gaia. I squeeze the silver pendant hanging around my neck—a constant reminder of all I've been through. I vowed that one day, I would destroy Finis Voras, the Dark King, and bring justice for my parents' murder.

Mya finishes gathering her belongings, drawing my attention back to her. If she's the Lastborn, I need her. I need her to help me destroy Voras. If her magic's the last trace of the forgotten Elemental Myrea, then she's the piece that I've been missing all these years. In time, I'll tell her what her true destiny is. For now, I won't spring it on her. She's already skeptical. I don't want to make her more skittish.

Getting her to agree to come to the Temple of Gaia for evaluation at all is a step I'm grateful for. I hope that when we arrive, Head Priestess Elera will confirm that she's the prophecy of the Lastborn, and allow us to seek refuge there. The temple is a safe haven—one that Voras wouldn't dare defile. At least, he never has before. We'd be safe there—at least for a time.

I watch her crawl out from beneath the ground, with her long, wavy, chestnut hair disheveled around her face, resembling a mole emerging from its burrow. I try to contain my amusement, but feel my lips curl.

"What?" she scowls, fury flashing in her eyes.

I shake my head, shrugging with a grin. "Nothing. Let's go to my place for the night. We'll leave at dawn."

"You think we'll be safe there? What if there are other Dark Knights in the woods?" Trepidation edges in her tone, and I can hear the fear under her words. She's alert, scanning the pitch-black forest.

"Don't worry, I'll protect you from the big, bad darkness," I tease. I turn on my heel and start toward my treehouse as I ignore the twist of irritation on Mya's adorable button face. I force myself to look away, though every part of me wants to do nothing but stare at her incredible beauty.

In less than a day, teasing her has become a pleasure. It's far too easy—just ruffle her pretty little feathers. I still can't believe she stripped bare in my bedroom last night. Like she owned the place. It's been hard to resist taking in the sight of her body. Yet, when I really looked, a twinge of sadness struck me at the sight of her ribs and spine showing from behind. She clearly lived on very little, and she's malnourished. Something deep in me wanted to feed her, protect her, and just keep her safe. Desire hits hard as I remember the kiss she pressed to my lips at The Dirty Fox. It plays over and over in my head.

Shaking the thought away, I lead Mya through the eerie woods on the outskirts of Sunhollow. I know these woods like the back of my hand. Even in familiar dark, my shoulders tense. I'm always on guard at night, but with Mya behind me, I wonder what might come to hunt us? The thought barely passes before I feel a rumble in the earth.

I pause, glancing back on Mya. Her copper eyes glint with fear. We stand in the tense silence for a second before another tremor vibrates through the earth beneath my feet.

"What is that?" Mya whispers.

From the shadows between the trees, darkness seeps forward, bringing more Dark Knights with it. I curse under my breath as they close in, circling us. I'm instantly at Mya's side, refusing to budge. I don't have my axes with me, but I have my powers—and I'll wield them relentlessly, just like before.

"Well, well." A deep voice rides the curling tendrils of darkness around us. "What have we here?" A hooded figure appears—the group leader, I presume—and stops before us. I know this man. Tall and lean, with dark peppered hair and a matching beard. His deep-gray, narrow-set eyes sit above a sharp, crooked nose—long ago broken. A scar runs down his left cheek, and a grin creeps across my face as I remember giving it to him with my dagger.

"Draegan Grimsbane," I drawl, the name a low sound on my tongue. "It's been quite some time, hasn't it? Hmm… can't remember how long," I pause, rubbing my head in mock thought. "Oh, that's right. It's when I gave you that nasty little cut on your face. Looks like its healed nicely."

The General sneers, his fingers brushing the scar on his face. "I see, River Dune, you haven't changed a bit since we last met. It's been years, and you're still as arrogant as ever."

"Only for you," I tease. "And what, may I ask, brings you and your brood to Gaia's Keep? You're a long way from home?" The Netherfields, and particularly its capital, Night Spire, are far from where they ought to be.

"You're not as clever as you think, River Dune. Hand over the girl and be on your way." It's a command that I won't follow.

"I think not," I shrug. "I kind of like this one. Find another girl on your trip back to the Netherfields. Surely, the Dark King doesn't care who he beds. Though, if you've come this far for a woman, he must have exhausted all his other options at home. Pathetic, isn't it?"

Draegan scowls taking a slow, threatening step toward us. I hold his stare, unyielding. "The King demands her." He nods toward Mya.

I throw an arm out in front of her, blocking the Dark Knight's General from advancing.

"He won't be satisfied until he gets what he wants."

"And what's so special about her?" I challenge—a brow perks up. "Do tell."

"It's none of your business, peasant," Draegan hisses through clenched, sharp teeth.

"Well, then, sorry. This one's mine. Finders keepers." Mya hasn't moved. She's frozen, speechless. I glance at the terror clear in her eyes, but she stays close, standing her ground.

Draegan stills, a sly smirk spreading across his lips. "You know," he begins, "you look so much like your father, River Dune."

My blood boils at the mention of my father. He has no right to speak of him. My jaw tenses; my fists curling tight at my sides.

"It'd be a shame if you to meet the same fate as him." He paces in front of us as his circle of Dark Soldiers gains ground. "It was almost too easy to strike him down. I didn't think it would be." He laughs—a low, haunting, sound that makes me swallow a ball of lead. It sinks into my gut. "But, once we had your mother, he yielded to anything we demanded—hoping to save her."

Rage boils as my teeth grind. I stay focused on Draegan—every muscle of my body tenses. In my periphery, Mya tries to catch my eye, but I don't let my gaze stray from the enemy at hand.

"Once we cut her down, he became a shell of a man. Broken, almost too easy to destroy. A weak, pathetic thing." His voice drips venom, and before he can say another word, I stomp my foot, ripping a crater open beneath him, sending several of them tumbling in. The ones who avoid the fall are met with a lightning strike, the shock stopping their hearts in an instant.

"Run!" I scream, grabbing Mya's hand, and we bolt in the opposite direction. Once we're far enough away, out of earshot, I speak again. "We have to go to my treehouse. I need my weapons, and yours are still there. These woods aren't safe. We have to leave for the Temple of Gaia, now."

Breathless, we rush to my treehouse.

"Who was that?" Mya pants as we move quickly through the woods.

"Draegan Grimsbane. One of the King's highest-ranking generals. I've crossed paths with him far too many times."

When we reach the treehouse, I scale the rope ladder fast. "Wait here," I order Mya. It's faster if I grab what we need alone. I snag my pre-packed rucksack, sling on my ax and scabbard, strapping it to my waist. A few knives wait in a holster, just in case I need them. I grab Mya's bow and quiver, then head down the ladder to her.

"Let's go." I hand her the bow and arrows, and her knife. We move at a fast pace to get a head start, away from the enemies chasing us. We head eastward to the Temple of Gaia. It'll be a week on foot, if we make good time. With a horse, it'd be faster, and far less brutal. For tonight, all we can do is put as much distance as possible between us and the Dark Knights. Two encounters in one night can't be a coincidence. The Dark King is upping the game. And the prize is Mya.

Chapter 6

Myalis

We tread all night through the forest, hoping to put as much distance as possible between us and the Dark Knights chasing us. Well, me, I guess. My feet ache, and just before dawn, we find a small cave hidden by green moss and foliage, and we decide to rest there for a while. With the sun climbing fast, we could only hope that the soldiers wouldn't find us. We laid our bedrolls on the hard, cold rock and, despite the discomfort, I fell asleep instantly.

I don't know how long I sleep, but when I wake up, River was already up, shoving his bedroll into a leather rucksack similar to mine. A pensive look falls on his face as I study him. Hearing the General talk about River's parents, I can't help but feel a pang of empathy. I wonder how much time has passed. Were his parents' deaths recent?

River clutches the silver pendant on his neck, closing his turbulent eyes. Perhaps memories haunt him. His jaw twitches, as if he's talking to himself in his head. He must have changed before I woke; he's now wearing a billowing tan linen shirt with the sleeves rolled up, but he keeps on the tight black leather pants—boots already on.

I sigh—too loudly—and it stirs him from his thoughts. River's head snaps around, and he offers me a stiff smile. "Morning," his voice is quiet, warm.

"Morning," I echo, stretching my aching back. I'm used to sleeping on hard surfaces, but it still hurts. Sleeping on the ground is never good, and something I've never truly gotten used to despite my years on the run. River stands but not to his full height, as the cave's ceiling is too low. I hold in a chuckle.

"Whenever you're ready, we need to keep moving." He grabs his bag, turns, and heads to the cave's entrance. "I'll wait outside."

I slept in my clothes, so there's no need to change. Not like I have a vast wardrobe anyway. My head still feeling groggy, I stand and roll my bedroll, thrusting it in my rucksack. I toss my quiver and bow around my shoulders and secure the knives to my belt. I run my fingers through my disheveled hair, braid it, and tie it off with a string of leather. Ready as I'll ever be, I stride out of the cave.

River turns, and heat creeps into my face. "I need to... um," I gesture awkwardly, and when River catches on, he coughs.

"If you don't mind," I shrug.

"Of course not," he nods. "I'll wait here. But if you're too long, I'm coming after you."

I roll my eyes and stroll around the cave to a secluded spot, hidden behind a tangle of bushy trees, where I can relieve myself. Once finished, I return to where River was, and we set off again.

The woods are dense, spread-out, and easy to get lost in. The world around us is alive with the fresh greens of an everlasting spring. Everything's in bloom. Trees bursting in whites and pinks. Bushes sag under the weight of bright red berries. Bees and other insects buzz about. I follow close behind River, trying not to let it all distract me.

"So," I drawl after the silence begins eating at me. "Your full name is River Dune?" River's shoulders tense at the sound of his name, and after a beat, he replies.

"Yes."

"River... Dune," I drawl, a chuckle slipping out my lip.

"What's so funny?" his voice is flat.

"It's just a funny name, wouldn't you say?" I tease. Payback for all the times he's teased me.

River scoffs. "I don't know. Why's it funny? It's just a name."

"River Dune," I repeat it, each time with a different emphasis. Each somehow funnier than the last. Finally, River spins on his heel to face me. A mischievous grin is plastered on his face, catching me off-guard.

"You know, the more you say it, the more I like the sound of it on your lips." He leans in, his lip brushing the curve of my ear, his voice barely audible, yet seductive. "The more I yearn for you to moan it." His blue eyes glimmer in amusement before he turns and continues down the path.

I freeze, heat pooling inside as arousal sweeps into me. A shuddering breath escapes me. Now all I need is a cold bath—his voice affects me far more than I'd like to admit. I force my legs to move, and I no longer say his name in jest.

For hours, we trek through the woods. My legs ache, and my feet throb as we haven't stopped once. When the sound of rushing water reaches us, River and I exchange an excited glance. We dash toward the sound, and come across a massive river snaking through the woods. We sigh in relief. Large rocks litter the shore, and a giant moss-covered tree has fallen across the current, its trunk jutting over the rushing water. The water is a beautiful blue green cascading over massive rocks and breaking into frothing rapids.

Parched, we race to the bank, bend over, and cup our hands in the cold refreshing water lapping up as much as we can. Once I've had my fill, I pull my empty canteen out of my bag and fill it. River does the same.

After a few moments of taking in the splendor of the area, I stretch on the ground and gaze at the sky. The rushing water hums like a pleasant melody in the background. As I close my eyes, my body relaxes for the first time in days. A meditative calm washes over me, one that I haven't felt in years. A breeze touches my hair, gently whipping up off the ground, as if trying to get my attention.

A loud splash snaps me into the present. I sit up and see River in the water. He's stripped his shirt and pants and jumped in.

His black hair is half tied up, too short to fit in his topknot, so wet strands hang loose around his face. He stands in the water, taking in the view, and when he turns, my jaw nearly drops. I shamelessly gawk at his muscled back. A sprawling Tree of Life tattoo dominates his upper back—the black ink, a stark contrast to his tanned skin. From a distance, I can't see all the details, but the art is stunning. When he turns to face me, I notice another tattoo inked across his left pectoral muscle. It's the same symbol as his silver pendant, the flowering spiral of Gaia—framed by the phases of the moon and slashed by a bolt of lightning.

I take in the sight of his rippling muscles and broad shoulders. His strong back tapers to his hips. My mouth waters at the sight of his god-carved body. Desire hits me as my core flutters. Embarrassed, I curl my knees to my chest and force my eyes away—but it's harder than it should be.

River smiles at me, like he knows I'm ogling him. "Come join me," he calls from the water.

He's waist-deep and I shake my head, even though I need that cold bath more than ever. "Oh, come on! The water feels great. Your muscles will thank you."

I pull my knees tighter to my chest, debating whether to take him up on it. It's not like we need to be near each other, right? There's plenty of room in a river this wide.

I toil with the thought for a moment before finally deciding to jump in. I feel River's eyes on me and tell him to turn around, which he does. I undress and wade into the water. It's colder than I expected, sending a shiver through me as I go deeper. When the water reaches my stomach, I dunk under, soaking my hair. After that, my body quickly adjusts to the chill.

My toes sink into the invisible sandy bottom—an occasional sharp rock bites at my feet as I swim toward the river's center. The current isn't rough, making it easy to wade through. The sun's warmth filters through the trees above, beating down on my skin. It feels wonderful.

I sink lower in the water, making sure River can't see my upper body. I don't need his eyes lingering there. He swims closer, sinking to my level until we're face-to-face.

"See? Not so bad," he grins. Sunlight glistens his wet, tanned skin, and I realize, after a moment, I'm ogling. Again.

"It's freezing," I scoff, trying to distract myself from the disturbingly handsome man before me.

"When your muscles are on fire from walking all day, this is a nice refresher," he winks; I roll my eyes.

"We should probably fish. We can eat, get some energy."

Fishing? Yeah, not my strongest suit. Hunting and setting snares, sure, but fishing? Not so much. Back in Dustfall, there wasn't anywhere to go fishing. Papa never got a chance to teach me that skill. Even while on the run, fishing never worked out for me. Maybe I'm too impatient... or perhaps I've never found the right fishing spots. Either way, fishing and I just don't get along.

My stomach growls at the thought of eating. We haven't eaten anything today because we've been on the move. It isn't unusual for me to go a day or two without food—doesn't really bother me. But, with all the energy we're burning, we need the sustenance.

"Food sounds good," I admit, my eyes drifting at the tattoo on his left pectoral. His chest is strong and sculpted. It's hard to resist the urge to reach out and touch it. River's body is a work of art—heat rushes inside me even when I'm in a freezing river, feeling ashamed for being unable to control my eyes. If his lower half wasn't hidden beneath the water, I doubt I'd manage to keep my eyes up at all.

"Like what you see?" River perks a thick, black brow. My face flushes.

I clear my throat. "Sorry, didn't mean to stare. I like your tattoo, that's all," I blurt the excuse, hoping he'll believe it.

"Uh huh," he smirks.

"It's true," I whine like an insolent child. "Maybe you can explain what it means."

River moves closer to me wading through the water, my breath quickens at his nearness. My heart races—he's only inches away. Even now, River towers over me, making me feel small. He traces a finger over the tattoo on his chest. "This is the symbol of Gaia. She's where my power comes from. Then I have the lightning bolt, the symbol of my greatest Gaian gift. The moons are the lunar phases, speckled with stars."

He stops tracing and instead reaches for my hand. River's hand is warm against mine as he takes my finger, tracing each small moon phase tattoo—then each star. His movements are slow and sensual. My breath slows, and my eyes linger on our intertwined hands.

His voice deepens as he speaks. "This one I got because it holds my future, my destiny." At first, I don't grasp his meaning, but as his eyes meet mine, something clicks within me. It's as if he knows what I am—what my power is. The tattoo marks a celestial being, that's what I call myself, though I'm too afraid to say it aloud. I don't know what it means, but as he traces it along the stars, a flutter rises within me. My stomach flips, a yearning building toward its breaking point.

A heated silence settles as he holds my hand against his taut chest. We're lost in each other's gaze. The desire to kiss him overwhelms me—his head leans closer. Our lips brush as we breathe in sync. Gods above! I want him. I barely know him, yet I want him more than anyone else in my life.

His other hand pulls me flush against his body. My skin on his wakes all my senses. I feel every ripple of muscle and gasp as our bodies meet. River's hand on the small of my back sends waves of desire through me. My head spins, senses swirling as I breathe him in. I close my eyes, feel his face near mine, our bodies melting together.

I realize my hand is slowly crawling up his chest, reaching to the back of his neck. I grasp loose strands of silky black hair between my fingers. Still, our lips had done nothing more but feather across the other's. It's like a duel; who will give in to the desire first? His mouth curls, lips still just out of reach. It's a taunt. He's teasing me.

"What do you want from me, River Dune?" I whisper against his lips.

"Everything." His voice is a caress.

"I don't even know you." I breathe, shaking my head. "We just met."

"There's not much to know," he admits quietly. "Orphaned at four. Raised by the priestesses at the Temple of Gaia. On my own since sixteen. Became an alcoholic at twenty-three. Now I'm just some random twenty-six-year-old living in a treehouse, waiting his Gods-given destiny. Which I think is you, Mya."

I pull away from his trance and stare into his eyes. They match the glittering green-blue of the water we're in. I release his hair and creep my hand back down to the tattoo on his chest. His Gods-given destiny? It seems too incredulous to trust fate that much.

My brows furrow. "You don't know me, River." I attempt to pull away, but his grasp holds firm on my back.

"Then tell me. Tell me who you are, Mya." His voice shakes with desperation.

"I don't know what all there is to tell. Our stories are similar. The Dark King killed my parents when I was thirteen, and I've been on the run ever since." I trust him enough with this information, but who knows if it's a good idea.

"Why is the Dark King chasing you?" Always coming back to this question.

I sigh and shrug. How long can I hold off on telling him? Half-assed answers won't last much longer. I relent, deciding to give him my story.

"When I was thirteen, my powers manifested. But they are nothing like any other abilities I've seen or heard of. My parents weren't Forsaken, so it was a surprise when I got them. When my magic surfaced, it felt like the world shifted. The earth shuddered all around me, as if I'd awakened something. A few days later, Dark Knights stormed our doorstep and demanded my parents hand me over to the King. They refused, and it cost them their lives. I escaped, barely avoiding them. Yet, they always find me, time and again. I don't know why he wants me, but I think it's because of the power inside me."

My shoulders slump, as does my head. I take a deep breath and close my eyes. "I always thought that my powers were some sort of mutation of Prometheus's— sparkling light magic twisted with fire. I never use it, because I don't want the Dark King tracking me." I meet River's gaze. His face is somber as I go on. "I don't want to hurt anyone. That's why I've stayed alone all these years."

I free myself from River's grasp, and head back to the shore. I don't care if he's staring at my ass. I've never bared my story to anyone before. It leaves me feeling raw, like I reopened a wound I've been trying to heal. I hear water splashing behind me as River catches up.

"You're not alone anymore, Mya." He places a heavy hand on my shoulder, stopping me. "Thank you for telling me about your past. You can trust me with it. I know we haven't known each other long, but I want to help you."

I have no more words for him. Only time will tell if he's truly trustworthy. I release a huff of air and head toward the riverbank. I grab my clothes and trudge into the forest—anything to escape River Dune's lingering eyes.

When I return, River is wearing his leather pants, but no shirt. His pants are rolled up and he throws a net into the water. I watch, curious. He must've had the net all along in his rucksack. With every motion, I glimpse rippling muscles and try to blink the sight away. Instead, I feel like a teenage girl who's just hit puberty, ogling him for the first time.

After setting the net, he returns to the bank and starts a small fire. I watch silently before settling close to where he works. His eyes meet mine, a slight curl tugging his lip. I watch his calloused hands spark fire with rocks and sticks. When the flint catches the sticks he gathered, he tends the growing fire. His lips form an "o" as he blows. Involuntarily, I lick my lips.

Once the fire burns strong, he stands and grabs his axe from his belt. "If you could keep this going, I'll grab more wood."

I nod as he strides past and disappears into the forest, leaving me alone. The rushing water soothes me, but the vast woods feel unsettling, especially since I'm not exactly sure where we are.

Much of Gaia's Keep remains unexplored and wild. It's the largest territory in Elemi, and no one knows what types of creatures lurk or what small villages or towns hide deep within the woods. My anxiety grows as I wait for River's return. The sound of wood knocking tells me he's not far away. It isn't long before he returns, carrying a handful of freshly chopped wood.

"Is that what you do for a living? Are you a woodcarver?" I ask as River returns to tending the fire and adds a log in it.

"Not really," he replies. "My parents were popular merchants throughout Gaia's Keep. They did a lot of trade within it, as well as in the Oasis Peninsula. In truth, I live off the wealth they left behind. Occasionally, I'll do menial tasks for those who need them. Sometimes I get paid. Most time, it's just out of the goodness of my heart."

A pang of sadness hits my chest. "I'm sorry about your parents."

River shrugs. "It was a long time ago. I barely remember them now. Perhaps a flash of my mother's dark hair. My father's blue eyes. I only really have their stories to keep my memory alive—I owe those to the Gaian Priestesses. My parents were close to them at the temple."

"Forgive me if this is insensitive, but do you know why the King killed them?" River shifts his weight as he sits. A flicker of pain crosses his face, a slight flare of his nostrils, a wrinkle on his forehead. His jaw tightens, sharpening his already hard features.

"Apparently, the people of Gaia's Keep liked them. They had strong Forsaken powers from Gaia. Stronger than any seen in years. The Dark King didn't like the idea of powerful Forsaken being so well-loved. He saw them as threat to his reign because of their influence as merchants. In a free world, my parents might have ruled Gaia's Keep. But here we all submit to Elemi's sole ruler. The Dark King crushed them before they could raise an army."

I shake my head in disbelief. "Do you think your parents would've done that? Raise an army to defeat the King?"

"I don't know. They were influential enough. With how well-traveled they were, and the power they held, it could have been a possibility."

"How did you survive?" I ask, hoping it's not too insensitive.

River takes a deep breath and closes his eyes. "I wasn't home. I was in the woods nearby when the Dark Soldiers arrived on our doorstep. All I saw was my parents dragged out and then the soldiers burned my home to the ground. I remember hearing my mother's screams before they were silenced." He pauses.

River shakes his head, lips thinning into a tight line. "I just remember running. Trying to get as far away as I could. The soldiers didn't even know I existed. I took sanctuary at the Temple of Gaia, on the outskirts of Everwillow. My parents were close with the priestesses. When I told them what happened to my parents, they took me in and cared for me. But as I grew older, all I wanted was vengeance. I've had quite a number of run-ins with the Dark Knights since."

"So that's why that General knew you last night?" I ask with a smirk. His grin returns as he looks at me.

"Oh yes. Draegan Grimsbane and I go back a long way. The last time we met, I gave him the beautiful mark on his cheek." River stands and returns to the river to check his net. He nods in satisfaction as he pulls it from the water. A few good-sized fish flap around inside it.

River quickly cleans the fish and forks them on a stick each, placing them over the fire. Fish isn't usually on my daily menu, but I'm too hungry to be picky. Eyeing the cooked meat, I bite into the crispy skin, tasting the flakey white flesh beneath. It's delicious, and I eat as ungracefully as possible under River's amused gaze.

"You don't really get to eat much, do you?" His question startles me as I chew the fluffy white meat of whatever fish this was—chomping the food in my mouth, savoring the flavor, and swallowing before I reply.

"Not really," I admit. "I don't need much, though. Most of the game I catch I sell so that I always have money—just in case I need to run again."

From River's physique, I know he ate heartily. Muscles like that don't come from diet alone.

"Hopefully, you won't have to live like that anymore." He mutters sullenly, finishing his fish. "Come on, we need to keep moving."

It's been a pleasant reprieve from the day's walking, but River's right. The more distance we put between us and Sunhollow, the better. Quickly, we clean up our spot, extinguish the fire, gather our things, and set off again.

Chapter 7

Myalis

After two days of walking, my body aches, is sore and my feet are blistered. It's been so long since I've been on the run that I'm no longer used to its strain. I manage to keep up behind River, despite moving slower than him. Occasionally, we pause for rest, which includes a nibble of jerky or nuts to keep our strength up. The breaks last anywhere from thirty minutes to an hour at the most. When we stop to sleep, it's never for more than four or five hours. My body is re-acclimating to the grueling pace of life on the run.

Thankfully, we haven't encountered any more Dark Knights, but it still feels like we're being followed. Maybe it's just paranoia. Not wanting to risk a run-in, River and I push ourselves as hard as we can. We hope to find a small village where we can buy horses, but luck hasn't been on our side yet.

Exploring the dense woods of Gaia's Keep is incredible. Sunhollow lies within Stormsbend Forest, a place well known even across other Elemental provinces. Then there's The Flowering Wood, also known to the outside world. However, what goes on in these vast forests is unknown to most. Even citizens within Gaia's Keep avoid wandering too far, fearing they'd be lost never to be found.

River knows the path well though. I watch in awe as he effortlessly navigates the woods, allowing the sun's position and the forest to guide him. Even though he shared his story, I sense there's more than he is leading on. Not that I suspect him of anything nefarious, but my curiosity about what he's hiding grows. I don't want to push him because we're still relatively strangers. Yet, I want to know him, and his full story. Hopefully he'll open up more as we go along.

When a clearing appears past the trees we've been endlessly roaming, excitement surges through me. A change in terrain sounds heavenly after the strain of trudging through the woods. All the roots, fallen trees, vines, and rocks on the forest floor, make travel exhausting. The weather is an eternal spring here in Gaia's

Keep, but today is warmer than usual; sweat drips from my brow, soaking the strands of hair clinging to my face. Despite the tree cover, sunbeams pierce through—casting bright light on the forest floor where we walk.

When we finally step into the clearing, River and I are awestruck by a giant meadow extending for miles. It's whimsical as tiny flowers dot the ground as far as we can see. Little bursts of yellows and whites amid the tall, bright green grass bring a wave of joy and rejuvenation. The scent of damp woods fades as the winds carry the fragrance of fresh spring wildflowers.

"If I'm not mistaken, we're near New Spring Farmstead." River announces as we enter the rolling, grassy hills. "Maybe we can finally get horses there."

Steadfast as ever, he strides through the high grass, leading the way across the meadows. The further we trek, the more uneasy I grow. If the Dark Knights return, we'd be sitting targets here with nowhere to hide.

After walking for an hour more, a large farming village comes into view. Quaint houses built on large plots of land bursting with new crops, some with barns and different animals. I assume this is New Spring Farmstead. When we reach the village center, it's bustling with people selling foods and wares. How such a quiet place is this busy is beyond my comprehension.

"Travelers from all over come to New Spring Farmstead for the produce." River says, almost reading my mind. "It's some of the best in Gaia's Keep."

Grassy plains surround the village, fading into dirt road that leads us into the center. Each building in the village center has a weathered thatched roof dwelling. Old-fashioned shops with small display windows line the street. There's a tiny tavern, and River and I decide it's the perfect place to rest for the night.

The place has a board with the name: Sweet Apple Inn and Tavern. From the outside, it doesn't look like much. Varying shades of gray stones make up the façade, and a pale straw thatched roof covers it.

Inside, the tavern room is small. Nothing like The Dirty Fox, and certainly nowhere near as rowdy. It's quiet, yet pretty. The scent of freshly cooked cinnamon apples fills the air. Ten wooden tables and a bar that can seat about eight folks fills the space. A large hearth built from the same gray stone sits on the left side of the room. Behind the bar stands a jolly, buxom woman with meat on her bones. Her pale blonde hair is woven beneath a cloth she's tied around her head. Her round face is red and healthily flushed. With only one patron at the bar, her face lights up as she sees us and she offers a wide smile.

"G'day, weary travelers!" she calls out. "Welcome to Sweet Apple Inn and Tavern. What can I do for ya?" As we approach the bar, I notice wrinkles set deep around her brown eyes and pink mouth. She rests her elbow on the bar and waits for one of us to speak.

"We're hoping to rent a couple rooms for the evening," River says smoothly, "as well as potentially buying two horses—if you know of anyone in the Farmstead willing to part with them." He perks a flirtatious brow at her. I roll my eyes watching them interact.

"Sure, sure," the woman says, her voice tinged with a thick accent. Leaning both elbows on the bar, she cradles her round chin in her hands. Her low cut, puffy-sleeved blouse accentuates her large bosoms leaving little to the imagination—she's certainly showing off for River. "I's gots a room." She raises an eyebrow at me.

"Two rooms, if possible," River states.

"Ain't got two, only one."

River hesitates, as do I. One room? We'd been traveling together for days, but I wasn't sure if I was ready for that. Sharing a room felt... intimate.

Finally, River nods. "That'll be fine." He fishes a coin pouch from his rucksack and tosses a couple silver on the bar. The barkeep's eyes go wide with pleasure.

She bows her head to River and then grabs a key. "You can have the last room upstairs on the left. Bathing chambers at the end of the hall should ya need it—and if yas in need of horses, see Farmer Dillson. He'll give ya a fair price. Just tell 'im ol' Lelah sent ya." She winks at River, and he bows his head in respect.

"Thank you for your hospitality."

She nods and returns to her patron at the bar, who was now growing impatient for his next drink.

River and I follow a narrow stairwell upstairs. Eight doors line the hallway—four on each side—and at the far end, a ninth door, probably the bathing chamber Lelah mentioned. We stroll to the last room on the left. River hands me the key.

"If you'd like to rest, I can go see about the horses." River says.

"You don't want me to come with you?" I ask, hesitant about staying alone.

"I'll be fine. I know you're tired. Rest up; we'll meet for dinner in a couple of hours."

Truth is, I can't refuse. The exhausting pace made me realize how weak my body had become. "Alright then, I'll see you at dinner."

River nods and heads down the hall, descending the stairs. I open the door to find a farmhouse-style bedroom. One bed. I gulp, trying to ignore that detail.

The room is small. The wooden bed, covered in a heavy quilt and fluffy cushions, sits directly across me on the far wall. To the left a small desk and chair is kept, topped with a lantern. A ceramic pitcher and cup, filled with water, rest on a tiny wooden bedside table. It'd be perfect for the night—if not for the fact that I have to share it with River. I can't remember the last time I slept in a real bed, well, aside from the night at River's. Stepping closer, I gently rest my hand on the soft quilt.

Quickly, I toss off my boots, rucksack, bow and quiver, and belt with my knives on it and climb into the bed. I rub my aching feet for a few moments before laying back. A sigh escapes me as the mattress and cushion engulfs me in a delicious comfort. A pleasant aroma of daffodils is present in the room, and as I put my head on the cushion, I realize it's the source. They must've laundered it in some type of oil from the flowers. Sleep swiftly claims me.

When I wake a few hours later, it's already dark. I curse under my breath, realizing I've probably missed dinner with River. Was I so deep in sleep that I didn't hear him return? I jump up, noticing his absence, and quickly rummage through my sack to pull out a fresh set of clothes. Luckily, I've got a lightweight, sky-blue, linen tunic dress with a pair of tan cotton pants—much cleaner than the ones I'm wearing.

With my clothes in hand, I slowly open the door to hear the sounds of the tavern below. Now that it's nightfall, it sounds much busier than when we arrived. I slip quietly to the bathing chamber at the end of the hall, grateful it was unoccupied. I shut the door behind me. An empty ceramic basin and a large pitcher of clean water are set in one side, on a table. In the corner, a large, round wooden tub is filled, though the water looks questionably used. The lavender scent is strong and clean in the water, but I'm hesitant to fully immerse myself.

Instead, I take one of the provided cloths folded on the wooden shelves. I quickly strip my dirty clothes and stuff them together in a bundle. I promise the next time we cross a river, I'd give them a wash. I'm tempted to dump them in the wooden tub basin right away, but I'd rather not abuse the facilities provided by my generous host. I wet the cloth and scrub my body clean as best as I can—arms, hands, feet, legs, and even my privates. I even dunk my long hair into the water to work out the tangles.

I pull a towel from the shelf, dry off and dress in my cleaner set. I pour some fresh water into the empty basin to wash my face and rinse my mouth. The feeling of being clean lifts my spirits as I step out.

I toss my dirty clothes in my room, lock the door behind me, and head downstairs. When I reach the narrow, rickety stairwell, I hear a familiar voice carrying up from below. I furrow my brow as I descend and spot River holding court with a large group. They were hanging on his every word of whatever tale he was weaving, especially the two well-endowed women glued to either side of him.

I frown, wondering what he's up to. He has a pipe in one hand, taking a deep inhale of whatever he's smoking. Laughter erupts around him as I make my way down, staring at River in disgruntled awe. Beer's scent wafts through my nose as I push my way between one of the curvy women—shining blonde hair in long waves, deep chocolate color eyes—and stand beside River, staring him down.

River turns to me, blue eyes swirling, and a bright smile crests across his mouth. "Ah, dearest Mya! You've finally joined me!"

Shit, he's drunk as a skunk—or perhaps high. I'm sure. "I thought we were going to have dinner?" I ask, my voice as polite as my frustration allows.

River's face twists in thought, his black eyebrows knitting together. "Oh right! I forgot," he slurs. "You see, I went to get us horses and when I came back, these lovely folks were all here and we started talking and drinking... and well, one thing led to another." River lifts his jug and takes a huge swig of whatever concoction is inside and then takes a long drag of his pipe.

My blood boils. "Well, don't let me interrupt your jolly time." I frown, leave his side and cross to the bar, taking a seat at it. Lelah is there already.

"I'll have whatever your special is and a pint of your house ale." I mumble, frustrated. I glance over my shoulder at River, but he doesn't look back. He's either too drunk, or he just doesn't care. I can't tell which.

"Of course." Lelah plops a pint of a caramel-colored ale before me. I smell the liquid, catching notes of apples, and take a huge gulp. It's delicious, with a hint of sweetness—like apple cider. I laugh at myself, remembering that I'm in the *Sweet Apple Inn and Tavern*.

Waiting for my food, I keep stealing glances at River. The pretty woman on his right with deep brunette hair and honeyed eyes whispers something in his ear. He laughs at whatever she says, and then draws on his pipe again.

My stomach twists watching him flirt. I get he's been stuck with plain old me for the past few days, but seriously? Have I truly been that boring? We stood naked and pressed against each other just days ago. He even admitted he desires me, but now I watch him woo another. I groan as I roll my eyes. Why am I so mad? I squeeze the pint glass tighter and take a large sip of cider.

My lips twist with frustration, and as I sip the drink again, it hits me. I'm jealous. Gods above, I am fucking jealous—of these women hanging on River, that he's reciprocating the attention. What in the underhells am I thinking? I scowl. Jealous? Could I really be?

Another sharp look over my shoulder and I see River's lips brushing the brunette's neck. A furious knot tightens inside me. Is he just a loose man? A womanizer? Does he bed every woman he meets? Granted, he and I haven't... but we could, if I wanted to!

Watching him makes my stomach sink. I feel sick. Maybe I misunderstood him—his words, his actions. Perhaps he isn't interested in me after all.

Raucous laughter fills the space as Lelah returns with a plate of pot roast and potatoes. The dish looks delicious, and I thank her. Though my appetite's gone, I force myself to eat. It tastes just as good as it looks and smells. The herbs tingle on my tongue as I savor the hearty meal. Lelah brings another pint of cider. After finishing my meal, I gulp it down in one swig. Then, I push myself up from the barstool and force my legs back up the stairs. I can't bear to look at River. I feel dejected and hurt, and I just want to be alone.

Once inside the room, I close the door quietly. A deep, humbling breath escapes me as my shoulders drop. Tears sting at my eyes, but I hold them back. I don't know why I'm so upset—I sniffle. What am I hoping for with River, anyway? He's taking me to the Temple of Gaia for sanctuary. Nothing more. Once we arrive, we'll part ways.

I shed my clothes again, throw them on the wooden floor, and crawl into bed. I stare at the ceiling for a few minutes before forcing my eyes shut, falling asleep quietly.

Chapter 8

River

I wake the next morning with a throbbing headache drool pooling beneath my face on the comfortable inn bed. I blink through the pain, groan, and roll onto my back. Last night is fuzzy—I clearly remember seeing Mya for half a second before she disappeared. What happened, exactly?

I recall the crowd around me, two women on either side. I was sure one was Mya, but was it really? The details blur as I sit up, clutching my head. I slept naked, but there are no signs of... well, coital bliss, which I suppose I'm somewhat grateful for. Especially since I'm trying to remember whether it was Mya's lips I was kissing or someone else. Great Gaia above, what the fuck is wrong with me?

Have I so easily slipped back into my old ways? All because of a little flattery, a little infamy? Disgusted, I swing my feet over the bed, hitting the wooden floorboards. The cold floor sends a shiver up my spine. I scratch my scalp, running my fingers through tangled black hair. I find my leather string, and tie the front of my hair back in a small bun.

I inhale deeply through my nose as I stand and stretch. The bed *was* comfortable—a step up from my bedroll. Still, I'm grateful for a safe bed, since today we return into the wilderness on our path to the Temple of Gaia. Speaking of "we", I notice Mya is gone from the room.

Mya. I need to find her—we've to get going. I quickly pull on my linen shirt, rolling up the sleeves. The deep V of my shirt reveals my Gaia pendant and a glimpse of the tattoo on my chest. I find my black leather trousers and pull them on, then grab my socks and boots and put them on.

By asking the locals around town, I managed to find Farmer Dillson. Though I asked for two horses, he was only willing to part with one. It wasn't ideal, but I was grateful nonetheless. The horse I got was a large, bulky beast, with brown hair and a gorgeous black mane and tail. He seemed strong enough to carry both me and Mya, so, I took him. Hopefully, Mya won't mind too much.

Luckily, I travel light and hadn't unpacked anything from last night. Yesterday in town, I picked up extra supplies, dried foods, and the like, just in case. They're safely secured in my rucksack. I cross the room and drink the entire pitcher of water from the small table before leaving the room. I march a few steps to the washroom and knock.

"Mya?" I call out, hoping she's inside. When there's no answer, I grow anxious. Where could she be? What if the Dark Knights found us and took her? And I, drunk dumbass didn't even fucking realize? My stomach drops as panic settles in. I dash down the hall, lurching two steps at a time.

Mya sits alone at the bar, a bowl of food placed before her. A cup of tea is kept beside the bowl. Lelah, the barmaid, is nowhere in sight. The Sweet Apple Inn and Tavern feels deserted. Relief washes over me when I see her there. I join her, observing to make sure she's okay. No signs of physical harm on her. All her belongings lie on the floor next to her, weapons included.

"Hey." I whisper, but she doesn't respond. She says nothing at all—just continues eating the porridge. "Is everything okay?" I ask, studying her. Physically, she seems fine.

Mya's hair is tied up. Wavy brown hair cascades down her back in a ponytail. She wears a pale blue tunic with short sleeves and a V-neck, that highlights her prominent collarbones, paired with tan pants and boots. She's stunning. Her nose is sharp but rounded at the tip; her full lips are slightly puckered out. Her large almond-shaped eyes are downcast, long lashes caress her cheeks.

The silence between us thickens, growing uncomfortable. I reach for her shoulder, but she snatches my hand away so fast, it startles me.

"Don't touch me." She seethes.

Shit. I wasn't kissing her last night, and she's pissed. I knew I messed up.

"Sorry," I breathe. "You just had me worried when you weren't in the room this morning. I didn't really get to talk to you last night—"

"And whose fault is that?" She snaps turning toward me. Her gaze burns into mine, a gut punch I can't dodge. I shake my head slowly.

"I'm guessing mine, judging by how you're acting." I reply.

Mya jumps to her feet, facing me. Her fierce expression pins me still. She stands close to me, her hands planted firm on her curvaceous hips.

I sigh. "Things are a little hazy. Sorry if I upset you." She shakes her head as she fumbles through a coin pouch on her belt and places a couple of copper on the bar for Lelah.

"Let's just go." She snatches her stuff from the floor and storms out. I take a few bites of the leftover porridge and follow her. Outside the door, she stands with her arms crossed, defensive.

Shit. What if I did kiss her—and she didn't want me to? I groan as the bright, spring sun blinds me, reminding me that my head still throbs from last night's drinking. I glance right and approach our new horse I tethered to a wooden post just outside the inn, beside a large trough. Quietly, I untie him and catching Mya's gaze from a distance.

"Where's the other one?" she asks, brow raised, arms crossed.

"I could only get one," I explain. "We'll have to ride together."

"Underhells, no!" she snaps, stomping her feet firmly.

"Mya." I say shrugging as I approach her.

"Don't *'Mya'* me. You were supposed to get two." Her face twists with irritation and after whatever I have done last night, I don't want to make her any angrier.

"Farmer Dillson wouldn't give two, I could only get one. It's only temporary. Just until we get to the temple. Traveling by horse will be much faster, and Buttercup here," I pat his neck and glance back at Mya, "is strong and sturdy. He'll get us there in no time."

A bemused smile crosses her face.

"Buttercup?"

I grin. "Yeah, that's his name." She fights back a laugh, her mouth scrunching in amusement.

"Did you name him that, or is that Farmer Dillson's doing?" She tilts her head.

I chuckle, holding his reigns. "I'd never name such a magnificent creature, Buttercup. But, Farmer Dillson said it's the only name he responds to. So, Buttercup it is."

The horse is saddled and ready. I'm not sure who to thank for that since I didn't do it. Maybe Lelah did it this morning?

I move to the horse's side and secure my gear to the saddle, then look back at Mya. "Shall we?" I ask.

She nods half-heartedly, handing me her things. I'm sure she'll confront me about last night when she's ready. For now, I just appreciate her yielding on this.

Shakily, Mya mounts the horse. Once she's settled in the saddle, I climb up behind her. It's a tight, uncomfortable fit, but we have no choice. Truthfully, I don't mind her close warmth against me. Her body tenses as her back presses against my chest while I grip the reins. I stifle a chuckle as we continue our journey to the temple.

I ease Buttercup into a steady trot. First, to get familiar with the beast; second, because Mya clearly isn't comfortable on a horse. The thought of her riding her own, especially so skittish, makes me laugh.

Once Buttercup and I both settle, I quicken our pace. We ride through the meadows, spring air whipping our hair around our faces. Mya's scent enchants me. I try to focus, but lean closer to her face more than I probably should.

Mya struggles to find where to place her hands, and though it amuses me, I wrap my arm around her waist to steady her. I'm skilled enough to hold both her and the reins. She tenses, as if she wants to pull away from my embrace. But with little choice, she settles into it.

After hours riding through the open meadows, we find a small stream. I stop to rest and let Buttercup drink and graze. It's been a while since I last rode, and my thighs burn as I dismount. A groan escapes my throat and as Mya slides off Buttercup, I hear her make a similar sound. My ass feels numb, and I stretch through the pain.

"How're you feeling?" I ask her. I rub my head, grateful that the hangover has faded during the ride.

"About what?" she snaps, still angry.

"Please just tell me what I did to upset you so we can move past this?" I plead as I approach. Women and their damn scorn.

Mya's coppery eyes glisten in the sun, glowing almost gold. But an emotion floods them as her brow tightens. Her cupid's-bow lips scrunch in irritation.

"Last night..." she hesitates, struggling to gather her thoughts together. "I just... I thought we were in this together, and you forgot about me." Her anger from before has softened, but now it's changed to something vulnerable. She's hurt.

"I'd never forget you—"

"*You did!*" she scolds. Her fists clench at her sides, her stance defensive. "You were supposed to come get me once you retrieved horses, but instead, you got distracted by booze! I'm sorry I'm not much for company. I've been alone too long. I don't know how to be around people. I'm a solitary person."

I try to grasp what she's saying but goes over my head. I shake my head, replaying her words in my mind. "You think I don't enjoy your company? That I was seeking others?"

She hisses—an incredulous look splatters across her face. "Those women certainly seemed to enjoy your *companionship* last night."

The hazy memory of me kissing a brunette flickers in my mind. My brow furrows, teeth grazing my bottom lip as I try to recall more. But the high of alcohol and wrathhog I smoked last night bring back everything in flashes and fragments.

"You were next to me all night." I say, but I doubt my words as soon as they leave my mouth.

"No, I wasn't." Mya counters. "I was with you for five seconds. You were too engrossed in your tavern posse, laughing and joking like old friends." Her words hit me like a cold slap.

"I'm sorry." I mutter, running my hands through my tangled hair. "I thought it was you beside me." My voice's barely above a whisper. Guilt washes over me. Had the alcohol and drug really strayed me that far from my path?

Mya exhales sharply, throwing her hands up in frustration. "Really? You expect me to believe that?"

I grit my teeth, "yes, I do. Because it's true, Mya. I thought it was you."

"You thought you were kissing me?" Her brow arches skeptically.

"*Yes!*" I repeat, taking a step toward her. "Is that so hard to believe?" A heated silence creeps between us as I realize what this is really about. A sly smile sneaks on my face. I narrow my eyes.

"Are you... jealous, Mya?" I tease. "Jealous that I kissed another woman?" Mya's cheeks flush pink.

"No." Her answer is defensive and immediate.

"Gaia above." I whisper under my breath. "You are. You're jealous."

"I'm *not* jealous!" The pink color of her cheeks deepens, and her knuckles whiten as she fists tighter.

I shift tactic and prowl closer. She's afraid. Afraid I don't like her company; afraid I'll abandon her. In my drunken haze, she saw me kiss another woman. And in that moment, she thought I'd leave her behind.

Little does she know that she is my destiny. I'd never leave or abandon her. Her presence stirs me in ways I'd never knew possible. I will never relinquish her. Last night, I thought I was kissing her, but my body knew it wasn't Mya. Especially when the brunette begged me to be taken to my bed. Something deep inside knew she wasn't the one for me.

No. We're in this together now, even if she doesn't know the full extent yet. I don't want her to doubt my feelings for her. I don't want her to think I'm that shallow.

I step close, barely inches away, staring at the top of her downcast head. She can't meet my eye. She won't admit she's jealous. It's okay because she doesn't have to. I cup her delicate face, my fingers to gently caressing her cheek.

When her gaze meets mine, her golden hazel eyes shine like glass, as if holding back tears. Are they tears of frustration or sorrow? I don't know. I brush my thumb along her cheek, ready to catch any that might fall. Her lips pout. My eyes fix on them longer than they should.

I wrap my other hand around her body and pull her against me. "You don't need to be jealous of anyone, Mya. I *am* sorry I hurt you last night. When I drink, especially with wrathhog, things tend to blur. I know it's no excuse. But truly, I thought it was you. I only want to kiss *you*. My wish is to worship you, and no one else."

Her lip quivers, teasing me and before I can think better of it, I crush my mouth into hers, stealing any reply she might've given me. Her body melt in my arms returning the kiss, with passion and hunger. Flashes of the first night we met at The Dirty Fox cloud my mind, and I remember her intense kiss. Since then, all I've thought about is kissing her again.

My body hums as I grip her tighter. Our tongues dance as I claim her mouth. She tastes sweet, like iced verdant cakes from Verdanta—the celebration day of when Gaia created Elemi. I want more—more of her, so badly.

When her hand lands on my chest, I freeze. Our lips part for air, and I inhale her. "Mya." Her name leaves my lips like a prayer. Perhaps it is. A prayer to the prophecy of the Lastborn, destined not just to save me, but to save us all. She doesn't know yet. Not yet aware of who she truly is.

I don't want to spoil this. I want to be selfish, even if it's just in this moment. She moves her hand to the neckline in my shirt, her calloused fingers skidding across my bare skin. Tracing the dark lines of the tattoo on my chest, I feel my heart race beneath her touch. My power hums just beneath my skin. My cock throbs as she lazily circles around one of the small moon shapes. Her touch sets my skin alight—desperate for release I can't name. My breath hitches as I gaze into her starry eyes. What's she doing to me?

I claim her mouth again, demanding her kiss. My hands tighten, pulling her body closer. My fingers roam the small of her back before gripping the curve of her round bottom. I grasp her firmly; Mya gasps in my mouth, drawing a feral moan from me. Gods above, I want to take her.

Everything about her feels perfect under my hand. The way she feels against my body, the way my hands easily caress and naturally fit around her curves like a puzzle piece. It's intoxicating. Together, our bodies hum— an ebbing, flowing harmony. My growing erection presses firmly against her, begging for release. The entire world fades away—there's only us.

The ground rumbles beneath me. For a moment, I think our pleasure triggered a slip of my power. Pulling away, I spot dark shapes in the distance. A line of Dark Knights has gathered at the meadow's edge.

"Shit." I hiss, releasing Mya, and sprinting toward Buttercup, grazing leisurely nearby. Grabbing his reigns, I shout for Mya, who's still in a lustful haze, but now angry at my sudden absence.

"We have to go."

Her eyes widen as she realizes what's happening. She runs toward me and Buttercup. Without a word, Mya jumps on, and I follow, immediately digging my heels into Buttercup's sides with a yell. Buttercup, displeased by the sudden command, bolts forward. In the open meadow, we're sitting ducks with nowhere to hide. Can we really outrun the Dark Knights this time?

I didn't expect the Dark Knights to chase us during the day; they usually move under the cover of night. But I should've known better. I never expected a Gaian Forsaken to serve in the King's Army. Fighting another Gaian pains me, but it also pisses me off—the fact that the King has supporters from Gaia's Keep.

The meadow behind us cracks open, a deep crevasse rapidly closing in on our heels. Mya glances back, but I already know this power well. The ground is about to collapse out from under us. I kick Buttercup hard and slap the reigns, urging him to run faster.

Deep down, I know we can't outrun or hide from them. Not out here in the open. Mya and I need to stand and fight. I spot a tree line in the distance, but we won't reach in time. No. I know what we need to do.

"We have to fight." I tell Mya, slowing Buttercup.

"Are you insane?" She panics.

"We're too far from the forest. Buttercup will tire before we lose them. It's our only choice. Use your bow; take down as many as you can. I'll handle the rest."

Buttercup halts. I dismount, facing our approaching foes. Time slows as I raise my hands to the sky, breathe deep, and prepare to summon my power.

Chapter 9

Myalis

I watch River's body tense as he opens his palm upwards, striding toward the ground between us and the marching soldiers. The once-blue sky scattered with fluffy white clouds, darkens overhead. Wind swirls around, causing the tall grass to sway unnaturally. Thunder rumbles in the distance, startling me. Recalling what River did the other day with his weather power, I leap off Buttercup, dropping low to the ground. I unlatch my bow and quiver from his saddle, throw them over my shoulder, bow in hand.

The Dark Knights remain undeterred by the storm as the ground shudders violently beneath me. Then I realize the earth isn't moving at River's command—I gasp, knowing we're in serious trouble. I nock an arrow from my quiver and raise my bow, ready to loose it at the first soldier who comes into range. I steady myself as River closes the distance.

Bolts of lightning crackle in his palms, illuminating the darkened space between us. Ear splitting thunder echoes as the meadow vibrates. River's broad, muscled back holds firm as he summons the lightning and wields it, showing no hint of pain. I watch in awe as he calmly advances on the Dark Knights.

The soldiers' cries pierce my ears, and the fight begins. River wields lightning with incredible, effortless skill. Sparks leap from the sky as he maneuvers it between the soldiers. I shoot my arrows, one, sometimes two, at a time, trying to keep them from reaching River, but they come in droves.

We're desperately outnumbered, but watching River fight for me inspires me. I know I can't run away. Not this time. For the first time, I stand my ground—approaching River, shooting arrows, knocking down men left and right.

At the meadow's crest, a harrowing dark shadow looms atop a black stallion. I can't make out who it is, but smoky tendrils reach out toward River and me. My breath hitches. A mix of dark and earth powers conjures creatures rising from the ground, stopping both River and me.

I stumble as the ground trembles, and strange creatures rise before me. Skeletal, grassy beasts form—wolflike in shape. Born of earth, they're brought to life Tazra Forsaken's magic. It's horrifying.

"Gods above." I whisper as dozens appear. Their skeletal wolf frames entwined with green, flowering meadow grass. A horrible fusion of life and death. Their eyes are pitch black and foggy as they fixate on River and me. An abomination.

River glances over his shoulder at me. His jaw is tense, his nostrils flare. He strikes a bolt of lightning into the grassy field, igniting a creature, but it keeps moving. I shoot for its misted black eyes, but my arrow pass through them without causing any harm.

"Run!" River commands. But where can we go? We're trapped in an open field. The creatures attack, their speed unnatural. Panic surges through me, and I bolt. River fights the soldiers with lightning strikes like branches of a massive tree. The soldiers drop dead. Only the dark creatures and their ring leaders remain.

River outpaces me, catching up just as the wolf-like creatures chase him. Plumes of darkness surround us, and I start hyperventilating as all the memories from my past come rushing back. The nightmares over the years fill my mind as the monsters' snarls echo around us.

I can taste the sweat dripping on my lips as I dash faster keeping up with River. "Come on!" He screams—he's now ahead of me. He grabs Buttercup's reins and waits for me to reach so that we can hop on and outrun them.

I trip and fall hard, the breath forced from my lungs. Darkness envelops me, and the grassy meadow vanishes from sight. I'm trapped—trapped in an orb of utter abyss. As the wolf creatures circle me, I shoot arrows at them, but nothing happens. They're impervious to my attacks. The skeletal creatures snap at my feet, circling as they wait for their master to claim me.

The silence around me is heavy and uneasy. I hear whispers, but I don't understand a word. A wolf creature snarls as a Dark Knight steps inside that orb of darkness. My breath just halts. It's the same man we encountered days ago. He survived whatever River unleashed on him. His narrow, gray eyes glow as he grins down at me.

"I finally have you for my King." The deep timbre of his voice, shaky with relief. "He will be most pleased to have you at his side."

Draegan Grimsbane's strong hand wraps around my throat, and I kick my feet struggling to break free. "Let me go!" I scream.

He says nothing as the darkness fades. River lies unconscious on the ground as the world comes back to view. The ghastly creatures sink back into the earth, their purpose fulfilled.

I struggle against the man's burly grasp, but Grimsbane's hold is firm dragging me toward his black stallion. I call for River, but he doesn't budge. My heart sinks, fearing if Grimsbane killed him. A personal vendetta finally coming to an end. My whole body goes numb watching River's still body getting further and further away from me.

Fury surges within me. My face twists. My blood boils, and I glare at Grimsbane. "Let go of me!" I snarl through gritted teeth, fighting back with all my strength. Draegan's hand tightens as he readjusts his grip around my throat.

Thinking fast, I pull out the knife from my belt and thrust it into a weak point, right under the armpit. He yelps, loosening his grip. I sprint to River but just as I reach him, another pair of hands seize me. Another man in black leather holds me back. Tanned skin with light hair, I immediately recognize him as the Gaian Forsaken who attacked us.

I fight him as well. Taking my knife, I strike where I can, but he blocks and dodges. When he captures both my arms, rendering me helpless, I scream into his face. My scream twists into an unnatural, terrifying sound. A sound I've never made before.

Everything slows to a crawl. Rings of light—like glowing smoke—steam out of my mouth. Both men are flung back, away from me. Startled, I watch their bodies contort unnaturally. What have I done? And how? I glance at my hands, and a subtle glow radiates from me. Horrified, I turn to River, who has lifted his head, stormy blue eyes staring at me in awe.

"We must go." Seizing the chance to flee, I rush to help him up. "Thank the Elementals, you're alive."

I don't know how badly he's hurt, but if we don't mount Buttercup and flee, there's no escape. River slowly mounts, and I quickly settle in front, taking Buttercup's reins. I've watched River handle him and hope I can manage. We need to get out. I've got to be able to do this.

"Hang on!" I shout digging my heels into Buttercup's sides to make him sprint. River wraps his hands around my waist, resting his weight against me. I push Buttercup to his fastest pace across the rolling meadows. We need to get back into the forest. We must put as much distance as possible between us and the Dark Knights.

Although terrified, it's up to me to protect us. River is weakened, and I need to keep us moving forward. We ride for hours, and my legs burn from the effort, but I keep pushing. I don't know if this chase will ever end. I want to cry over the year of peace I had—and that now it's over.

When we reach The Flowering Wood, relief floods me. It's easier to hide here and the further we go into the woods, the safer we'll be. I wish we'd find a town or village for refuge, but all that awaits is the Temple of Gaia. We're in her home woods—the residence of the Elemental.

The Flowering Wood takes my breath away. An expansive forest teeming with diverse foliage and fauna. Flowers scatter the dirt path and adorn the towering trees above. A bouquet of fragrances hit my senses as I slow our pace. Now that we're deeper into the woods, I hope we've put enough distance between us and the Dark Knights.

Various flowers bloom around us. Their bright colors delight my weary eyes. Whites, yellows, and pinks scatter around. It's peaceful and beautiful, especially after what we have just gone through.

As the sun sets, I stop Buttercup and dismount. I nearly collapse as my feet hit the ground. My legs are weak and numb, my body physically exhausted from earlier. River slides off the horse and joins me by my side as my ass hits the ground.

"You alright?" I finally ask, scanning his body to see where he's hurt. "How bad is it?"

"I'm fine," he says, though I doubt it's true. "Just tired. I tried to enter that orb to get you, but it was some sort of sleep magic. The moment I touched it, I passed out."

River's eyes lock into mine as I catch my breath from the exertion of the long ride. He stays silent, a goofy look on his face. After a beat too long, I snap, "What?"

"Your power…"

My brows furrow. "*What about it?*"

"When you screamed," he explains, "the light that came from the vibrations… that's your power."

I shake my head and stand. "I don't know what you mean."

I turn to leave, but he grabs my arm.

"Yes, you do." His voice is gentle this time. "Talk to me."

"There's nothing to talk about!" I snarl. "I don't know how to control it or use it. I can't even explain what it was." Frustration overwhelms me, "and now that I have used it, the Dark King can track me again. He's already sending waves of soldiers after me. That Draegan Grimsbane guy was going to deliver me to him. We have to reach the Temple of Gaia and fast, otherwise, I've a feeling I'll be seeing the King much sooner than I want."

River's shoulders slump. "Let's rest briefly and then continue. It's not safe to stay in one place for too long. I'll hold the reins while you sleep."

I open my mouth to protest, but River lifts a finger and tuts. "No buts. I'll be fine. Let's drink some water, eat something, and let poor Buttercup rest for a moment. We'll move again in half an hour, okay?"

"Fine." I agree reluctantly. River's right, we can't stay here to sleep, even though I desperately want to. We can't waste the time we fought so hard for. I don't know what my power did to the General and his Gaian Forsaken, but they didn't follow, so maybe they're no longer a threat.

The realization I killed people today finally hits me. I start to tremble. During my time on the run, I'd avoided killing people. Today, that changed.

River is suddenly beside me before I even notice. "You alright?"

My chest heaves, heart thundering. "I killed people today." My voice is so small, almost inaudible.

"Shit." River huffs, then wraps his muscular arms around me, holding me steady. "It's okay. They tried to hurt us. It was self-defense, Mya." I nod and take a few deep breaths. River doesn't let go. He simply holds me, grounding me. "Don't get in your head about it, okay? It's alright. It's all going to be okay."

I don't know how long we stand there, but when River's sure I'm okay, he lets go. He heads to Buttercup, grabs a small pouch, and hands me some dried meat. Hesitant, I take a few jerky sticks even though my appetite is gone.

My mind wanders to our destination. I'm uncertain about what awaits at the Temple of Gaia. Still, I look forward to the solace that waits for us.

My body aches as the adrenaline fades. I want to sleep and let myself rest, but River's right. We don't know how far behind the next wave of Dark Knights is. We sit in silence, drinking water and resting. Soon, we'll continue to the Temple of Gaia, and I pray we get there before anything else finds us.

Chapter 10

Voras

A cold silence fills the throne room. I sit on the black gilded seat on a raised dais. The chamber is empty as I absentmindedly trace my jawline with my forefinger in thought. There's been no word of the Starlight Princess—the celestial wielder—and my impatience grows. Despite that she's re-emerged into Ulnisi's reach, I'm no closer to capturing her. The seer's visions are useless, and my Dark Knights keep failing me.

I need Myalis Lucernas—the so-called Lastborn, heir of Myrea—to solidify my rule. If the Lastborn prophecy comes true, she'll destroy me, and I can't allow that. The shadow of the prophecy looms; I aim to control it. After generations of rule, I refuse to be the Dark King who falls. Still, the weight of potential collapse presses on my shoulders—burdening me.

Keeping peace in the world of Elemi hasn't come easily. The Dark Kings before me ruled with iron fists and vicious laws—traits I admire. My father ruled with bloodshed and terror, and I've continued his cruelty as a ruler. Yet, none of the previous Dark Kings had to contend with a prophecy, which I envy.

I fought my way to this throne, killing my own brothers after my father died. I live with it every day, but that's the price of being the Dark King. It was bloody, brutal—but I never cowered. When the battle ended, my powers grew—solidifying my sovereignty and reign. It was a sign of approval from the great Elemental, Tazra, mother of darkness.

I'm a direct descendant of Tazra—the chosen heir. My duty is not only to continue the dark reign, but to prolong the lineage. Yet, I find that part difficult. Killing my own kin for the crown scarred me more than I care to admit. So, when my advisers present "suitable brides," I am wary. My counselors urge me to marry and produce a strong, worthy heir to succeed me. I groan whenever the subject arises. That shouldn't be for a long time, so I push it aside.

When I heard of the prophecy and existence of the Starlight Princess, fear crept in for the first time. I wondered what would become of me. I worried the Lastborn could destroy me and the darkness—just as foretold. But everything shifted when I discovered her identity. Myalis Lucernas—Princess of Starlight, the reincarnation of Myrea's powers. A new idea struck. A way to bend the prophecy in my favor. I will claim her. She'll be a worthy queen, helping me fulfill my duties as the ruler of Elemi. With our powers combined, our rule will be unbreakable. Together, we'll produce an immensely powerful heir, one ready to take the throne when the time comes. Yes. It will all go according to my plan.

The massive iron doors to my throne room swing open, and one of my senior guards walks in alone. Clad in the black leather armor of the Dark Knights, he approaches the dais and bows.

"My King, General Grimsbane has returned," he announces, voice flat. He waits silently for my response.

"Well, show him in." I reply, my voice calm. The soldier shifts uncomfortably. I raise a brow reading his hesitation. "Must I repeat myself?" I tilt my head, studying him. He's middle-aged, brown hair streaked with gray. Dennen is his name. His brow furrows and I see beads of nervous sweat forming on his large, wrinkled forehead.

"Of course not, my King, it's just... the General is unwell. Something happened to him and his men."

My curiosity is piqued as I rise from my onyx throne, studded with diamonds and rubies. "Bring him in." I hiss through gritted teeth. The guard gulps and nods.

I'm growing tired of this—so many incompetents in my service. Dennen disappears behind the throne room doors, returning with a group of Dark Knights carrying General Grimsbane in—more like, dragging him.

One of my most trusted generals lolls his head against his chest as two Dark Knights support him, dragging him forward. Puzzled, I step off the dais and approach as they reach the base of the steps. The men clumsily bow while holding him, but I cock my head, studying the limp Grimsbane.

"General Grimsbane." I say, testing if he's conscious. "What happened? Any news of the girl?"

He's silent but gives a weak shake of his head. I can't tell if it means yes or no. Frustration grows within me at this sorry sight. I take a deep breath, casting my gaze at the men holding him.

"Does anyone know what happened to the General?" I ask, meeting each man's eyes in turn. An eerie silence falls over the throne room; no one answers. My shadows lengthen behind me, the darkness taking over. They tend to fluctuate with my mood. I clear my throat, perk up a brow, and lace my fingers together, waiting for some sort of answer.

"They found the girl." One of them speaks up. I turn to face him—a young soldier, probably early twenties, brown eyes partly hidden by blonde hair. I approach slowly, halting when I tower over him.

"And?" I prompt, waiting.

The young solider takes a breath. "Apparently, she did this to him."

The news surprises me, but I keep my face composed. I can't let my subjects see me caught off-guard. Last I'd heard, Myalis Lucernas hadn't used any magic in recent encounters. Grimsbane gave me little details on their last encounter, only that he was in pursuit.

"I see." I step back toward the motionless, useless man before me. "Perhaps, I should see for myself what happened."

I raise my hand inches from his face and let the darkness within to penetrate his mind. Dark tendrils come out from my palm, snaking into General Grimsbane's ears.

I close my eyes, diving into the General's memories. Flickers of his past surface, and his most recent memories are the sharpest.

I see her. The Starlight Princess—Myalis Lucernas. She's grown; quite a beauty now. Her coppery eyes, flecked of gold, blaze with anger as she fights Grimsbane and his men. Her bow-shaped lips press into a thin line as she evades them. Wisps of her chestnut hair fly across her face as she screams at a Dark Knights. The sound immediately deafens the General. As she continues, light pours from her, her screams wield a power I've never seen. The Dark Knight who gripped her collapses, his ears and eyes bleeding. Soon after, General Grimsbane succumbs to a similar fate.

Delving deeper, I find another familiar face with Myalis in Grimsbane's mind. A man who's long been a thorn in my side. Though he vanished for a while, the name comes easily. River Dune. I remember my father having his parents killed years ago for threatening the crown. They'd grown so renowned in Gaia's Keep that they nearly raised an army to overthrow my father. He couldn't allow that. Therefore, he made an example of them.

At the time, no one knew they had a child. Supposedly, he wasn't home when the knights arrived. It wasn't until years later that I learned my father had left a trace of the bloodline. At least, that's what River Dune told me. Since then, he's done everything to weaken me. He attacks my outposts, kills my soldiers, and burns villages, mostly around Sinsport, on the border of the Netherfields and Gaia's Keep.

River seems to have become a rogue warrior in the recent years. Muscular and tall, he'd be a valuable asset to my army. Especially with his Gaia-given power. Maybe I can persuade him to my cause someday soon.

I withdraw from Grimsbane's mind, content with what I've seen, and turn to my subjects standing in line. Knowing River and Myalis work together, I sneer. Myalis is beginning to use her celestial powers. I'd hoped to intervene before this. Surely, River is encouraging her. Or at least teaching her to wield them.

"Get him out of my sight." I seethe, waving away the men with Grimsbane. "Bring me Ulnisi." Another soldier bows, and I stalk back to my throne to sit on it.

Once more, I rub my forefinger on my chin in thought. Now that I know Myalis isn't working alone, I need a new strategy. If my men fail, I must retrieve her myself. I rarely leave Night Spire now. I haven't needed to. My Dark Knights have handled tasks, but she's too important to leave to them. The Starlight Princess *will* be mine. I only need to retrieve her.

Moments later, two guards bring Ulnisi into the throne room. The beautiful seer is chained, led before me. Silvery white hair falls over her face, hiding the whites of her blind eyes. She seems kissed by moonlight; her skin pale and alabaster. Ulnisi's slender form is draped in shimmery, silver, sheer gauze, gathered at her waist. Much of her body is on display—open to all eyes, though members of my court know better than to stare at my pet.

I remember when Ulnisi was gifted to me as a coronation present from a high lord. He found her in a brothel, recognized her talents, bought her from that wretched place, and thought she'd be useful to the crown. She was young then, but has since matured into an invaluable asset. Ulnisi's gifts alert me to any disturbances and foretells what's coming. Though she's my pet, to do with as I please, I do try to treat her well.

"My Lord." She bows at the dais, her velvety, alto voice, a caress to my ears.

"Ulnisi," I reply. "I'm in need of your services. You see, I need to know where the Starlight Princess is heading. It seems General Grimsbane failed in his duty and I must retrieve her myself."

"Of course, My Lord." She nods and rises. "Allow me to sit; I shall do as you ask."

My lips curl. "As obedient as ever, Ulnisi. I'll allow you your preparations." I watch her sit on the dark gray stone floor, palms turned upwards resting on her legs. Even blind, she closes her eyes, and breathes deeply. My eyes drift to her supple bosom, then away to her sensuous mouth moving in silent whisper.

Ulnisi's eyes snap open, glowing white as she enters a trance. I'm no longer unsettled by her seer trance, but I recall how startled I was when I saw it the first time. I watch her trance last several minutes before her body shivers and she returns.

I wait. She recovers, then stands and bows. "My Lord, the Lastborn heads to the Temple of Gaia. But be warned, should you follow her there, you shall fail."

I scowl. "What do you mean? I won't capture her there?"

"Wait until she crosses into the land of sand. There you'll find what you desire." I hate her riddles.

I repeat her words, slowly understanding. "Myalis is traveling. I can capture her somewhere along the way?" Ulnisi nods at my question. I feel relief at the thought of having the Starlight Princess within my grasp. I can be patient.

"You have pleased me, Ulnisi," I praise her. "That will be all."

My guards escort her away as my mind dives into planning. Knowing Myalis's path, I can deploy my spies across the kingdom. If I can capture her sooner, I will. But for now, I'll wait anxiously for her to fall into my trap.

Chapter 11

Myalis

For two exhausting days, we ride on Buttercup's back in tense silence, still unsure if the Dark Knights are pursuing us. Fatigue consumes me to the point that I can barely stay on his back. Since I'm not familiar with the dense forest, I'm not sure how much longer it'll be before we arrive at the temple. River leads the way being familiar with the path, and I obey his command without a word, too tired to fight or argue or question.

"Let's rest here for the night." River mutters as he stops Buttercup. "I don't think the Dark Knights are following. Tomorrow we'll reach Everwillow and then the Temple of Gaia."

Dark circles surround River's usual bright blue eyes, now looking dull with exhaustion. I don't know how much he'd slept in the last two days. I know his amount was lesser than mine, and I could only get a few hours. River slides off the horse, patting him on his muzzle.

The past couple of days, we've come across little streams here and there to refill our water supply and give Buttercup some rest. But even Buttercup needs some time to recover. As I slide from the saddle, my legs give out and I crumple to the floor. Buttercup snorts and lowers his head, fleeing free to feed on the low grass.

River kneels at my side. "You alright?"

I nod, panting. "Yeah, just tired. My legs shake from sitting on the horse for two days straight."

River's dry lips curl in a hiss. "Same." He stands, fetches our supplies from Buttercup, then returns to where I was sinking beside me. He places his leather rucksack into his lap and opens it, pulling his canteen out to quench our thirst and the familiar pouch of jerky. He eases the cork free and drinks greedily from the canteen. I stare as he licks the drops of water from his lips, heat coiling low in my belly at the sight.

I scoff at myself. I'm so delirious, my malnourished, exhausted body is turning to sexual urges. Ugh, what the fuck's wrong with me? My priorities are completely messed up. River quirks a brow as he studies me.

"What's wrong?"

I quickly shake my head. "Nothing, just trying to figure out how to sit on my ass without hurting." I remain on my knees, my palms still pressed to the ground. I haven't moved since I fell here.

River chuckles, some of the light returning to his eyes as he looks at me. "Want me to set up your bedroll? You can lie down and rest till morning."

A smile sprawls across my lips as I peek at him. "Thank you, but you've done enough these past days. I can at least pick up my lazy self and set up my own bed."

Groaning, I haul myself up and grab my sack. Unbuttoning it, I open the flap and pull out the thin blanket that serves as my bedroll. I'm grateful the past few days have been warm so we won't freeze out here tonight. Especially since a large fire would easily draw unwanted attention.

I spread the woolen blanket, and I sit on it mimicking River's way. I take a sip from my canteen and nibble on some nuts. It's not much, but it's enough to fulfill my needs. Well... most of them anyway.

I avoid River's burning gaze, though I feel it on me. Why am I so sexually drawn to this man? I don't know.

Yes, he's incredibly good-looking—carved by the Elemental gods themselves, and all, but I haven't known him for that long. The past few days since my birthday have been a whirlwind, I don't really know what I've gotten myself into.

I agreed to journey with a stranger to the Temple of Gaia—for what? For the priestesses to tell me I'm magically gifted? To let them define which Elemental I descend from? To train my powers? Is this *really* what I need? Especially while the Dark King hunts me. My entire life, I've avoided him, yet now it feels like I'm walking right into his wrath.

I don't know if it's the right thing. But now that I've chosen this path, and my reprieve is over, I feel it's the only way. I trust River. Despite his flaws, the man seems decent enough.

My mind drifts to the Sweet Apple tavern, to the moment when he kissed the other woman. How deeply that hurt me. His drunkenness, ignorance, and his stupid, manly aloofness. I shrug it off. How long can I hold a grudge, especially since River and I are... what? Nothing to each other, really. Just travelers sharing the same path. And despite our recent transgressions, I can't fool myself into thinking it'll ever be something more. No matter how real it felt in those brief intimate moments.

Munching on the last of my nuts, I take another sip of water. Exhaustion overtakes me, and I lie down on my bedroll.

"Well, goodnight." I don't meet River's eyes. I hear him inhale as if to speak, then pause.

"Goodnight," his husky voice flitters in my ear.

I wake to the sounds of birds chirping and the scent of fresh morning mist on the earth. I squint against the soft light. The sun barely peeks through dense green leaves overhead. Coming to my senses, I search for River, but he's nowhere in sight. Panic rushes through me. I sit up, my body still aching from riding Buttercup, but I force myself to get up and look for him.

"River?" I call out into the dewy foliage. Buttercup has wandered nearby, doing upright. "River." I call again, urgency sharpening my tone.

My breath catches. *Oh, Gaia above, where could he be?* I steady myself, taking in my surroundings. Buttercup's here, so I'm not worried that he left me. I redirect my thoughts. If there was a nighttime fight with the Dark Knights, surely, I'd have heard? I look around for his rucksack, but find nothing.

My huntress skills kick in; I observe the ground closely. The disturbed morning dew reveals a set of boot prints heading into a path between two large flowering bushes. Tension in my shoulders eases. Maybe he's gone hunting. Or maybe he had to relieve himself. I shake off my worries and roll up my bedroll up to pack it away.

Moments later, River rustles through the trees, a rabbit in hand. His dark hair falls over his eyes as he silently approaches. He rubs the scruff on his chiseled jaw before our eyes meet. Gaia above, he's gorgeous.

"Good morning." I say, my face flushing.

"Morning," he replies with a small smile. Silence grows as I shift on my feet.

"You had me worried." I admit.

His thick brow arches. "Did I? Why's that?" He teases.

I bite my lips and shrug. "I thought something might've happened…"

His grin broadens, playful. "Nah, I'm tougher than that. But I did find us some breakfast. If you want, you can start a small fire, and I'll clean it for cooking."

"Sure." I nod, wandering off to look for sticks that would do. It doesn't take long to gather what I need. We don't need a long-lasting fire, just enough to cook the meat. Back at camp, I set about lighting it.

River readies the rabbit, skewering it over the fire I started to cook. "So," I break the silence, twisting my tangled hair into a messy braid. "Did you manage to get any sleep?"

"I did." He replies calmly. "Enough, anyway. You?"

"Me too. I slept like a rock." I scoff.

"Good, because another long day awaits us. We should reach the temple by nightfall." River says, pulling the rabbit from the flames and picking the meat apart. He offers me a piece, and I instantly put it in my mouth. Freshly cooked meat sends a pleasurable shiver down my spine. The scent, the flavor, the juices slither down my throat bringing contentment. My stomach growls, demanding more. River and I devour the meat, practically sucking the bones clean. The nutrients restore me. When finished, we snuff the fire and continue to the temple.

Buttercup doesn't when we mount on his back, but my body aches from the stiff posture. I know a long ride lies ahead, but I'm not sure if my body will endure. I lean into River—against his strong chest and try to relax. He stiffens but remains silent.

Watching River navigate the Flowering Woods fascinates me. Perhaps his attunement comes from being a Gaian Forsaken. We never stray or get lost amidst the trees that all look the same. River leads expertly, as if these woods are a familiar territory. Perhaps they are, having been raised at the Gaian Temple.

There is a reason that the Flowering Woods are seldom invaded. Everwillow, the capital of Gaia's Keep and home to the Temple of Gaia, is so well hidden that only a few people can ever find it. It's also protected by Gaian Forsaken warriors. Being one of Elemi's oldest cities, no one wants to take a chance on such a sacred place. Which makes me wonder how the Dark Knights breached River's home when he was a child. Thinking of the past sickens me. I know too well the horror of losing a parent.

As we proceed, I absorb the woods' beauty. Wisteria flowers flutter above, scattered through the trees. Their pleasant, light scent invades my senses. I haven't ever been this deep into the Flowering Woods and feel humbled to visit the ancient city. Maybe after my journey and once I learn to use my magic, I'll find a home here. Everything I need is within this vast forest.

Maybe River and I can build a cool treehouse here, like the one he has back in Sunhollow, despite my fear of heights. I shake my head, refusing to get lost in daydreams. They're too dangerous. Too full of hope. Especially since I don't know what lies ahead.

Chapter 12

River

We reach the outer gates of Everwillow, the capital city of Gaia's Keep, just as the sun dips lower in the sky. Tall, gray-brown stone walls rise high, fortifying the forest civilization that shelters the Temple of Gaia. As the gates open, two Gaian Forsaken guards come into view, stationed at their post.

"State your business." The guard's green eyes rove over us, sharp and assessing.

"I'm River Dune, and this is Mya. We're here to see the Head Priestess Elera at the temple."

The man's skeptical gaze falls over me as he rubs his hand along his jaw. "Dune?" He recognizes the name, as he should.

"Indeed." I reply coolly, my patience thinning with fatigue. "Head Priestess Elera and I go back a long way. I'm also Gaian Forsaken. Do you need me to demonstrate?"

I summon a crackle of thunder in the distance. Both guards glance skyward before exchanging looks with each other.

"There's no need for that." The other guard, older with shaggy blond hair and weary, brown eyes, interrupts quickly. Wrinkles crease around the eyes. "I remember your parents well. You're always welcome, River Dune."

I nod and nudge Buttercup forward. Once inside the city, I let out a sigh of relief. We'd be safe here—at least for a while.

"I didn't think they'd let us in." Mya says suddenly. She's been quiet the past couple of days. And although I steal glimpses—sometimes catching her returning the gaze—I can't help but wonder what's on her mind. Is she nervous over our circumstances, or simply tired like I am?

I wanted to bring her to the temple, but now that we're so close, anxiety gnaws at me. First, it could confirm what I've long hoped, that she is indeed the Lastborn, the prophecy that I've been waiting for. Second, I'm not sure how she'd take the news, especially since she's been so suspicious of coming here.

Over the past few days, I've let the awkwardness between us linger. Still, I can't help those dirty little thoughts that creep in my mind—our bodies in the river, flushed together, skin on skin. The feel of her in my grip had electrified every sense in me. I crave more. I crave everything. But first, we have to survive this hurdle.

She has to choose to help me defeat Finis Voras. I can't force her. Without her, the reign of Dark Kings will never end. If she chooses to embrace her destiny, then maybe—just maybe—we can build a future together. I can almost see it. Our happily ever after. Mya is everything I could hope for in a woman. Strong, brave, resilient. Her beauty is unlike anything I've ever seen, and I love the hint of wildness in her. The thought makes me stifle a chuckle as we continue deeper into the city.

Having her seated in front of me for the entire journey has driven me insane. My body wants to take her, and it's taken every ounce of self-control I've got to keep myself in check. I try to shake it off, think of anything else, but my dick certainly won't let me forget the press of her back against me. The scent of her hair brushes my senses every time the wind blows. I only hope Mya hasn't noticed how easily she unravels me.

"It's good to know my family name still carries some weight around here." I finally say realizing I've been lost in my head for far too long.

Everwillow is unique. Rustic, yet seamlessly embedded within the surrounding forest. Homes rise within the trees, cascading overhead, similar to my treehouse in Sunhollow. These homes, however, are much more elaborate and beautiful in their craftsmanship. Rope bridges link home to home as though spun from the branches themselves, sprawling from one tree to another in arcs. It's been so long that I'd been here that I'd almost forgotten its wonder.

While homes interweave into the sprawling branches high above, the dirt path below—the main street in Everwillow—thrives with shops. The wide pathway bustles with Gaian citizens going about their day, just like any other. Bakeries, flower shops, clothing establishments, blacksmiths, tanners, butchers—anything you could dream of is a shop along the road.

"It's incredible." Mya whispers looking around. It takes me a moment to realize she's likely never been to such a populated city. From what she's told me, she's spent her life on the run, hidden in the wild, living simply and away from civilization. Though I myself made Sunhollow my home and lived in isolation, I'd at least traveled to far off regions of Elemi and seen grand cities before.

"This is where I grew up," I admit, nostalgia hitting me. A man with dark skin pulls his cart piled high with vibrant vegetables. The crowd's beginning to disperse as the sun sinks lower. "When I was a boy, I'd sneak out of the Temple and roam Everwillow and the surrounding forests. I kept the head priestess on her toes."

Mya chuckles softly. "Ever the trouble, even then."

My lips curl at her comment. "Even then."

At the end of Everwillow's main dirt road, similar paths branch into the forest's shadow. We take the left trail. The trees grow denser as the path narrows. The Temple of Gaia is close.

The sun descends, turning the sky above us gold in hue, and the green foliage radiates its shine. The forest falls quiet, and I know we're near the sacred Temple of Gaia. Anticipation stirs as I return to the place where I was raised. I haven't been here in years, and truthfully, I was nervous about bringing Mya. When I left, it wasn't on the best terms.

But now I need Elera to confirm whether Mya is really the Lastborn. Only a priest or priestess of the highest order can know—and the only one I trust is Elera.

Elera never supported my ambition to destroy the Dark King. In fact, she openly frowned upon it. I can't say I blame her. As the one responsible for peace in Gaia's Keep, she's as close to a ruler as you can get in our twisted dictatorship. If the Dark King ever wishes to impose a law, he comes here to the Temple, and instructs the head priestess to enact it. To Elera, all my talk of overthrowing him was pure blasphemy, something she refused to even hear.

When I left, I think she was relieved to get rid of me and my ideals. I scoured the world searching for any weakness Finis Voras could possess. After years of fruitless searching, I found the Oracle Athenaeum, an ancient library hidden deep within the Red Wastes and guarded by jebbucha—massive sand worms that protect the land. Vicious creatures, their bodies stretching over fifty feet, with maws lined by thousands of razor-sharp teeth. Even now, I wonder how I managed to escape their grasp. But beneath the sand, in this ancient library, I found a tome that spoke of the prophecy of the Lastborn—the only force destined to destroy the darkness.

I remember the excitement I felt bringing this news back to Elera, only for her to tell me to leave it be. She urged me to let go of my vendetta against the Dark King and move on with my life. Anger got the best of me and instead of heeding her advice, I left determined to chase this prophecy. It took years before I finally admitted Elera might have been right—that the prophecy wasn't real, or at least not meant to come true in my lifetime.

That's when the depression set in. The hopelessness. The endless drinking, and the smoking of wrathhog. I stumbled into Sunhollow, The Dirty Fox, and that's where I stopped. I settled down. Built a life for myself. Did menial tasks around the village for anyone who needed it. Mostly, I paid Badger's bar tab with the beer and cider I downed. My life felt purposeless, until I saw Mya. And now, bringing her here, back to the temple, nerves twists within me.

A clearing opens before us and in its center stands the ancient Temple of Gaia. Built of cream-colored stones, worn with age and moss. Towering trees ring the sacred space, their vines winding up the temple walls. Butterflies drift lazily around us, landing on wildflowers that bloom between the grasses. The clearing hums with a quiet peace—ethereal, calm, peaceful, like a breath of fresh air.

At the temple's entrance, I dismount Buttercup and extend a hand to help Mya down. The temple is exactly as I remember. A giant statue of Gaia stands before us, hands folded in prayer, and I can't help but lock my gaze on her. Countless times I prayed to her for strength, and now, standing here again, I feel like it's all been worth it.

The courtyard at the entrance blooms with ever-blooming flowers. In the distance, the soft trickle of the stream encircling the temple reaches my ears.

"It's breathtaking." Mya sighs, her eyes fixated at the massive structure before us. From the outside, it resembles a ruin—beautiful, foreboding, like a forgotten relic left to crumble with time. It blends into the nature surrounding us, but the inside is what's truly breathtaking.

"Come on." I nod toward the entrance. The massive wooden door is intricately carved, another homage to Gaia. The Tree of Life spreads its cascading branches across the wood, surrounded by etched creatures and beings.

The temple itself is usually closed to the public, however, people can freely roam the outer gardens of the temple in prayer. Its doors only open during Elarenai—or what we call Verdanta— the celebration of the day Gaia created Elemi. During Verdanta, the citizens of Gaia's Keep bring offerings to honor Gaia and the Tree of Life, which stands proudly at the center of the courtyard. The only other time people enter is by a persona invitation, or for a hand-fastening.

I pound my fist against the door, uncertain if anyone inside will hear me. Even though Everwillow is a peaceful place, I'm surprised that there wasn't a Forsaken keeping guard outside.

"Who goes there?" a deep male voice calls from behind the door.

"River Dune." I reply, curious if I need to elaborate. A latch scrapes open form the other side, and Mya and I share a curious glance. The heavy door creaks open just enough for a sliver of green light to catch—a pair of bright green eyes staring back at us.

"Why are you here?" his voice is even deeper now, resonating through the crack.

"We seek an audience with the Head Priestess Elera and hope for refuge." I explain calmly. The man turns and whispers to someone unseen within.

"You may enter. Wait here until you are granted permission to see the head priestess." The man swings open the door, allowing Mya and me into the temple's antechamber. Once we're inside, he closes the door behind us and stands silently, waiting. I examine him from the corner of my eye. He's not quite my height, but broad and muscular. Definitely a Gaian Forsaken warrior. A green robe is belted at his waist, and his blonde hair tied with a brown leather string atop his head. A massive dagger rests at his side, and I know better than to make him an enemy.

My gaze drifts to Mya as she shifts uncomfortably in her place, her hand toying with the end of her braid, curling dark strands around her finger. Her copper eyes scan the space, as if searching for another exit should things go poorly. I notice her biting her bottom lip, tension written all over her face.

I take in the space. It hasn't changed since I was last here. Smell of stale flowers and incense waft through the air. Two long stone hallways with windows allowing the last of the natural light to seep in, stretch at either side. Intricate gold torches, resembling vined flowers decorate the walls, glowing in readiness for nightfall. Ahead stands another set of wood doors, leading to the giant courtyard, where the ancient Tree of Life resides. Sacred and eternal, it's Gaia's symbol and where many priestesses come to pray. The courtyard is a vast garden of roses, sculpted hedges, and ponds alive with fish. I spent countless hours there in prayer. It was also my favorite place to cause mischief as a child.

Footsteps echo down the right-hand hall. A group approaches, led by a familiar face that makes me smile. As she enters the antechamber, she extends her arms toward me.

"River Dune. What a joy it is to see you again, especially after all these years. My, you've become a man." Elera's voice is motherly and kind as she eyes me up and down. "Quite roguish, too." She grins, revealing the wrinkles around her mouth.

Elera looks just as I remember, though her young face has now aged a bit over the years. Her long blonde hair, now streaked with silver, is tied up in a bun on the back of her head. She wears a cream-colored robe with a V-neckline and long cascading sleeves, adorned with a golden chain belt around her narrow waist. A dark green cape drapes her shoulders, fastened with an intricate gold clasp, matching the gold necklace around her neck. A simple gold circlet rests on her head, the mark of the head priestess.

"The pleasure is mine." I bow my head respectfully as we part from our embrace. "It has been a long time."

Elera's green eyes shift to Mya. "And who, dare I say, is this?"

Just as I'm about to speak, Mya cuts in. "Myalis Lucernas. I am River's travel companion."

The use of her full name catches me off-guard. *Myalis*. Such a beautiful name. Now, I feel stupid for never really asking much about her. A twinge of guilt floods me.

"We're hoping you'll allow us refuge. It's been a long journey." Mya explains, an uncertain smile tugging at her lips.

"I see." Elera arches a golden brow at me, suspicion flickering in her eyes. "Very well. I wish to hear all about it. Come, follow me. I'll see you to suitable rooms." She nods to a fellow priestess, who hurries off down the hall.

The cream-colored stone hallways at the temple's entrance are humble, neither extravagant nor ornate. Its true beauty lies deeper within, in the vast gardens at its heart. Elera leads us through the hallways, and I catch Mya gazing through the glassless windows into the courtyard. Even here, the smell of roses drifts in the air.

"So, tell me," Elera breaks the silence. "Where do you hail from, Myalis?"

I watch Mya's shoulders tense. She shared little about herself during our travels, and I've respected her privacy, knowing she preferred not to talk about the past. Mya's copper eyes reflect off the setting sun as she glances at me.

"I was born in Dustfall. It's a tiny village on the southeastern border of the Netherfields. Hidden away in the part of the territory known as the No Man's Land. Practically forgotten, if I'm honest." She explains.

"Do you still have family there?" Elera probes, her tone gentle.

Mya shakes her head. "No. My parents are dead, and I was an only child. As far as I know, I have no family left. Both my grandparents had already passed before my parents died and they never spoke of siblings." She pauses, as if reaching for a memory, her face growing pensive.

"Though it was years ago, I remember life in the Netherfields was hard. Dustfall is poor. Papa was the village butcher, and he taught me everything I know about hunting and cleaning animals. Mama worked as a seamstress in the village clothing shop, and she always wished that I would do more girlie things. But I always chose Papa's way instead."

A genuine smile sprawls across Mya's face, and I find myself grinning with her. It's rare and stunning, enough to steal my breath away. Her words reveal her deep love for her father, and seeing her talk about him with such fondness makes my heart swell.

Mya sighs tucking a loose strand of wavy hair behind her ear. Her gaze drifts back to the windows we pass, her full lips twitching. "When I turned thirteen, I was playing out in the fields by our home. It was nighttime and I wanted to watch the stars glitter above. I always felt a deep connection to them. I remember, it was such a perfect and clear night. I lay in the tall grasses and wildflowers, lifted my hand to the heavens, and traced the constellations above me, and like magic, the stars shifted at my motion."

She pauses, staring at her hand. Elera halts mid-step, and the other priestesses falter behind her. Elera's brow knit—her green eyes intensely focusing on Mya.

"At first, I thought that it was just a trick of the eye. That I was seeing things." Mya lets out a soft chuckle, still studying her hand. "But then when I drew it back, it was as if a universe had formed in my palm. Like, I'd pulled the stars down from the heavens. I remember staring in awe. At least... until the earth rumbled beneath me."

Elera darts toward Mya, and I instinctively step in between them.

"*River*," Elera's voice is a demand for me to step out of the way. It was how she used to chide me as a child. We stand off against each other, but only for a moment. "This is what you wanted, isn't it?" she says.

Mya lifts her wide, confused eyes to me. My chest tightens, but when I look back at Elera, I nod and step aside.

"River?" Mya whispers, her voice small. Elera steps in front of her, lifting her palm with gentleness.

"This won't hurt, child." Elera's voice is pacifying as she presses her palm to Mya's forehead and closes her eyes. I can see Mya's body tense, torn between flight and frozen fear. She stands motionless, as Elera's hand glows, light spilling from her palm and flowing outward, weaving between the two of them.

In the narrow hallway, the two women blaze into blinding light. I raise an arm against it, squinting, straining to see what Elera is doing to her. The head priestess's green eyes roll back, glowing gold, her mouth agape as she presses her palm against Mya's forehead.

"River!" Mya's panicked voice cuts through the radiance as she remains frozen in place. I ache to help her, but I can't. This is Elera's power as the head priestess— only she can determine if Mya is truly the Lastborn. Mya pleads, but I force myself to stay rooted.

Then as suddenly as it came, the blinding glow dissipates before us. Elera steadies herself, her eyes locking into mine the moment she returns to herself. "You cannot stay here."

Chapter 13

River

My gaze narrows on the head priestess. Her face is etched with worry, green eyes blazing with fear, lips pressed in a thin line.

"What? Is it because of me? Did I do something wrong?" Mya's voice quivers with layered emotion as Elera and I lock eyes.

"River knows why." Elera says, her words striking like a knife. There's my proof.

Mya shakes her head, her brows crease in confusion.

"I don't understand. What does she mean, River?" Mya's gaze flicks between us. My jaw clenches, my fists curling tight.

Elera's brows lift in sudden surprise. "She doesn't know?"

My stomach drops. I never told Mya about the prophecy—and this isn't how I planned to tell her. An uncomfortable silence falls between us. From the corner of my eye, I see Mya shaking her head, puzzled.

"River, what is going on? What don't I know?" When I fail to answer, she turns her attention back to Elera. "*Please*, we have been traveling for days. River said we'd find refuge here."

Only then does Elera truly look at Mya, her gaze sharp and searching as she studies the Celestial Forsaken. "I'm sorry. But I cannot grant you refuge. He was mistaken." The head priestess shakes her head, guilt shadowing her eyes.

"*Elera*," I growl in warning.

"Why not?" Mya's voice rises, sharp with frustration. "What aren't you telling me?" Her copper stare pierces through me, cementing me in place.

"The Dark King hunts you," Elera says firmly. "I will not draw his wrath upon this temple. They have searched for you for centuries, and I will not risk the lives of my priestesses nor the others within this temple. Not even for you, River. I told you long ago: I do not support this vendetta that you carry."

Elera, Mya and I stand in the center of the hallway, not even past the temple's threshold. We stare one another down, waiting for the other to speak.

"*River.*" Mya's stern voice snaps my attention to her. "What is she talking about?"

I exhale, shoulders heavy, knowing it's time to tell her the truth. Hesitant, I finally meet her eyes. "You know the story of the Elementals, our great creators?"

"Yes, of course. Everyone does," Mya retorts impatiently.

"Well, the story you know is wrong." My words hang heavy. Mya's eyes widen, as if she misheard. I shift on my feet, glance at Elera, and swallow before continuing.

"Thousands of years ago, the Elementals lived peacefully in the celestial plain." I begin. "Prometheus, God of Fire. Hydros, God of Water. Gaia, Goddess of all things bountiful and earthly. Tazra, Goddess of Darkness. But there was another, the one erased from our history. Myrea, Goddess of Order." Mya freezes, lips parting in shock.

"What?" she breathes, looking between Elera and me. Elera's gaze falls to the floor, her mouth set in a hard line as I continue.

"Together, the five Elementals lived in harmony, until one day, Prometheus grew bored. He longed for something new—an entertainment. So, he created mankind, along with the sun and fire to provide for them. Gaia created Elemi for mankind to reside in. She created vegetation and foliage for them to eat. Hydros created the lakes, oceans, and streams for them to thrive. Tazra created night so they may rest and rejuvenate. And Myrea created stars to give them hopes and dreams. It was a beautiful world, and the Elementals delighted watching the humans live and grow. Yet, as the years passed, Prometheus grew jealous and wished to walk among them. He wanted to live among them and so he did."

I pause, glancing at Mya. She listens intently, her anxious eyes fixed on me. Elera side-eyes me, and then looks to the other priestesses gathered around her.

I rake my fingers through my hair and draw another breath. "Prometheus enjoyed having a human form. He flaunted his powers of fire and metal-wielding to anyone who would watch and of course was recognized as a God of Elemi. Tazra and Hydros were next to join the humans, for they too wanted glory and recognition. It took a while, but in order to maintain peace, Gaia and Myrea joined them eventually.

Soon, the Elementals began having affairs with the humans and produced offspring. While most offspring were human, some were born with extraordinary powers. Half-human, half-God. Once discovered, this pleased the Elementals and the offsprings were thus named Forsaken Elementals."

Mya and I meet each other's gaze. The air in the hallway seems to still. "Years passed and although Forsaken children lived extended lives to that of humans, they were not immortal like the true Elementals. When this truth spread, jealousy festered. Many turned against them, hunting the Forsaken. Battles and wars began to rage upon the once-peaceful Elemi. Soon, territories were divided, temples built to help protect the deities, such as this one. But there were too many humans and not enough Forsaken.

Then, Tazra began to take things into her own hands. She deemed that with her powers, she could control mankind and that they, she and her Forsaken children, should rule Elemi by force. Hydros agreed with Tazra, that perhaps their children should establish order. Prometheus and Gaia started to believe that they should leave Elemi altogether and leave mankind to their own devices, but Tazra couldn't imagine abandoning her children. Myrea, being the tiebreaker for the Elementals, ruled that the Elementals should return back to the cosmos, and allow this world to settle things themselves." A silence falls between us as I pause, trying to gauge Mya's reaction.

"So... what happened?" Mya's voice fades to a whisper, and I barely hear the question. She bites her bottom lip, wringing her hands in front of her.

"War," I state matter-of-factly. "Tazra declared war. She wanted to rule Elemi and she selected her best child to help her do so. She refused to follow Myrea's command and deemed that she wouldn't bow down to her whim. Myrea, however, only wished for peace. She did not want a war with her kin. But Tazra didn't care.

For two centuries, they fought. There was endless bloodshed, and one day, Tazra managed to kill Myrea. No one knows how. I wasn't able to find any scriptures explaining what happened. I did find that soon after Myrea's murder, Tazra hunted and killed all Myrea's Forsaken children as well so that there would no longer be any indication of Myrea in the world. Tazra established her power and the right for her Forsaken to rule Elemi. She put the Dark King in power, selecting her strongest and most powerful child to rule. She then forced the other Elementals to obey her command or suffer the same consequences as Myrea. They bowed before her and began to draw up territories."

Elera clears her throat as she looks at me solemnly. Mya's face echoes Elera's, processing everything I said. I knew it was a lot to take in. I pause shifting on my feet again.

I'd forgotten just how tired I was, the exhaustion sinking into every part of me. I'd hoped Elera might be more accommodating when we arrived, that we wouldn't be thrust straight into this. I would have preferred to sit in the courtyard with tea and food, watching the sunset. I wanted to ease gently into the story of who Mya is. Instead, here I was, spilling it all. Exhausted. Hungry. Aching. And Mya staring at me with a look I can't quite figure out.

Snapping out of my thoughts, I force myself to continue. "Tazra told the other Elementals their Forsaken would remain safe if they stayed in their territories and allowed her and her new Dark King rule. Prometheus, Hydros, and Gaia agreed, not because they believed her, but because now they feared her given that she destroyed Myrea. Thus, the new world order of Elemi began.

Hundreds of years later, the Elementals all but left this world, unexplained. Back to the cosmos, like Myrea had originally wanted. However, now, there was no longer any knowledge of the forgotten Elemental. Mankind was left to their own, with the Tazra heir as their king. Once the Elementals left and the people began living on their own, the memories began to fade altogether. Elementals' presence became myth and legend, yet the Forsaken remained. Some Forsaken found "mates"—or properly known as astrelles—with other Forsaken which continued the lineage of the gods' powers, but Forsaken Elementals eventually became less powerful over time and humans became the dominant species. Everything continued exactly as Tazra had desired, until one day, a seer announced a prophecy."

I gulp, nervous to relay this part. Mya's intense gaze catches mine and her brow creases deeper than before. *"There will come a day, when starlight returns, a forgotten one whose power shall overcome. Darkness shall fall, the Lastborn shall remain."* I recite the prophecy exactly as I'd read it years ago. I pause, waiting for Mya's reaction, her chest rising unsteadily. Elera and I exchange glances.

Realization hits her, and Mya's chest rises and falls in uneven breaths. "What are you saying?" she whispers, hand clutching her chest, as if to steady its frantic rhythm.

"The Lastborn is a being of celestial power, the reincarnation of Myrea's essence." I reply, hesitant.

"No." Mya shakes her head, her breath quick and shallow.

"It's you, Mya," I confess softly. "Elera just confirmed it. It's you we've been waiting for."

"*No.*" She repeats, stepping back from me.

"*You* are destined to defeat the Dark King. *You* are the Lastborn."

Mya's copper eyes lock with mine, glassy with unshed tears. Her face twists in confusion, her lip trembling. "You lied to me."

My stomach fell at her words. "What? No... I didn't lie—"

"You *lied* to me!" She yells. "You said we need to come to the temple to understand my powers. You said I'd be safe here, that I'd finally have refuge."

"That's all true." I say calmly, trying to hold myself steady.

"*It's not.* She already said I can't stay because of what I am." Mya's voice sharpens with disgust. "You don't care about me. You just want to use me. Use me for your own vendetta against the King." Her step falters as she clutches her head. "I'm such a fool… a goddamned fool!"

Mya bolts, sprinting down the hall toward the atrium. She throws herself at the massive door, pulling hard.

"Mya, wait!" I yell, but she flees out the door. I lunge after her, but Elera's hand clamps around my arm.

"*This is not how I wanted her to know*!" I shout at my former caregiver. Elera's grip loosens, and her eyes soften.

"I'm sorry, River. I can't risk my people. But she has a right to know what you've been trying to do. If you really cared for her, you would've told her sooner." Elera's tone is gentle, but it sets my blood boiling.

"You have no idea how much I care for her. It's none of your business, Elera. I want to protect her. I have to find her before she's caught." I wrench free from her grasp and dart toward the door.

"River—" she calls, and I pause, turning back toward the head priestess.

"Should you find her, bring her back here. You may stay a few nights, enough to rest. I see how exhausted you are. Unfortunately, I can offer no longer than that." I study Elera's thin, guilt-ridden face—her eyes full of genuine concern. My shoulders sag as I stare at the woman who raised me like a mother. I nod once, then push through the doors in search of Mya.

Chapter 14

Myalis

My heart pounds against my chest as I struggle for breath. I fled the safety of the Temple of Gaia. I couldn't stand another moment inside, not when everyone seemed to gawk at me as if I were nothing but a spectacle.

Night has fallen, and the once-enchanting green forests around the temple now feels ominous. I don't care. I keep rushing through the dark woods, desperate to put as much distance as possible between myself and the temple.

Where will I go? I don't know. Anywhere but here. Maybe someone in Everwillow to would take me in for the night. I run until my exhausted body gives out, and I drop on my knees.

Everything River said crashes over me, stealing the breath from my lungs. Tears sting in my eyes as the truth stares me in the face. I'm the Lastborn. Whatever the fuck that means. A goddamned prophecy meant to defeat the Dark King. As if I could. I can't even control my powers, let alone use them to kill an all-powerful wielder of dark magic.

Gods, I don't want this. I want peace. I want quiet. I don't want to be chased, or hunted, or shackled to some impossible destiny. Why me? Why was I chosen? It has to be a mistake, right? Surely, another celestial being will rise one day. I can't be the only one. I won't be the only one... will I?

Tears spill down my cheeks, warm and salty against my lips. I wipe them away and sniffle, lifting my gaze to the night sky. Stars peek through the tall trees above me, as if whispering it's all true. They glitter like Myrea herself watches from above, reassuring me that she chose me for a reason. It strikes me how often I'd look to the sky for guidance. The stars guide me. They always have. I curse under my breath wrapping an arm around my stomach, while my other hand claws at the hard earth beneath me. My chest heaves, air coming too fast. I'm on the edge of breaking. "Keep it together." I whisper to myself.

A rustle behind me snaps my body tight. I twist, falling hard to the ground as I turn to toward the sound.

Scrambling, I kick backward, forcing myself to get back on my feet. River appears from the brush, sympathy etched across his disgustingly handsome face.

"Mya—"

"Don't." I lift my finger cutting him off. Still, he approaches slowly, as if I were an injured fawn being stalked by a hunter. From down here, River's stature seems massive, his rugged exterior a harsh contrast to his gentleness in his. He offers me his hand.

"Please, Mya, let me explain," he pleads.

I push to my feet, refusing his hand. "Why should I? Everything you have told me, everything you've said, has been a lie."

"I never lied to you—"

"Withholding the truth is same as lying, River." I snap.

He chuckles nervously. "I didn't—"

"You did! Why wouldn't you just tell me? If I wasn't a pawn in your personal vendetta against the Dark King, then why not just tell me?"

River steps closer until our bodies are just inches apart. I meet his turbulent blue eyes with mine. "You never would have left with me if I'd told you outright. You would've stayed in your little hovel. I needed confirmation that you were the Myrean Forsaken. Elera needed to see you first. I didn't want to scare you."

I nod slowly, lips pressed thin. I draw a sharp breath. "It *is* scary, River. Going up against the King is suicide. If I fail, you walk away free, and I die. But you could give a shit less about that—"

"That's not true," River growls, long and rough. I shake my head in disbelief. He'll really say anything to keep me tied to this bullshit plan of his.

I take a step back, then turn on my heel. "I'm going home."

River lunges forward, seizing my arm and, spinning me back to face him. "And do what, Mya?" he grits out. "They've found you. They know where you live. They won't stop until Voras has you… then what?"

I ball my fists, straining against his grip. "The only reason they found me, River, is because you *exposed* me. I was fine until you barged in and shattered my peace."

He hisses. "Oh, please. They would've found you eventually, Mya. You were on borrowed time. You still are. Please, let us train you. We'll find a way. Don't you want to defend yourself? Don't you want to know how to wield that magnificent power buried within you?" His voice softens as his grip eases. His thumb gently brushes my arm in a soothing rhythm.

"Look," he sighs. "I know this isn't what you want. I know you never asked for any of this. But from what I've seen, I'm in awe. You are so much more than you believe. Even before I met you, I felt our destinies entwined. I can't explain it, but I knew, deep in my soul that we were meant to do this together. Please."

My shoulders sag. "I don't know. It's too much for one person, River."

"Don't think about the prophecy right now," he concedes. "Just focus on learning to use your magic. That's all I'm asking. Once you understand how your magic works, we can figure out what to do next, okay? I'm not pushing you to fulfill a prophecy for my sake, Mya. I don't want you hurt. But, if it's your destiny to defeat the darkness, then you need to learn how to keep yourself safe."

When I meet River's eyes, I see raw sincerity. But can I believe him? How well do I really know this man? As much as I'm drawn to him, my trust in him falters. He's a smooth talker—a man who could charm the undergarments off any woman. He'd managed to get me all the way across Gaia's Keep to the Temple of Gaia. Was I a fool to think he was telling me the truth? How many times will he mislead me before I finally walk away?

"Okay." I relent. "I'll try to learn my powers. But that's all." I only hope that I won't regret trusting him again. Just because I agree to learn more about my magic, doesn't mean I'll trust every word he says, or forgive that he *withheld* the truth from the start. But I'll try.

River's entire body slackens with relief, a smile curving on his face. "Thank you," he breathes, before pulling me against his solid frame. The embrace is warm and tender, and my insides flutter, but I keep my guard up.

"I'm not doing it for you." I murmur as he lets me go. I press my hand against his chest to push him away, but he grabs it. A sensual touch. My eyes meet his, and the heat in his gaze lingers. My cheeks flush as I look away, his hand still holding mine.

"I know you're not," he replies softly. "Come back to the temple with me. Elera offered us shelter for a few days to rest."

The words surprise me. "All right."

River turns, leading me the way he came, my hand caught in his. I let him guide me. Follow him blindly. I have no idea where I lost myself in my haste to escape, but River knows these woods, this temple. He grew up here. It doesn't take long before we return to the ancient building that looks more like beautiful ruins than a residence, yet still alive within. With night settling over the forest, I'd have been lost on my own. For that, at least, I'm grateful for the fortress walls around me again.

Inside, torches flicker along the walls as River leads me down the hallway we'd barely gotten through before River's story unraveled, the truth about who I really am. Without sunlight streaming through the open windows, the temple feels far darker now.

"Come this way," River murmurs, his voice low as we walk the corridor. "It'll lead to the rooms where we'll stay for the next few days."

I follow him in silence down a series of winding halls, all of them nearly identical to the one we first entered. River had spoken of the temple's beauty, but so far, the looming stone only unsettles me.

"Here you go." River stops at a small wooden door. "You'll sleep here. I'll be a few doors down."

"Thank you." I say, stepping forward to open the door.

"Sleep well." River lingers a moment, then shakes his head and moves down the hall toward his own room. For a moment, with our hands on our respective doors, we gaze at each other from a distance, and then disappear into separate chambers.

I inhale deeply as I step into the space that will be mine for the next couple of days. Small, quaint, nothing extraordinary. A bed. A little desk. Likely a priestess's quarters—simple, functional. I slide off my bow and quiver, almost forgetting that I've been wearing it. They've become another limb, so much a part of me I hardly notice the weight. Though, once I set them aside, the ache in my shoulders catches in. Honestly, my entire body throbs— everything. It's in moments like this, when rest comes, that I truly feel it, especially once the adrenaline wears off.

On the bed lies, a white shift dress, clearly meant to sleep in. My rucksack was placed by the door. I'd left it on Buttercup, but someone must have brought it in when I left. Too tired to rummage for my old, dirty night shirt, I pick up the clean shift from the bed instead. Peeling off my travel clothes, I grimace at the once-sky-blue tunic now stained and grimy from the road. I reek, and I long for a bath, but I'll ask in the morning. I'm too tired to care about it now. I unbraid my hair, running fingers through it, massaging my scalp until the sensation soothes me. I take a few deep breaths. I sit on the small bed and lower myself onto it, all my muscles screaming in pain. The softness is a relief so sharp it almost hurts. Within moments, sleep claims me.

The following morning, I wake to the sound of a gentle knock. Groaning, I wipe the drool from my face, prying open my crusted eyes. "One moment." I grumble, pushing myself upright. My bones ache as I force them into motion, step by step, sluggishly, toward the door.

I stumble to the door and unlatch it. A priestess stands waiting, a small tray balanced in her hands. She wears the stunning green robe of a Gaian priestess, belted with a slim gold chain. Her deep brown eyes are warm, her mahogany hair shot through with a few silver strands, braided neatly down her back.

"Good morning, Myalis. I'm Nani, one of the priestesses here. I've brought you a simple meal. May I come in?"

I nod. "Of course." Stepping aside, I let the graceful woman in. She places the square wooden tray on the desk across from the bed: a tiny teapot, good for maybe two servings, and a plate with bread and eggs.

I smile with gratitude. "Thank you."

"Of course," she replies with a slight bow. "Would you like me to launder your garments or perhaps draw a bath? We can provide robes in the meantime."

"A bath sounds heavenly. Could you show me where to go?" My cheeks flush in embarrassment as Nani glances at my filthy tunic and leggings discarded on the floor.

"Yes. I'll let you enjoy your food and return shortly. In the meantime, I'll take these to the laundry." She smiles as she grabs my soiled clothes. Embarrassment prickles my skin, but I appreciate her thoughtfulness.

"Thank you," is all I manage before she nods and slips out. I sink into the chair at the desk and pour myself a cup of tea. The first sip surprises me, the citrus orange and honey flavor awakening my senses. It's delicious, a brew I plan to savor alongside the meal. The eggs and rolls are freshly made, simple yet perfect. How such a simple meal can satiate me, I don't know. Perhaps it's because it reminds me of the mornings with my parents.

I shrug, my mind wandering to the past. What would they think of all of this? Me being the Lastborn, destined with celestial powers. What if they knew? What if that's why they put their lives at stake to save me? Maybe they knew what my destiny held. I spiral into a haze of "what ifs" until a soft knock pulls me back. Nani's voice filters through the door.

"Myalis? May I come in?"

"Yes." I call, taking another sip of tea. Nani steps in, carrying a white cotton towel and a bright green priestess robe.

"If you're ready, I'll escort you to the hot springs for a bath." Nani's voice is warm, almost motherly. It's hard to place her age. She carries a youthful glow, yet faint lines crease her eyes and brow when she smiles.

"Yes, thank you." I nod, then pause, suddenly self-conscious in just a plain nightgown. Nani stills, eyeing me up and down.

"Of course, how foolish of me. Would you prefer to change into something else? You're welcome to wear this robe." Nani extends the folded green fabric to me. I consider it for a moment, then sigh.

"No, it's fine. I'm clothed enough. Surely the priestesses are used to the female form." I gesture at my nightgown.

Nani stifles a chuckle. "Of course. The hot springs aren't far. We can take secret way, if you're up for a little adventure."

My brow perks up in curiosity. "A secret way?" Nani nods.

"Yes. The temple is threaded with tunnels, built as precautions. But rarely ever used." Nani explains as we step out the door. I follow her in silence down the narrow hall lined with wooden doors, just as I'd walked with River last night.

River.

Passing his door, my thoughts snag on him. Frustration flickers, boiling up. But, it's hard to stay mad at him. Deep down, I've already forgiven him. He's infuriating, and I shouldn't be so accommodating, so trusting, and yet, I am. Somehow the man has ensnared me in ways no one ever has. It's maddening. What is it about River that leaves me at my wit's end? He's vexed me more than any other man I've ever known. And last night, I agreed to his demands. Agreed to learn my magic, whatever it even is. My mind churns with arguments and doubts. How are we even going to train? What am I supposed to do? How will I evoke my powers in a safe way?

I start to feel the tension crawling up my neck as I follow Nani. We enter into a room, one similar to mine, only bigger and with bookcases and tapestries upon the walls.

"These are my chambers," she says, approaching one of the tapestries hanging on the wall. It's a beautiful mural: an enormous, flowering tree, with deer and woodland creatures gathered beneath its boughs. Above, Gaia herself is stitched among the stars, watching over the land from the cosmos.

Nani pulls the tapestry aside, revealing a narrow door hidden behind it. I eye it suspiciously. "You weren't kidding when you said a 'secret' way."

A soft giggle escapes Nani's lips. "No exaggeration. Come. This leads straight to the hot springs. My own little path."

Blindly, I follow as she pushes open an ancient wooden door, its iron hinges rusted and ready to give away. The loud, groan it makes hardly feels discreet for a "secret" passage. She waves me inside, shutting the door behind us, and we fall into utter darkness.

A wave of panic consumes me as my eyes struggle to adjust. Darkness has always haunted me, and here, in this confined space, my chest constricts. I've followed a near stranger into an unknown passage. My sense of self-preservation is clearly lacking. My breathing quickens as I stare at the endless void before me.

"Follow my voice." Nani's hypnotic voice cuts through the dark, grounding me. She hums softly, and I follow the sound down the corridor. I stumble and trudge through, praying I won't fall flat on my face.

"Why don't you have a torch?" I finally ask, irritation flaring as my eyes refuse to adjust. So far, it's nothing but a narrow hall that seems to lead nowhere.

"You could be our light," she replies, still humming.

I frown. "I don't understand."

"You're a celestial. Your power is light. You can bring it forth to illuminate the darkness before us." Nani's voice lilts in a sing-song rhythm, weaving with her hums. This priestess is strange and unease pricks at me. What if I'm being led into a trap?

"I don't know how." I admit.

"Sure you do. It's your natural gift. Just feel it within you." She continues, "It's like any other Forsaken's power. It's a part of you. You only need to summon it."

"Summon it?" I whisper, more to myself than to Nani. My palms cling to the rough stone walls, afraid to let go of their frail security. I pause, weighing her words, then peel my hands away from the walls. Nani's voice falls silent, leaving me alone in pitch black. The only sound is my own unsteady breathing. I clench my fists and close my eyes. Is it really so simple? Can I just summon my powers on my command?

I draw a deep breath, and picture light. I think of the stars. How beautiful they are, how I often feel drawn to them in my loneliest hours. I remember the full moon, grand and luminous, a beacon in the darkest nights. Warmth. That's what I always felt beneath its glow, wrapped in starlight, safe.

Without realizing, I extend my palm. My breath steadies, and a tingling sensation overcomes me. When I open my eyes, a tiny cluster of glittering stars pulses in my palm, glittering like captured fireflies. My lips curl into an incredulous smile. Nani's face glows in the starlight, her expression alight with pure delight.

"See?" is all she says turning gracefully and continuing down the narrow passage.

She's right—the power feels natural, effortless. Her confidence in me burns far brighter than my own, though she barely knows me. I hold the power of starlight in my palm for several more bends of the tunnel, until we reach another door. Nani opens it, and sunlight bursts through, forcing me to squint. The passage led us out behind the temple, into the woods. The starlight in my palm dissipates as we step out into the greenery, swallowed by the day.

"The hot springs lie just beyond this strand of trees." Nani says, continuing ahead. Ancient trees tower around us, their branches almost touching the blue sky and casting deep shade over everything below. The sound of trickling water threads through my ears as we near the springs.

Chapter 15

Myalis

A pool of deep blue water glitters among the rock formations cradled by the dense woods. A small waterfall trickles into it, keeping the water fresh and moving. Morning sunlight filters through the canopy of trees above, steam evaporating off the water's surface. Birds chirp in melody above us as I take in the sight.

"It's beautiful." I whisper, stepping closer to the rocks and dipping my fingers into the water. It's deliciously warm.

"It is," Nani beams. "It is our main spot for bathing. The spring rejuvenates us, deepens our bond to the land, and to Gaia herself. There are soaps on the rocks, handmade from the forest. Please, help yourself. I'll leave your towel and robe here for when you're done."

She sets the items on a carved wooden log. "There's no need to rush. Take your time. I'll return later."

With that, Nani departs, leaving me alone with the springs. As her figure disappears into the tress, I lift the white shift over my head, and step into the hot springs. The steam kisses my skin, heat enveloping me, and I let out a sigh as I sink fully into its embrace.

The water though tinted a dark blue, is translucent—my naked body visible to anyone who might happen upon me. But the forest stands quiet, desolate, and I know I'm alone. I push the thought aside and let the warmth soothe my aching muscles, finally relaxing.

The hot springs snake through rocks, pooling deeper than I expected. Small waterfalls cascade gently across different levels, their low, constant music filling my ears. I settle against a large, flat boulder, stretching out my arms before closing my eyes.

Nani was right, it is rejuvenating. I breathe deeply, filling my lungs with the scent of dew-damp leaves, fresh earth, and clean water. A smile at my lips as I enjoy every sensation of the warm water. I've never had a moment like this before. It's a rare taste of pure luxury.

"Well, look who I found." The voice startles me, and I jolt upright. My eyes lock into bright blue ones filled with delight. A mischievous grin spreads across his handsome face—he stands there with nothing but a white towel slung around his waist—accentuating the deep "V" of his abdominal muscles.

"River," I breathe.

"No need to be shy, Myalis. This is a communal spring." River's brow perks in amusement, and I realize why he's grinning. My entire being is exposed. I cross my arms over my chest, but the translucent water betrays me, revealing the rest. Heat floods my face as I throw a hand down there, trying to grasp at my last shreds of modesty.

"I can leave." I say, exasperated. "Just turn around and I'll get out." My gaze darts to where Nani left my towel and robe.

"Oh please. No need for that." River chuckles, tugging the towel loose and letting it fall—revealing the stunning expanse of his nude body. My face flames as I fight to hold his gaze, resisting the urge to look downward.

River steps into the water, sinking into the steam, and my eyes drift down to his chest. Muscles as though carved by the Elementals themselves gleam beneath the mist. I force myself to look away, clearing my throat before my eyes wander any further. He wades forward, closing the space between us until he's suddenly there—towering just in front of me.

For a long moment, silence stretches between us before a nervous laugh escapes my lips. "How do we always end up naked in water together?" My arms remain locked in place, shielding myself.

"Would you prefer we be naked together elsewhere?" His question steals the breath from my lungs. Heat pools low in my body as my thoughts travel to sensual desires. River tilts my chin upward with a single finger, forcing my gaze to his. "Well?"

He waits. I shake my head. "I don't know." I whisper, breathless, unsure, my heart pounding against my chest. What is it about this man that unravels all my resolve? Since meeting River, I've felt myself changing. The walls I built so carefully around me are weakening, crumbling. I no longer feel the wholly self-sufficient woman I once was. Instead, I feel reliant on this man. A man who tricked me into his quest for revenge, I remind myself.

"Tell me, Mya... the first night we met, when you kissed me. If you hadn't blacked out, if our kiss hadn't been interrupted, would you have taken me for your own desires?" The question startles me, yet River's voice is smooth, hypnotic, his lips brushing the shell of my ear. "That day in the river... it wasn't much different from this. You broke away, but your body sang to mine in that moment before. Say it. Do you want me like this? Bare before you, with my hands touching your body?"

The question ignites me, turning thoughts to haze. Coherent thoughts flutter through my mind. Before I can utter a word, River's finger drifts beneath my chin down my neck. The touch sends shivers down my spine. His hand lingers along my collarbone, his strokes gentle, causing my breath to hitch.

"You confound me." I stutter as my eyes flutter closed. River's hand grabs the small of my back, drawing me flush against him, and I gasp. Every nerve sparks alive. The feel of his calloused fingers slowly lowering down my back evoke a convulsion within my core. His pectoral muscles firm against me; the air in my lungs seeming to dissipate. The feel of his erection pressed up against my stomach crumbles me.

"Then let me be clear, Myalis." His lips trail to my throat and my head tips back. River plants feather-light kisses down my neck moving lower to the hollow of my collarbone, which he'd been tracing. His soft lips tingle my skin as he goes. With his one hand on my lower back and his other laced through my damp hair, pleasure builds within me.

I wrap an arm around his neck, while my other hand rests upon his chest. My fingers trace circles around the tattoo.

Our lips linger near an inch of each other's. The anticipation of it climbs within the swell of my core. Sharing breath with this man works like a drug. River consumes my mouth—heat, hunger, and need crashing together. My body thrums with desire. His grip on my ass tightens letting a moan escape from my mouth. We kiss hungry, our tongues intertwining as if they've been starving a lifetime. My head becomes dizzy with desire. River's arms hold me up as my knees weaken.

He pushes me toward the boulder I'd been lounging on, leaning me up against it. "You're so beautiful." He holds my face in his palms, his eyes seem like they're staring into my soul. I'm naked, but now I feel raw before him. The heat in his eyes looks like a storm swirling, ready to wreck me.

I wrap my legs around his waist, hands pressed firm on his chest. "What is this feeling?" I whisper, my voice breaking as I wonder what it is between us. This yearn, this pull between us.

"Destiny." River breathes as he kisses me again, passionately, as our hands roam and grasp at every inch of each other's bodies. His skin on mine, surrounded by the hot water electrifies our senses. Water sloshes around us as we sink into it. Wrapped in River's strong arms, his lips trail down my neck, the scratchy gruff of his beard leaves a tingling sensation as he goes. When his mouth captures my breast, my lips let out a low groan.

River knows how to please a woman. I'd known this since I first met him. His charm is magnetic, pulling the women around him like flock to fodder. But this, experiencing him, feeling our connection, it consumes me. I'm lost in pleasure. His light tongue brushes my tightened nipples. And when River thrusts himself into me, the world around me fades away as I savor the ecstasy. I gasp with the feel of him inside me, his girth unexpected, hitting right where my senses explode.

He slowly pulls out, and I groan feeling the loss. Still mourning the feel of him inside me, I try to steady before he thrusts again, filling me back up. My entire body lights up with pleasure. It's him and I—like we're on another plane entirely. With stars in my vision, I moan as we move as one. River's grip tightens on my hips, and my nails dig deep into his muscled back scratching him.

River's hand moves lower, slowly working my clit with his thumb while thrusting within me. My body convulses as the orgasm starts building.

"That's it. Fuck, you squeeze me so good," he groans. "Come for me, Mya. Let go."

I explode a release, my muscles spasming. My body burning with aftershock as River shudders through his own release. The stress and ache of days' travels that once weighed me down has gone limp with bliss. Our breaths mix as River brings his forehead to mine. His strong grip relaxes, and his fingers tenderly stroke my sides. I lace my fingers in the back of his hair, running them through it as we hold on to each other.

"Why did that feel like the best thing I've ever known in my life?" His voice was soft, almost reverent.

I whisper, shaking my head, "I don't know... it was... amazing. Gaia above." Heat clung to me by both the water and his lingering touch, beads of sweat sliding down my temple.

"Let me get the soap." River breaks contact moving away. The loss of his body and warmth gives me a chill. He quickly returns with a bar of soap. He begins to lather it between his hands.

He arches a brow nodding toward me. "May I?"

I nod, uncertain what he means, until he moves in close, working soap into my skin. His fingers massage my scalp, sending shivers down my spine. His chest presses against my back, his frame overwhelming, and silently I let him wash me. When he rinses my hair, his soapy hands glide lower over my body.

"Are you trying to get me worked up again?" I joke, eyes closed, though my body hums with desire again.

River chuckles, lips almost touching my ear. "Well, I did enjoy watching you come undone." I shudder and turn my face toward him.

"You're cruel," I tease.

"And you're a goddess. One I hope to worship for the rest of my days."

I give a nervous laugh. No one has ever spoken such romantic things to me. "You only flatter me to get me to do whatever you want." The words are a joke, but an awkward pause creeps between us.

The moment the words are out, I feel the weight of them. The truth. I turn fully to him. His expression is flat, his jaw tense beneath dark stubble, brows knitting low.

"Oh, Gods." My shoulders collapse beneath the realization. He seduced me. He *used* me. Was this his plan all along? Flatter me, force me to give into my desires so that I'd feel safe with him. Then use me to fulfill the prophecy? He'll probably spin it to sound like it's my choice. He'll convince me to go along with him. I fell for the manipulation. Again.

Shame creeps up my cheeks. I've fallen for it again. I'm embarrassed to even look at myself.

Mortified, I surge out from the water, rushing to grab the towel and robe Nani left. "I have to go."

"No, wait. Mya—"

I snatch the items and run, retracing the path Nani brought me, desperate to find the mysterious door that we'd used. River calls from behind, his voice chasing me—closer and closer. I push myself faster. I need to get out. I need to leave the Gaian Temple, leave him. Grab my rucksack, vanish, run as fast as I can from River and his constant manipulations.

The back of the stone temple comes into view, and with it, the little wooden door. I yank on the iron ring, managing to pry it open. Once inside, I slam it shut sinking to the ground. Warm tears run down my face and a sob cracks through me. How stupid am I? How utterly foolish. I knew River was a selfish womanizer. And yet I allowed myself to fall for it.

Naked, I curl on the cold stone floor, knees pressed to my chest, arms clutching tight around me for warmth to stay. When the tears finally run dry, I drag in a shaky, deep breath and put on the green priestess robe rolled in my hands. Then, I summon the starlight back into my palm allowing it to guide me back to Nani's room.

Luckily, the priestess isn't there. I see myself out of her private room into the maze of hallways. My pace quickens as my chest constricts. A priestess walks beside me, curiosity written all over her face, but she doesn't stop me as I press on, desperate to find my little chamber.

But I become lost in the temple's endless halls. I try to recall every detail. Any sort of identifying piece to help me remember where I'm supposed to go. A tapestry of nature, a painting of Gaia—it doesn't do me much good.

Relief washes over me when I nearly bump into Nani, carrying my freshly laundered clothes. "Ah, Myalis," she greets. "I was just getting ready to bring you back from the springs."

"I need to get back to my room. I have to leave." I blurt quickly.

"Goodness, is everything all right?" she asks, turning on her heel to guide me. I fall into step behind her.

Thinking fast, I lie. "Yes. It's just... the Dark King hunts me, and I don't want to bring his wrath upon this temple for harboring a fugitive. I know Head Priestess Elera was worried about that."

"Oh, I see." Nani doesn't seem convinced. "Shall I fetch River as well?" she asks, innocently enough.

"No," I snap—too sharply. "We've decided to go our separate ways. I won't endanger him any further." Another lie.

I couldn't give two shits about what happens to him. I hope that the Dark King ends him before I see him again. My anger only grows.

"Oh. I see." Nani's voice dips solemnly. "I'm sure he's disappointed about that." My brow knit in confusion.

"Why would you say that?" I ask as we reach my chamber. Nani opens the door, letting me step in first before slipping in after me and closing it.

Nani's brown eyes kindly regard me as she places my clothes on the bed. "Because, I think he's quite smitten with you. He's never spoken of women before. And you're all he's been talking about."

"You and River are… acquaintances?" I pause, taken aback.

Nani nods. "Yes. I helped raise him, trained him as a boy. I am a fellow weather wielder. I took pity on him, being so young when he lost his parents. I took care of him any way I could. Once he left, he learned more on his travels. River surpassed my abilities long ago. But I'm proud of the man he's become. Honest. Loyal. Fierce. Passionate. A true protector of his kin." She smiles, crooked teeth flashing.

I laugh outright at her description, and Nani tilts her head, puzzled. I can't stop myself. He isn't any of those things. He's a manipulator. A deceiver. A liar. I shake my head in disbelief.

"Forgive my outburst," I manage at last. "If you'll excuse me, I need to change and be on my way. But... thank you for your kindness."

Nani stays quiet for a moment before folding her hands in front of her, quietly seeing herself to the door. She opens it, its hinges squeaking, but before she steps out, she speaks one final time.

"Go to the Altar of Water... they'll show you how to use your magic. Learn it. Harness it. Claim your power and use it."

Chapter 16

Myalis

I leave the Temple of Gaia without letting anyone notice, but take Buttercup with me. Trying to command the gigantic horse on my own is harder than I thought, but I'm getting the hang of it. With only my rucksack, arrows, and quiver, I travel lighter than before. I'm not sure if I'm heading the right way, so once I reach Everwillow, I ask a few passing townsfolk for directions—either to the Oasis Peninsula or the Altar of Water. Most shrug, but I eventually find an older man who points me toward a path. It's all I have.

Before leaving the bustling town, I gather a few supplies for the journey ahead, and force myself to leave hoping to never see it again, despite how incredible it is. River doesn't follow me—thanks to the gods. I don't know what I'd do if I saw him again. Perhaps stab him with my dagger. One day, I'll seek retribution. But today isn't that day. Nor tomorrow, or the next. The Dark King still hunts me, and I need a new place of refuge.

For hours, I ride in the direction the Everwillow gentleman showed me. My legs already ache. The ride is more strenuous than before, since River's been the one guiding Buttercup toward Gaia's Keep. Now, it's all on me. All I can do is grit my teeth, endure the pain, and learn to do it efficiently.

I'm not sure if I'll be able to find my way to the Oasis Peninsula, yet I plan to stay in the direction the man had shown. He seemed trustworthy enough, although, my recent judgment in men seems to be lacking. The gentleman said that the Peninsula is about four-day eastward ride on horseback. I'll know I've reached the border between Gaia's Keep and the Oasis Peninsula when I see Jade Lake straddling between the two territories.

I have to navigate the woods and whatever other terrain until then. For the past ten years, I've managed to travel across the continent of Elemi. Mostly staying within Gaia's Keep and the mountainous region that borders the Scarlet Lands, I've never needed directions. It was easy to find shelter—be it a cave or a hollowed tree—close to a village or town, and I'd stay there. I roamed freely. Free of responsibilities, except caring about my survival, picking up a little money here and there when I needed it. It hadn't been a glamorous life, not that I knew what glamour is like, but it was enough to keep me alive.

I'd stayed hidden and alone for so long. Now, after traveling with River, being without him feels like something is missing. The realization creeps in—I did like his companionship. The witty banter, the shameless flirting. The pull of lust and desire. What I thought were mutual feelings of admiration and want. I shake my head, frustrated. I need to forget him. He's done nothing but lie to me and manipulate me to get what he wants.

Hours of the day proceed into night. Another day comes and goes. I rest for only a few hours at night, still terrified of the darkness. Especially alone. This deep into Stormsbend Forest, the tree foliage has turned dark green. The tree barks look almost black, with gnarled branches mimicking menacing hands reaching for me. Humidity swells around us. Murky water twists through trees towering high above me branches draped with hanging vines. The terrain has completely transformed before my eyes. I frown at the unfamiliar land racking my brain to recall if I'm supposed to pass through this swamp on my way to the lake. Now, I can't remember if the man ever mentioned it.

I sigh and urge Buttercup forward, despite his trepidations. Maybe it's animal instinct I should be heeding. Buttercup isn't a frail horse—he's muscular steed with opinions of his own. Talking to him as I ride helps pass the time. I feed him, let him rest and rehydrate, as I do so myself. We have developed a kinship, he and I. A fucking horse. Is this really my life when my only true and noble companion is an equine?

As the swamp and evening alike darken, strange sounds chirp and caw. Everything else falls silent, leaving only the sway of branches and rustle of leaves. The air reeks musty and dank, like stagnant, moldy water. I don't know how deep the water runs, or what creatures might lurk beneath it. I steer Buttercup onto what little dry land I can find. We've to keep moving so we don't get stuck. This is the last place I want to spend the night. I pray to the Elementals above that I'm not lost.

There isn't much ground left, and Buttercup's hooves begin to sink deeper into the mud. If I'm not careful, I could hurt him. Putrid water splashes around us. Buttercup whinnies, skittish by the unstable land beneath his hooves. I tug his reins and murmur at him.

"There, there," I stroke his neck. "It'll all be okay."

It calms him, though I'm not sure if he'll be okay. I don't know where we are or how far the border of the Oasis Peninsula is. I fight off the despair creeping in. I can do this. I can find the Altar of Water. I can navigate as well as River could. The stars will guide me. They have to. After all, I am the Myrean Forsaken. My power won't lead me astray... right?

Branches snap in the distance, startling me. Buttercup's ears flatten and he huffs anxiously. The ground shudders beneath as stomping and the crack of breaking trees increases. I halt Buttercup and frantically search for the source of the sounds. My breath quickens as my heart starts to race. For a moment, I desperately wish River was here.

Trees crack all around us and movement stirs above us. Panic rises in me.

"Go!" I whip the reigns, but Buttercup's too spooked, and rears upwards. My inexperience sends me falling backward, flat on my back into the shallow, murky water. The air leaves my lungs as Buttercup bolts away in fear. "Wait! Come back!" I yell, water splashing into my mouth. But he's too terrified, too panicked to do anything but save himself. I gag on the stale water, fighting the urge to retch.

As I sit, water ripples around me. The sounds draw closer, followed by a loud roar. Birds take flight, cawing warnings as they scatter. As the ground shakes beneath my hands, I struggle, stuck in the muck. I try to follow the birds' direction, hoping to escape, but the sticky mud bogs me down. My limbs slug and it exhausts me trying to stand on my feet. Dense foliage and darkness pull the birds quickly out of my sight.

I groan in frustration. The cracking of trees grows louder as I finally stand. My leather boots slap the ground as I try to put distance between myself and whatever lurks nearby. It seems like a swamp creature. A creature I've no desire to encounter. I need to find Buttercup and get out of the swamp. Otherwise, I might never reach the Oasis Peninsula at all. *Keep moving*, I urge myself, stumbling forward. Even though I crawl through the mud, I just need to keep my feet going.

Another crack snaps behind me and I turn—just in time to see a massive tree trunk hurtling toward me. "Shit!" I duck, narrowly dodging the flying lumber. A roar echoes. And I see it—a giant swamp creature. An ancient tree beast, at least twenty feet tall, emerges from the shadows. Its black, moldy bark and branches let it blend into the surroundings. Thick, gnarled roots act as appendages, and it moves in a horrifying manner. Patches of deep green moss cover the creature's thick girth of a body. Glowing blue eyes, void of emotion, narrow upon me.

The hairs on the back of my neck stand upright as I steel my gaze on the creature. I have never seen anything like it—and I have no idea how in the underhells to fight it. Quickly, I shoot an arrow. It strikes the enormous creature, but does nothing. The thing isn't even bothered. I pivot, thinking of the only thing I can do. Flee. Maybe I can outrun it. But it moves effortlessly through the terrain, where I struggle.

"You cannot escape me," a calm, seductive voice fills my mind. I turn as it roars, revealing a monstrous mouth lined with sharp, jagged, wooden stakes as teeth. Did I imagine the voice? There's no way this creature could have possibly sounded like a human.

I snap out of it and keep running. I hop over dry patches and leap fallen logs, avoiding the swamp's murky water and mud.

"Come to me, Myalis," the voice coos again in my mind. I shake my head, causing strands of hair to fall in my face. Who's speaking? Is this tree a vessel for a darker force?

I shout, unsure whether it was loud or in my mind. "No!" The earth trembles as the tree monster relentlessly chases me. I tire, struggling through the harsh terrain. My chest heaves; the humid air feels thin as I force myself forward. I need to get out, but it surrounds me with no escape in sight. This ancient beast rules here. I am the outsider.

Sweat trickles down my temple, through my face, stinging my parched lips, only deepening my thirst. My limbs burn as I pour every ounce of energy into running. I can't stop. The ground shakes: I hear cracking before a tight grip snags around my ankle, pulling me down into the mud.

The last of my breath leaves me as I'm dragged backward, closer to the beast. "No, no, no, no." I thrash, struggling to escape its rooted clutches. I claw at the dirt, nails cracking. Tears stream down my face. My mind races for a plan. How long before this thing kills me?

A dagger. I have one. I reach for it at my belt but miss. Moments later, I remember—it's secured in my boot. "Fuck." I shout, hope fading—the roots tug at the boot holding my dagger.

Panic surges as I'm hoisted into the air. A scream escapes as I flail wildly. I curl, struggling to free my ankles, but exhaustion and pain weigh me down. The creature's grip is strong; the gnarled roots splinter my fingers as I claw at them.

I flinch, crying out as I flounder helplessly. The tree beast raises me to eye level. Void, glowing blue eyes stare down at me. Something alive watches from within, curiously studying me.

"Submit," a voice caresses my mind. "Submit, and this will end."

I thrash, limbs dangling, but the roots hold tight. Looking down, the height makes waves of nausea wash over me.

"Leave me be. I mean no harm." I yell. "I won't submit, no matter who you are."

I hold my breath as silence stretches. The beast remains still, seeming to consider my words. Its timber brows furrow and wooden fangs gnarl; a roar vibrates through me. Suddenly, I'm shaken violently in the air. My back cracks loudly as the world blurs.

Then I'm hurled through the air—thrown by the beast. I hold my breath, hitting a tree and falling to the marshy ground. Mud coats me and my body throbs in sharp pain. I groan as the ground rumbles, the water puddles rippling. I know the beast is coming back. I try to push myself up, but my strength fails me. My limbs feel like rubber. I hiss, forcing my body upright. Blinding pain rips through me. It's life or death, and I need to get on my feet, despite being in pain. My legs shake beneath me as I steady myself.

I glare at the beast once its blurred silhouette comes into view. For a moment, I think of my powers. How I warded off the Dark Knights days ago, and how I'd created light from my palm. I remember Nani's words. Could it really be that simple?

My chest heaves; a wheeze accompanies every breath. With all that's happened, it feels like my bones rattle. Determined, I stand tall and face the monster. I clench my fists, my arms drop at my side, teeth gritted. I focus, channeling my powers. Warmth spreading from my core, growing outward. An electric current hums through me, igniting my insides.

"You will leave me be," I whisper. The beast's gnarled roots stride closer, but I stand, staring at its glowing blue eyes, unyielding.

"Leave me be." I command with force. The power within me takes charge of my body, ready to explode, and all I need to do is let it out.

As the beast lunges, a guttural cry rips from me, and I thrust my hand forward. My entire body unleashes a blinding light. Everything slows. My soul leaves my being as my mind goes blank. I feel possessed in a way, entranced by my own celestial powers.

After that, I don't know what happens. The creature is a blinding blur; my body collapses as the light pours out of me. Tears stream down my cheeks, breath quickening, before my knees buckle and darkness consumes me.

Chapter 17

≈

Voras

I startle, stumbling back as I'm released from the Larkfury's mind. Myalis's power is awe-inspiring, igniting a thrill from within me—a sensation I've missed. I breathe heavily, reveling in her raw strength. When I collect myself, I stand tall, refusing to show weakness before those present.

Dark Knights and Ulnisi are gathered around me. They observed as I infiltrated the Larkfury's conscience and bent him to my will via the looking glass. Thanks to Ulnisi, I briefly glimpsed Myalis's whereabouts within Gaia's Keep. Though it's not easy, but well within my power. Knowing her location let me dispatch the Larkfury after her.

I meant her no harm, nor wished to scare her. Yet sometimes, when controlling another's mind, echoes of their being leak through. Usually peaceful, a Larkfury turns alarming when provoked. The solitary creatures are territorial—with her stumbling upon his swampland I could only do so much in means of control.

Myalis, however, stood her ground, quite bravely I must add. She's alone, which means I can seize her now. The last vision showed her magic draining her strength. Even from a brief glimpse, I sense her untouched potential. She's unused to wielding her powers; they deplete her quickly.

"My Lord?" A quiet voice stirs me. I turn abruptly. Jurikson stands there—my oldest friend and the General of my personal Dark Knights. His dark hair curls at his ears; brown eyes focused, waiting for orders.

"Quickly, I must portal." I say striding from the looking glass chamber into the hall. The group follows as I march through the castle toward the throne room. I ignore candelabras dripping wax and the tapestries hanging on the dark stone walls, all depicting Tazra's power. My black cloak flutters behind me as I quicken my pace. Footsteps and Ulnisi's chains clatter behind me, trying to keep pace. Servants swing open the throne room doors as I arrive.

"Where are we going?" Jurikson asks while I mutter, readying the portal. Do I need to answer him? No.

He'll know soon enough. But I won't send my friend in blindly.

I pause mid-incantation. "The Wild Swamps of Gaia's Keep. I'm retrieving the Starlight Princess."

I resume chanting, eyes closed, palm outstretched, crafting the portal before me. It's a rare skill. One passed down through my bloodline by the great Elemental Tazra herself. When the dark mist finishes forming, I open my eyes and turn to those behind me. "You'll be silent when we arrive. Bring Ulnisi, keep her close. I will approach the princess alone."

I step into the shadowy portal. Cool mist brushes my skin as my knights follow, Ulnisi's chains clattering against the dark gray marble floor. Silence reigns in the abyss, but as I emerge, the croaking of frogs and rustling of leaves fill in my ears.

I open my eyes and I'm right where I intended, the Wild Swamps. Darkened trees sprawl overhead and the moon's bright glow flitters through the foliage. Soft footfalls sound behind me; my knights emerge from the portal. Squishy green moss cushions my feet—a small gratitude. Our arrival is silent.

I scan the swamp, searching for Myalis. Where had she fallen? Outwardly composed, inwardly I start to panic. Did I miss the exact spot? I step forward—surrounded by dark, green, murky water. I scowl in disgust. My nostrils flare as I try to think hard. Could she be underwater?

Fuck. My eyes skim the water, but I can't see her through the dark surface. How deep is the swamp? What other creatures lurk below? I know every territory in Elemi, but not every single creature in them. Do I really want to risk myself here? I glance back and point to one of my knights.

"Tread forward." I command. Immediately, he moves ahead plunging his black boot into the dark, foreboding water. He sinks to the knee, but no deeper. Carefully, he moves forward, hardly making a sound as the water ripples around him. I continue to scan around, and, in the distance, I see the Larkfury I'd controlled. At least, what's left of it. The creature lies lifeless—its hulking body splintered into shards littering the ground.

If the beast fell here, then Myalis can't be too far. I rush toward the broken carcass, brushing away bushes and branches in my haste. I break through the dense greens and freeze. Not more than thirty yards ahead, a familiar face stands before me, although preoccupied.

My brows furrow as I hold back a growl. River Dune. Fucking hells below. Would this man ever not be a thorn in my way? He holds Myalis Lucernas. My princess. In *his* arms. He must've retrieved her, so she wasn't alone after all. I could end him right here. It would be easy.

As I step forward, a hand grabs my arm. I turn sharply. My body tense, I snarl. My snarl fades as I meet Ulnisi's pale, unseeing eyes. Her white hair falls across her face; she gently shakes her head, lips flattening. I search her expression, hoping for a reason to heed her.

"No, My Lord. Do not pursue," she whispers. "When they cross into the land of sands, there you will succeed." The same words she spoke days ago. The vagueness only makes my blood boil. Do the fates think I can't best one man? I frown, nostrils flaring, eyes fixed on Myalis and her apparent savior, River Dune.

River stiffens as if sensing me. With Myalis propped in his arms, he turns, and from a distance, we lock eyes. Our gazes meet; I straighten, holding his stare. I glare, letting him see both me and my knights lurking in the mist. I'll let him think he's won. His ego will be his downfall. I want him to see that I know where they are, and that I'm hunting them. I won't stop until I claim what's mine.

Chapter 18

Myalis

My head throbs as I wake beneath glittering stars in the night sky. I'm wrapped snug in a bedroll, dressed in a clean, dark green, long-sleeved tunic and brown trousers. Wool socks warm my feet; my boots sit next to them. My hair falls in loose waves around my face. My body aches, shocks of pain shooting through me as I stir. The scent of medicinal herbs and creams lingers in the air. I assume they've been applied on my wounds.

The details are foggy, and I don't remember what happened. The sound of crackling fire shoves me back to reality and I jolt up, panicking. I groan, teeth clenched, as pain radiates from my back. Every muscle and bone of my body screams as I slowly turn my head in the direction of the fire. The golden-orange glow illuminates River's silhouette. Firelight catches his features—strong jawline, dark beard closely shaved. He sits hunched by the fire, elbows on his knees, hands clasped.

My shifting draws his attention and he's on his feet. "Hey, there. Welcome back," he says, voice calm and soothing as he approaches. But all I can think about is how angry I am—memories of our last encounter rush in my mind. I attempt to stand, even though collapse feels inevitable. He stands before me, relief on his face. My legs are trembling, but I use all my energy and slap him hard across his smug face. A yelp escapes me as pain from the slap reverberates through my sore muscles. I huff, watching shock taking over River's face. Silence falls as I ready another slap. River catches my wrist in a firm grip.

"Not exactly the thank you I was expecting." A wry smile crosses his face.

I try to slap him with my other hand, but he catches that one too. Exasperated, I grit my teeth and yell. My remaining energy fades and I collapse to my knees before I react. The pain overwhelms me. River holds my wrists raised above my head, then releases them and looks down at me.

"This isn't how I was expecting you to be on your knees before me for the first time," he chuckles. Anger boils as tears start to well.

"Shut the fuck up, River. Haven't you caused me enough pain?" My palms fall weakly onto the grass. I feel utterly weak, barely able to hold myself up. My arms tremble, pain searing through my body. It's grueling, and my muscles have a horrible ache. Reluctantly, tears fall and River kneels in front of me.

His large hands cup my face gently, his calloused fingers rubbing my cheeks. "Hey, I was joking. Don't cry."

My chest heaves, the fight leaves me. "If I had the strength, I'd have your throat at my dagger's end right now."

River smirks. "Sounds fun. Maybe I should give you your dagger back then?" He quirks a brow. I press my lips tight into a straight line, unamused.

"I'm not joking, River. I'm dead serious." I pull back and push his hands away.

"So am I," his tone deepens, growing solemn. "Look, I know you're mad at me, but what happened at the hot springs... I never meant to betray your trust, Mya. I do have genuine feelings for you. I'm sorry I didn't know how to react when you accused me of using you. Your words stunned me. I was speechless."

I exhale, staring straight into his eyes, shaking my head in disbelief. Am I really going to believe another lie? I know he'd say anything to keep me on his path. But honestly, what the hell am I doing? Where am I going? What am I really trying to accomplish?

My shoulders slump as the truth settles in. "I believe you." I do. I believe he cares for me. He wants me to master my magic so I can protect myself. I know his intentions are good. His expression says it all.

The truth is, I *do* want to learn my powers. I want to understand what I'm capable of. I don't feel driven by revenge for my parent's deaths. I just want to end the source of my pain and fear. I'm tired of running, tired of sleeping with one eye open. I want to live my life and feel safe—secure. Not hiding underground, or in a tree, or outside. Whatever I desire in my future, I want that. But to get there, I know I must end the Dark King's reign. River is right—I must kill him.

I shudder as River approaches. He wraps his muscled arms around me guiding me back onto the bedroll. "Lie down. You're still healing." He moves me gently onto the bed, like a rag doll. It's then I realize that he layered both our bedrolls together so I'd have more cushion. He gave up his comfort for mine. The gesture warms my heart. A weak smile spreads across my lips.

A soft chuckle escapes River's throat. "And what has caused you to grace me with that little smile?"

"Nothing, just glad to lie down. My body aches." A harmless lie. He doesn't need to know that he made me smile. "What happened? My memories are fuzzy."

I remember fleeing Gaia's Temple with Buttercup. I was on my way to... somewhere. The Altar of Water? Clearly, I hadn't made it. I remember the swamp. That disgusting swamp. And the giant tree creature. Gaia above, what the hell was that?

"A Larkfury." River replies softly as if reading my mind.

"What?" I ask, turning to him as he sits beside me. He runs his fingers through my hair; the sensation eases my headache. "You got yourself into the Wild Swamp." He breathes deeply, gazing at me. "At the hot springs, when you ran off, I knew that I had to let you go, but I also expected you'd get lost. I'm not mocking your sense of direction. Just that those unfamiliar with this part of Gaia's

Keep tend to vanish forever. I didn't want that for you. So, I let you get ahead and followed you."

I sigh and roll my eyes. "Of course you did."

"I'm glad I did," he says, all humor fading. "If not, you'd be dead or in King Voras's grasp."

"What?" I sit up, alarmed. Air deflates out of my lungs and my ribs aches. "The Dark King?"

River nods. "The Larkfury chasing you was possessed by him."

I try to remember everything, but it's blurry. I faintly recall words, but they're unclear now. Closing my eyes to remember only worsens my headache.

"How did you find me?" I ask River, hoping that he can fill in the gaps.

River gives me a sympathetic look and shrugs. "Obviously, you had a head start, and I needed to get supplies and a horse since you took ours." He smirks at me. "I didn't know which way you went, but I guessed you'd try heading to the Oasis Peninsula. It was tough, but I was lucky enough to track Buttercup's hoofprints. I followed the tracks until you entered the swamp, but it got harder after that."

My heart grows heavy as I watch pain flash across his face.

"I wasn't sure if I'd find you. It was getting dark. Any hoofprints I'd found disappeared in pools of water. I roamed aimlessly but kept trying. I knew I couldn't give up on you. Hearing the roar, I suspected it was you and that you were in danger. Ash and I followed the creature's voice. Thank Gaia it carried those cries. I found you just as you glowed, delivering a final blow to the beast."

Missing pieces begin clicking into place as some memories return. I remember the tree beast. I guess its proper name is a Larkfury. The largest creature I've ever faced. More terrifying than the bony wolf creatures from the meadows. Time slips away. How long have we ridden through Gaia's Keep? How long have I been out after fighting the Larkfury?

"Ash?" I ask, confused by the name.

"It's the horse I took from the temple." River says, pointing behind him. Near the fire where he sat stands a sleek spotty gray stallion. She's lithe, much smaller than Buttercup, who grazes nearby. Relief washes over me that River found him, or maybe Buttercup found River. Regardless, I'm glad he's safe and with us again.

I think about River's words—the Dark King controlled the Larkfury. How does River know the creature was possessed by him? My brows knit together. Several thoughts consume my mind. "I remember its eyes glowing blue. It whispered to me. But, in my mind. How's that possible?"

"Voras possesses many, if not all, of Tazra's dark gifts." River explains.

"Why do you think it was Voras and not just the Larkfury defending its territory?"

River shifts uncomfortably beside me. He sits in the grass, legs crossed. He covers my hand with his and squeezes gently. "Because, Mya, when I pulled you from the water, he was there."

My entire freezes as I hold my breath. "What?" I whisper.

"If I hadn't reached you first, he would've. And I'd have lost you." River tightens his grip on my hand.

"How? How was he there? Did you fight him?" My voice trembles with racing thoughts.

A horse whinnies, drawing our attention. A gust of wind sways the tall grasses around us. Silence lingers until River speaks. "Voras can portal wherever he wants."

I'm stunned. Unsure how such a power can exist. I've never heard of it, not even among Tazra Forsaken. It makes me feel small, realizing how much I don't know. I pull my knees to my chest, pain flaring with the movement. I feel as if I need something to keep myself grounded. The world tilts, and I want to close my eyes and shut it out.

"He let us go without a fight, which makes me more suspicious." River admits.

"Why?"

"It's a scare tactic. He knows where we are. Voras is following us, but he's waiting, biding his time. That worries me more."

I shake my head. "If he wants to kill me, why wait?"

River lets out an exhausted breath, forcing himself to his feet. "I don't know. But after seeing him, something tells me that he may not wish you dead after all. Anyway, you need to rest. We'll continue toward the Oasis Peninsula and the Altar of Water tomorrow if you're feeling well enough to travel."

I don't know if I can ride, and sore as I am, I slowly start to doze off. I have so many questions, especially now that River thinks Voras wants me alive. It terrifies me. What could he want from me? My power, maybe? Is there a way he can extract it from me? Gods above, is that possible? And, if he does, would it kill me?

Chapter 19

Myalis

I try to sleep, but toss and turn, shifting uncomfortably on my bedroll. After what feels like hours, I decide to get up and stretch my legs. My body aches from the injuries I sustained. Everything is sore, one reason why I struggle to sleep.

I stand and look around, realizing we're somewhere else. Not where we were when I last fell asleep. I steady myself, trying not to panic. How did I get here? My breath hitches as stars glitter overhead with a bright, white crescent-shaped moon hanging high above. The sky is clear, no dark clouds in sight.

Around us are rolling foothills, sparse trees scattered here and there. Wildflowers ripple in tall grass with the night breeze. A scent of lilac drifts through me. Turning, I see a huge sparkling lake not far from where I stand. Mist cascades over the water, the sight enchanting. I inhale deeply. It's beautiful and serene.

I step toward the lake, searching for River, but don't see him anywhere. Have I been taken? My heart pounds as I notice a fire dwindling to glowing embers. It's dark, and I can barely make out anything beyond the lake. My aching legs move forward and once I'm at the fire's edge, I sit and pull my knees to my chest.

My muscles throb with the movement, and I exhale. Whatever River gave me for the pain, combined with the rest, has helped. But fear gnaws at me—not knowing where I am or where River could be. There's no sound out there other than that of nature. I stare at the lake and notice large white flowers scattered across it. Its surface reflects the stars above like a mirror. It's breathtaking. I feel my magic thrumming inside me.

A small smile skirts across my face as I realize I'm on the outskirts of the Oasis Peninsula. This must be Jade Lake. A frown replaces the smile as I realize I was unconscious. I don't know how long or if River brought me here. A sinking feeling grows as I wonder how River managed it, if it was him, who moved two horses and my unconscious self.

Despite my fears, it's peaceful sitting by the lake. Crickets chirp and frogs croak around me, calming me. A snore stirs me from the left. My eyes dart toward a mature weeping willow. Its vine-like limbs graze the lake's surface. Quietly, I move toward of the sound. At the tree, I push vines aside to reveal River—sleeping, shirtless, back against the thick trunk of the tree, his arms crossed.

I thank Gaia it's him here, and not some stranger or the King. I'm relieved by his presence. I study his sleeping form. He's gorgeous, even asleep. It infuriates me how beautiful he is. River looks young, despite the dark scruff along his jaw and upper lip. Small wisps of his almost black hair fall across his face. He's tied half of it up in a bun at the back of his head, the rest falling in waves, that barely touch his shoulders.

I watch his chest rise and fall at a slow, steady pace. The silver Gaian pendant hangs between his pectorals. My eyes settle on the chest tattoos—intricate moon phases done swirling over the Gaian symbol.

Staring at his taut chest, I stifle a laugh. He must shave his chest; it's deliciously smooth, hairless. I want to reach out but fear the desires it would spark. Desires I'm desperate to keep in check.

He sits relaxed, and I kneel before him. I bite my lip holding back a sharp noise as I squat. Surprisingly, he doesn't wake. His long legs cross at the ankles. River's boots lie to the side— I realize he's not wearing them. He's wearing tight black trousers, front laces loose. They reveal much of his abdomen. Muscles taut, the "V" carved deep, a light speckling of hair apparent—delving lower beneath said laces. Desire surges within me.

The longer I watch him, the more I'm certain. He must've taken a swim in the lake. That explains his state of dress and why he'd sleep, hidden by the weeping willow.

For some reason, my body edges closer until, before I know it, I'm straddling him. My legs on either side of his—but I manage not to touch him. At least, not yet. His snore is soft, drawing my gaze to his frowning lips. Lips I devoured not so long ago. Elementals above, his kisses were intoxicating. The memory alone heats my skin.

I weigh whether to let the sleeping dog lie. I don't want to wake him. I only want to look at him. Really look at this man. River Dune. Once a stranger. The man who convinced me to travel a perilous journey to learn about my powers. The man who lied to get me to follow. A man who betrayed me for what he wanted. And yet... he's the man I hate to like. The one who cares what happens to me.

The man I'm starting to seek out. The man I might—can I even admit this? Care about? Is that what I'm feeling?

Am I falling in love with River? His jaw twitches; his brows furrow. I go still on top of him, heart thundering. I shouldn't be doing this. I'm still aching from the Larkfury. Straddling a man and gawking isn't helping. Against my better judgment, I trace his tattoo with a fingertip. Barely grazing his skin, I draw lazy circles around the moon phases. A firefly glows at the edge of my vision, drawing my gaze.

The firefly distracts me—then River's arms shoot around my waist, dragging me flush to him. His eyes open, slow and lazy, a boyish grin spreading across his face. "Are you admiring me, Mya?" he whispers, voice husky. His deep voice stirs something carnal in me.

"Sorry," I say, breathlessly. "I didn't mean to wake you." I shake my head, cheeks burning.

River tilts his head, our lips nearly brushing. "Then what were you trying to do?" Desire thrums through me. I have no answer. I don't know what the fuck I was doing. He caught me, red-handed, touching him and straddling him while he slept. I feel like a lovesick idiot. What was I thinking?

I try to get up, but River holds me fast, not letting go. His strong arms keep me pressed to him. I glance down, noticing the bulging veins along his forearms.

"I'm sorry I woke you." I repeat, unsure what else to say.

"I don't give a shit that you woke me." River says. "I want to know what you planned to do to me." His voice is a sensual caress, and the heat in my core ignites. My body craves him, missing what we shared just days ago. I swallow, nerves tight, eyes dropping from his.

"You're right." I confess. "I was admiring you. I couldn't help myself."

If it were daylight, River would be laughing at how red I'm turning. I feel like a fool for giving into my fantasies. River's hand slides up my back fingers curling in the hair at my nape. He brings his lips to my ear, and I stifle a gasp, biting my lip.

"I think you would've done more than *admire* me if I'd let you go longer," he whispers. His husky laugh makes my toes curl. Gaia above, I am doomed.

"Do you wish to ride my cock like this?" He plants a kiss right below my ear and I can't help the moan that escapes. "Straddling me, or should I get you on all fours and take you from behind? Is that what you want, Myalis?"

Shit, the way he says my name gets all my juices flowing. I shake my head, trying to deny it, but my body betrays me, melting in his grasp.

"Tell me your desires and I'll give them to you." He plants a trail of kisses down my neck before he reaches the hem of my tunic. Clothes become an obstacle—I want them gone, want to feel him against me. His hand leaves my hair and drifts to the collar, moving it aside. The neckline isn't forgiving. River kisses the base of my neck, then pauses.

"Want me to rip these clothes off, so I can worship you like the goddess you are?"

I nod, breathless, and River rips my tunic over my head and tosses it aside. Still straddling him, I gasp as River's mouth finds my bare breast, sucking gently. My head falls back, and I moan. Muscles between my legs flutter and tighten. Gods, he knows how to worship. His warm tongue flicks my nipple, toying, before he moves to the other one.

His calloused fingers trail down to my waist, finding the knot of my trousers. Effortlessly, he undoes the string and slides his hand between my thighs. We groan as his mouth claims mine. I grab the back of his head, fingers lacing through his damp, silky hair.

His skilled fingers rub the ache at my core. Desire builds as my body spasms under his slow, steady strokes. There's still pain, but pleasure wins, and I surrender to it. He slides a finger inside, I inhale sharply. My body pulses around his digit.

"Gaia above Myalis, you're so fucking wet." He groans into my neck. When he slips a second finger, my world teeters on the edge. I can't help but meet his thrusts with my hips.

"There you go," he croons. "Take what you want, my goddess." Those words undo me faster than I ever anticipated. A moan shatters the silence of the night around us as River continues to thrust in and out of my body with his fingers. As I ride the waves of pleasure, he throws me onto my back, and hovers over me. The pain is gone, replaced with pleasure. He pulls his hand from me, and then puts those fingers in his mouth to suck my juices. River groans as his eyes roll back. Then, with both hands, he pulls my pants off me.

He spreads my legs apart and puts his mouth on my core, delving his tongue into my throbbing center. My body jolts from the sensation. I've never had a man go down on me. The shock, and the way of River laps and sucks on my clit leaves no room for shame or shyness. Instead, a stimulating thrill pulses through me, one that I've never experienced before. Fuck, I've been missing out.

My limbs curve as he works my core with his tongue and mouth. Both his hands grasp my hips, fingers digging into my bare skin. A rush of electricity thrums through me. My arms splay out, my nails clawing the ground as River fucks me with his tongue. I can't even put into words what my body is doing. The pleasure spikes and a cry of ecstasy rips through my throat not even sounding like me. A tidal wave of pleasure floods through me, and my body becomes limp.

My breathing slows as I drift back down from the high. My eyes flutter open and when I look at River, his stormy eyes seem alight with glee, a mischievous grin spread across his face.

"You're a demon in disguise." I tease, boneless.

He laughs, crawling slowly up my naked body. When his face reaches mine, I can see my juices glistening on his mouth. River licks his lips in a way no man ever has—downright filthy.

"Perhaps." He shrugs and brings his mouth to mine. The kiss is gentle, sensual; unlike the passionate fervor from before. "But if I were a demon, I'd demand more of your body. I'm a gentleman, and you're still healing. I won't take further advantage of your gorgeous body. Not tonight."

As I stare at River, I push my questions aside. I don't want to think right now. I roll my eyes as he catches my chin, resting his forehead against mine. "I mean it. You're gorgeous and I'll enjoy worshipping this body for eternity if you'll let me."

I scoff, propping myself on my elbows. "You'll tire of me eventually."

River's grin lights up the darkness. "Never. Now come on, let's take a dip." He stands, stripping off his pants. It takes everything I have not to stare down there. River offers his hand. I take it.

Chapter 20

River

We ride for two days through the Oasis Peninsula. The air is thick and humid, sweat pouring from my forehead as we travel beneath a blazing, barbaric sun. It's a stark difference from the pleasant spring weather in Gaia's Keep. Hardly any trees grace our path. Instead, it's open, rolling fields of tall grass.

Myalis and I navigate through the edge of Hydros's territory without trouble. After all the chaos at Gaia's Keep, I'm grateful for the calm. My thoughts drift back to the moment when Voras watched me pull Myalis out of the swamp. It unsettles me how easily he let us go. I was sure that he'd fight me for her. I don't know why he didn't, but I don't like it.

We've come a long way since the Wild Swamps and Jade Lake. Mya's confidence has grown riding Ash. She suits her better than Buttercup ever did. With two horses, we can travel farther in a day, and faster. It's sped our journey up immensely.

We're close to the pathway to the Altar of Water. I've never seen it, but I've heard the tales of the treacherous trail required for passage, and the nefarious creatures lurking in the waters. I don't know exactly what we'll face when we arrive, but I hope we'll handle whatever comes.

Mya still doesn't trust me. Not after all that's happened. I understand why she feels betrayed, but it was never my intention to use her or her body to get my way or to lure her into something she doesn't want. I'll never be able to forgive myself for making her feel that way. I remember her face at the hot springs after we made love, her expression when she thought I'd used her. My heart still shatters every time I recall that. I just hope that I can fix what I ruined.

I want to be better for her. My only desire is to make her stronger. Give her a chance against Voras should it ever come to that. And after seeing him in the Wild Swamps, I know one day, it *will* come to that. He'll come for her again. When he does, we have to be ready. We need to train, hone our skills. Mine have grown rusty over the years when I gave up on the quest to find the Lastborn. My vices—smoking, drinking—took over everything else.

Now, I have purpose again. Myalis and I found each other. I found the Lastborn, the shooting star that I've been chasing ever since I first discovered the prophecy. Nothing else matters but her. She doesn't realize it yet, but she's going to be our savior. *My* savior. I just need to help her claim her destiny. She will defeat the Dark King.

The sky darkens above, gray clouds shifting as I lift my gaze, embracing it. Weather, after all, is my strongest wielding ability. As we continue, the terrain begins to change from lush green grass to a hard rocky trail. Rolling hills turn to stony mountains around us as we enter into a pass. Rain falls—the heavy pour, a cooling reprieve from the heat.

"Are we still going the right way?" Mya's voice calls from behind. We've been quiet all day, trading only simple pleasantries, and occasional pauses. Since leaving Gaia's Keep, our pace quickened. Mostly because I want to get as far away as possible from the Dark King.

"We are." I call back, trying to ease the tension in her voice.

"Do you think the weather will be a problem?"

Her words make me laugh. I feel her glare burning at the back of my head. "You do realize who you just said that to, right?" I turn and quirk a brow. She sighs, and I'm sure she rolled her eyes.

"Do you think we'll be safe in the pass at night?"

I stop Buttercup and wait as Mya falls in beside me. She warily stares at me, her golden-flecked eyes filled with confusion.

"What?" she snaps.

"We'll be fine," I assure her. "The temple path is just ahead and as long as we stick together, there shouldn't be a problem. Hopefully, we can make it before nightfall."

Her eyes shift to the path ahead, trepidation settling in. I nudge Buttercup with my heels and take the lead. "It's not far now," I say, then fall silent. I'm grateful for my sense of direction because just like Mya, I don't want to be stuck in the pass overnight. The hooves clop over rocks, rain echoing in the pass.

"Are you sure nothing's hunting us?"

Mya's been on edge since I told Voras came for her in the Wild Swamps. But we haven't seen or heard from him since. I've tried to calm her, but I remind myself she's new to this part of Elemi. She's mainly stuck to Gaia's Keep, never venturing deep into the Scarlett Lands, let alone to the Oasis Peninsula.

"Nothing's hunting us, Mya. This place is mostly unlivable—just reptiles and mountain goats," I explain.

We press through the mountain pass for hours. Luckily, the rain tapers off. Trickles of water run alongside us, running over rocks beneath hooves. When we emerge from the gap, a vast lake sits in a valley, stretching as far as the eye can see. We reach a rocky, stone-filled shoreline with deep blue water so still, it feels unreal. The sky darkens; thick clouds gather, threatening a storm.

"We're here." I say calmly, dismounting Buttercup and patting his neck. Mya follows suit.

"Where?" Mya scans the empty space, confused. "There's nothing here." Her sharp brows knit together, lips scrunched in frustration. I want nothing more than to grab those lips with my own and claim them. When silence drags, I shake my head, breaking her spell.

"The Altar of Water. We're here." I repeat, gesturing toward the water. "We have to pass a trial before it reveals itself." I cross my arms, staring over the vast water.

She sighs. "What *kind* of trial?" Mya opens her rucksack strapped to Ash's saddle. She pulls off her bow, quiver, and leather dagger sheath, securing the last to her thigh before gearing up. Watching her arm herself makes my blood run hot. The huntress in her awakens, making her look so damn sexy that it's hard for me to concentrate.

I take a staggering breath and pull out one of my ax harness from my bag, strapping it along my back. "I don't know. The books never said what it was. I guess it depends on the person."

She scoffs. "Well, that's helpful." Mya paces the shoreline, biting her lip in thought. "Do you think we'll face separate trials, or stay together?"

Mya's overthinking, worrying for nothing. Before she digs herself a hole in the rocky sand with her pacing, I step close, gripping her arms. Her eyes peer up at me through long lashes, and I tuck a strand of hair behind her ear.

"It'll be fine, whatever it is. We'll face it together." I say, confident. Her body loosens, and I cup her face, before pressing her lips to mine. The kiss is gentle, barely a whisper. The sensuality makes my dick twitch, and I can't help the smirk as I release her, hoping she doesn't realize how she affects me.

"So, what do we do until then?" Mya whispers, lifting her big eyes to mine.

I shrug, taking a seat by the shore. "We wait. Wait until the trial finds us." I pull my knees up resting my arms over them, hands dangling. I stare at the dark lake—lifeless beneath the surface, eerie in its stillness. The sky grows darker above. I wonder how long we'll wait for whatever is meant to find us. Should we build camp, or just wait it out?

Myalis sits beside me in silence. She sighs, her impatience clear. I stifle a laugh. The horses' chuffs fill the quiet. From the corner of my eye, I watch Mya's leg bobbing up and down. A grin spreads across my face.

"Not good at waiting, huh?" I tease.

She sharply turns her head, shooting a pointed glare. "I'm just not used to sitting still for long."

Her face falls as she exhales. It takes a moment for me to catch her meaning. "Tell me about it."

"About what?" She doesn't meet my gaze.

"About hiding from the King. How you survived eleven years on the run. Being in constant fear for your life. How did you do it?"

She purses her lips, fingers running through her hair. "I don't know. I just kept moving. Hid wherever I could. Under tree roots, beneath brush, caves. Anywhere for shelter. Sometimes I was safe for weeks, other times only days. The Dark Knights were relentless. Honestly, I don't know how I fled them long enough to get myself a year's respite."

Mya's shakes her head, thinking. "I hunted and set traps when I was in secluded. It took time to learn to live on my own, provide for myself. I was only thirteen when I started running. Thankfully, Papa taught me to hunt and prepare game. Mama tried to teach sewing, but I didn't take to it. I learned the basics, simple stitching. Alone, I mended clothes and hunted to eat. When I found villages, I'd hunt extra, sold what I could. It helped keep me alive."

"That sounds tough." I admit.

Mya turns offers a small smile.

"I can't imagine what that must have felt like, being so young. You're brave, Mya. Stronger than you realize."

She waves me off. "You're just trying to sweeten me up." The statement playful as she looks away.

"It's true." I shrug. "Even though I was reckless as a child, I don't know if I could've endured being chased by the Dark King at the age of thirteen."

Myalis laughs. "I'm sure you would've been just fine. You're a strong and capable fighter. I can only imagine how rambunctious you were as a child."

I laugh too. "I did give the Gaian Priestesses a hard time. That I can admit. They didn't usually take in children. I think sometimes I turned the whole temple upside down."

We both burst out in laughter. When it dies down, silence fills the space again. I sigh. "I'm sorry I didn't get to show you my favorite part of it."

"Of what?"

"The Gaian Temple," I state. "I wanted to show you the Chamber of Gaia. It's my favorite room. It's covered, floor to ceiling, in beautiful stained-glass windows, depicting the story of the ancient Elementals and everything related to Gaia. The seasons, the territories, all our powers. It's beautiful. I spent a lot of time in there growing up."

I fondly think of my childhood home. The temple where I was raised after the King killed my parents. Even though I missed them, I was so young when they died that I saw Elera and Nani more as mothers than my own, unfortunately. It's been so long, I can't even picture my parents' faces. I hadn't called the Temple of Gaia home in years, but returning to it, even just for the day, brought back happy memories. I think on that now sitting by the dark, hidden lake in these mountains, wondering what's next for Mya and me.

Myalis needs to learn her powers. That's why we're here. In hopes that the Priests and Priestesses of the Altar of Water will be bold enough to take her in and train her. I pray they won't fear Voras's wrath if he learns they're sheltering a "fugitive" of the crown.

"It does sound beautiful," Myalis says. For a second, I forget what I said. "I'm sorry I didn't stay long enough for you to show me."

Our eyes meet and a spark ignites in me. Something tugs at my soul, indescribable, that I've never felt before. I don't know what it is about Mya that brings this on. Is it the wonder of being in the company of the Lastborn, or that she's the only Celestial Forsaken? My earth magic feels

harmonious with hers. I'm captivated by every part of her.
All of her. Every bit of her being that she's let me see.

My heart skips, and I lean closer. She subconsciously sways toward me. Our lips nearly meet, then a melodic tune flutters from the water. A voice sings out, drawing our focus. Ripples break the dark lake, but I can't make out what's approaching us. I rise, taking a step toward the edge, my boot's tip dipped in water. Mya joins me, as we watch the surface.

The song is haunting, hypnotic. Sung in an old language—one I don't understand. A creature skims the surface in the distance. I squint, trying to see. Realization slams into me.

"Fuck," I mutter.

"What is it?" Myalis whispers.

"A seareniss." I state. Mya shakes her head—she doesn't know. "A water guardian of the deep. They were said to lure travelers to their deaths with their voices. I didn't think they lived in lakes."

As I finish, the creature emerges. Long, black hair crests the water, shrouding her face as she rises. Her skin is ashen gray, slick and slimy. The top half: a voluptuous, hauntingly beautiful woman. The bottom—something inhuman, hidden beneath the surface.

"Travelers…" Her voice is low, hypnotic as she tilts her head. Wide-set eyes—deep, blood red. An angular face with full lips. When she speaks, sharp, pointed teeth flash. It's an eerie beauty. Alluring and terrifying. The kind of face that haunts dreams.

"What brings you this way?" she asks.

Only then do I notice the black spotted tentacles rising around her as she props herself up with human seeming hands and arms.

"We seek asylum at the Altar of Water. We hope the gracious priests and priestesses will train the Lastborn." I say, steady. My hand rests on my ax as her eyes flick between Mya and me.

The seareniss's expression shifts as she studies Mya. "The Lastborn?" Her tone is curious, not surprised.

"Yes," I affirm. "The head priestess at the Temple of Gaia confirmed it. But she can't yet control her powers. We hope someone here will be willing to train her."

The seareniss seems annoyed that I'm speaking, but her gaze stays fixed on Mya, who's frozen under the stare.

"I know not what the Hydros's priests and priestesses would decide in regard to training the Lastborn. Especially since she is a Celestial Forsaken. That kind of power hasn't been seen in thousands of years. But they might offer refuge. I assume you seek asylum from the Dark King?"

Her eyes turn back to me. I nod, catching Mya's gaze briefly before looking back at the seareniss. When she glances at Mya again, my fingers twitch, fists clenching. I've no idea what she'll do next.

"You may enter," the seareniss says, parting the water beside her, revealing a stone path into the lake.

"Thank you," Mya murmurs, bowing in relief. Was it really that easy? She steps onto the path, and I watch, holding my breath.

"Yes, thank you for your generosity," I say, moving to follow Mya down the path.

"Oh, no." The seareniss's eyes snap to me. Mya stops, turning toward me.

"I don't understand," I say, approaching the haunting creature. A cruel, exaggerated smile sprawls across her face, showing how horrifying those sharp teeth are. Her black tentacles curl above the surface.

"She may enter. *You* must face a trial."

252

Chapter 21

Myalis

"Wait." I force myself to speak. "Why does he have to face a trial, and I don't?"

I step back to shore, away from the path to the temple. Her red eyes shift back toward me, that predatory smile still curling her lips.

"You are worthy of passage to the Altar of Water. He, however, is fogged. Blocked from my sight, my ability to judge his worth."

I frown and glance at River, who stays impassive.

"What does that even mean?" I ask, stepping closer to the half-human, half-tentacled creature. I've never seen such a thing before. River calls her a seareniss. She's haunting, and I don't want to be in her presence longer than necessary.

She turns her attention back to River. "This man claims he found the Lastborn. He harbors a star." Then to me. "I want one too."

River and I stare, confused. I don't understand, but River speaks first. "A star?" His voice is low, sending a shiver down my spine.

"Indeed," the seareniss hisses. "Bring me a star to call my own. Fail and well…" She trails off, the threat clear. Death. I inhale sharply and watch River. His jaw tenses, lips thinning, Adam's apple bobbing as he swallows.

"Hurry, dear… you have fifteen minutes to bring me my star."

"What?" I shout, heart pounding. "He has fifteen minutes to do the impossible. How are we going to bring you a star? It's not even night. There aren't any stars in the sky."

The creature shoots me a look so menacing it freezes me in place. "*You* will do nothing. He must complete the task. He alone."

"*River*." My voice is desperate, and I take two steps toward him. He meets me, cupping my cheek with his hand.

"It's fine. Searenisses hoard treasure. It's in their nature. I'll figure it out." He reassures me, bringing his forehead to mine. "But whatever happens, go to the temple. Get the training you need."

My heart aches as I look into River's eyes. Why does this feel like goodbye? I grab his wrist, pressing into his touch. "I won't go on without you." I whisper. "We've come this far together."

Heat flashes in his eyes before River kisses me—fierce, possessive, his tongue caressing mine. We crash together, his fingers tangling in my hair like it's the last time he ever will. I gasp and he devours the sound with his mouth. When our lips pull apart, and River steps away, I feel the loss. He turns back to the searenis.

Determination sets in as he glares at the water creature, searching for a way to grant her impossible request. It's as if the two of them are involved in a staring contest. Neither of them takes their eyes off each other.

"Hurry, pretty one, your time is dwindling," the seareniss taunts, mouth twisting in a wicked grin. Her sharp, jagged teeth glint. The sight is deeply unsettling.

River's brow furrows as his gaze skims our surroundings. He's searching for an answer—to figure out what the seareniss truly wants. Could she mean a literal star? How could anyone do that without magic? Can I create a star in my palm and give it to her?

My heart races. "River," I call. He steps toward me, as if time isn't slipping away. "What if I create a star with my powers? You could give it to her." I whisper, keeping my voice so low the seareniss won't hear.

His eyes glint with amusement as he stifles a laugh. "I love that you want to help," he murmurs, "but I doubt she'll let you complete the trial for me. She already told you not to interfere."

My body sags with disappointment. It was the only solution I could think of. River lays a heavy hand on my shoulder, his smile not quite reaching his eyes, before turning back to the water.

"Time is running out Gaian Forsaken." The seareniss coos. "Where is my star to keep?" I haven't kept track of how long it's been, but I know that River doesn't have much time left. I rack my brain, trying to figure out if there's anything else that I can do. Anything I can think of that might help.

"Take me." I blurt out.

"What?" River barks, sharp and alarmed.

"I'm the Lastborn. I can create celestial magic. Please, take me and let River go." I plead, moving closer to her.

"Absolutely not!" River snaps, stepping between us. "That would mean sacrificing your life, Mya. I won't allow it. You're too important."

I grit my teeth, frustration bubbling. "What other option is there?"

"While your offer is generous," the seareniss hisses, "again, *you* are not the one who needs to complete the trial. Find a star to call my own, Gaian. You have five minutes left."

River lowers his gaze. "What other option is there?" he echoes softly, almost to himself. "Another option." His eyes flick to the water, then back at me. Suddenly, he bolts, plunging into the dark waters with a deep breath—gone from sight.

Horrified, I gasp and run to where he dove. "*River!*" I scream. "*River!*" My heart flutters, my stomach drops as I look for him in the murky waters.

What the fuck is he doing? I don't know what creatures live in this lake, but if there are things like the seareniss, who knows what else lurks beneath. I pace the shore, frantic. No sign of him. After a minute, panic seizes me. Has he drowned? Gaia above, I'm about to be sick. I scan the lake, hoping River's head will pop out any moment, but he doesn't.

Time stills, the world shrinking until all I hear is pounding in my ears. Everything else fades but the lake. The longer I stare, the more it crushes me—River isn't coming back up.

Warm tears well as I pace the shoreline. Even the horses are silent as I stand there, waiting. Rage builds inside me when I see the seareniss, watching me with a satisfied look on her haunting face.

Nostrils flaring, I yank my dagger from its sheath and march toward her. I seize her slick, black hair exposing her throat, blade pressed hard to her ashen skin.

"Where the fuck is he?" I snarl. "What did you do?"

She smiles, and her blood-red eyes upturn in amusement. "I did nothing. He entered the Dread Lagoon by choice. There are never promises of return."

I growl, pressing the blade harder. A bead of black blood trickles down, but the seareniss doesn't flinch. She almost seems to enjoy the threat.

"Tell me, Lastborn, what do you know of your travel companion?"

She stares directly into my eyes. "Is he really who he says he is? You follow him blindly, let him steal your body and heart and yet... what has he told you of himself?"

I frown, caught off-guard, pulling back. "Well, I—"

"He is fogged," she repeats. "Clouded from my judgment. And while you trust him now, just remember what you don't know."

Another riddle. One more to dwell upon. The splash of water and a sharp gasp draw my eyes to the lagoon. River emerges like a Forsaken of Hydros himself. Relief floods my senses, but a seed of doubt takes root. He moves slowly toward the shore, the seareniss studies him, as if she's granted him passage.

"Your timing is impeccable, Gaian. You had twenty seconds to spare. But tell me, have you brought what I seek?" Her suspicious eyes roam over him, catching on something in his hand.

My gaze drifts there too. River holds out a sea creature, a bottom-dweller shaped like a star. Its smooth surface shines pale, illustrious gold. I squint, awestruck by the tiny thing, unsure what it means.

"A starfyn," the seareniss states, amusement curving her angular face.

"Indeed," River confirms. He flips it over, revealing soft bristles underneath, and a hole at its center. River sticks his finger into it, and I wince, wondering if it hurts it. Carefully, he digs and pulls out a golden, star-shaped pearl.

"A golden pearl to keep forever in your horde. Here is your star." River proudly states holding it out. I look at him in awe. Stunned that he knows such a creature exists. The seareniss nods, accepting the pearl.

"Congratulations, Gaian. You've passed your trial. You and the Lastborn may enter the Altar of Water." With the wave, the stone path reappears through the water. River bows and heads to our horses to gather our rucksacks, then returns to my side.

"Ready?" he asks. I stand in shock, mouth agape. So many questions swarm in my mind, but they'll wait. The path to the Altar of Water awaits.

I nod slightly and watch River step onto the path—water parted by the seareniss. The path leads down into the lagoon, walls of water rising on either side as we descend.

"This is creepy," I whisper, watching water walls tunnel overhead. River leads unaffected, deeper into the bowels of the Dread Lagoon. The world dissolves. No more rolling hills filled with summer trees. Not even our horse remains in sight.

Further along, the water walls collapse behind us, sealing the tunnel to the temple. I realize this place is magic. Hydros himself must have created this as a safe haven for his people. There's no other explanation for such ancient power sustaining itself here.

River and I move silently in the endless Dread Lagoon path. I wonder how deep we are and how far it descends until we reach the end of the tunnel. Only the sound of our breaths fills the unnerving and eerie silence. I clear my throat, fighting off the claustrophobia.

"How did you know a starfyn would suffice? I've never even heard of one." I mutter.

River chuckles, shrugging. "I've traveled all over Elemi and been to many ancient libraries. I've read about all sorts of creatures during my travels. Once while I was rummaging through the Gaian Temple's library, I found a text about Elemi's different sea creatures. I had read about starfyns long ago but remembered that they lived in salt water. When I saw the seareniss, I knew it was a saltwater lake. Searenisses like to boast and brag about shiny trinkets. It was a long shot, but the starfyn was the last thing I could think of. I'm just glad I found one."

"I'm also glad you found one." My mind drifts to what might've happened if he hadn't, then to the seareniss's words while River was underwater. I'd hoped we'd moved past betrayal and lies, but now, I'm not so sure. "How *were* you able to find that creature in the dark water?"

River turns his head briefly, his chin dipping over his shoulder. "I control weather. Because of that, I can sometimes wield water. The starfyn shines with an illustrious sheen. I could barely spot the bottom feeder."

Incredible. Almost too incredible. Maybe River isn't who he says he is. I raise my guard back up again. I grunt, understanding what he means, but I'll never know how he did it. If it had been me, I would've failed the trial. I would've probably died or become imprisoned by the seareniss. Who knows what she'd have done to me?

Then I realize just how intelligent River is, and how much I lack. I've come so far, but I'll never be as knowledgeable. Never as skilled. My stomach churns as we cross a cave's threshold.

Inside, the sight stops me cold. My jaw drops as I take in the Altar of Water.

Chapter 22

Myalis

The giant rock cave towers high above us. Water drips from stalactites, a steady music to my ears. A broad rock path leads up to the ancient water temple, perched on a crystal-blue lake. Waterfalls cascade off the side in all directions, disappearing into a dark abyss below. I dare not look over the edge as one misstep means death.

I gulp as River leads on toward the entrance of the giant sandstone temple. A massive central tower boasts a waterfall cascading down its face. Flanking it are two domed towers, their pointed sparkling spiral tips reaching toward the cavern's ceiling. The palace is magnificent, awe-inspiring. It's so enchanting that I don't know how Hydros conjured it.

Crossing the black abyss onto the crystal-blue lake, I notice how still and shallow the water is. The sandy bottom is clear beneath, schools of small iridescent fish swimming around. The closer we get, the wider the lake spreads out.

"This is unbelievable," I whisper as we near an archway. Two men stand guard, dressed in dark blue loincloths and opalescent armor on either side of the entryway. War paint covers their faces. Nervously, I meet their gaze.

"Who seeks entry to the ancient Altar of Water, Temple of Hydros, sacred place to Hydros Forsaken and place of gods?" One guard barks; his voice deep, authoritative. His timbre echoes off the cavern walls. The reverberation shakes my bones.

"I am River Dune, Gaian Forsaken, from Gaia's Keep, and with me, I bring Myalis Lucernas, the Lastborn, a Myrea Forsaken." River's voice is as commanding as the guard's.

The two guards exchange a glance before the first speaks again. "And what is your business here?"

"We seek refuge, and hope that the priests and priestesses will be willing to aid the Lastborn in learning her powers." River's words cut to the chase. I bite my lip, praying they won't react like Elera did at the Gaian Temple.

I hope to find rest here, sleep in a bed for longer than one night. Eat food that tastes good. Maybe even bathe regularly. I don't want to be turned away again. My body and mind can't take it.

The guards exchange another glance before one speaks. "I will take you to the head priestess. She will determine whether or not you can stay."

Relieved to gain an audience, we fall into step behind him as he guides us under the archway and toward the overwhelming temple. My stomach drops and a sense of dejá vu hits. We ascend stairs leading to massive wrought-iron double door—the temple's entrance. The doors are beautifully crafted, studded with dark blue jewels and pearls. An image of a giant sea creature is depicted—a long slithering body with sharp gnarled teeth. I assume it's Hydros himself, perhaps in sea beast form? It's a stunning work of art. The doors open as I continue to admire the craftsmanship.

We step into a large receiving room. "Wait here," the guard orders heading toward two wooden doors, guarded by two more soldiers dressed in identical attire. They nod, allowing him entry. He disappears quickly, leaving River and me with two soldiers who eye us suspiciously.

I take in the space around us. The room is dark, lit only by a chandelier made of seashells. River steps close, his pinky finger brushing mine. My breath catches at the gentle touch. Our eyes meet. I wonder if River feels as nervous as I do.

Before we speak, the guard returns and gestures us inside. We enter a giant space, and I'm dazed by its beauty. Sandstone walls frame the space with gold and pearl chandeliers hanging high above. Archways line our way through the giant room, and in the front is a dais with a large silver chair. Tepid waterfalls cascade from the ceiling, falling into small pools on either side.

A stunning woman sits in the throne chair, flanked by dozens alongside her. She's dressed in a flowing gossamer dress with a deep V-neckline. The sheer fabric sparkles and as we approach, I realize that the dress leaves nothing to the imagination. She doesn't seem human as I look at her face. Her skin is pale blue—so pale, it's almost ghostly. Her large oval eyes, deep blue in color, and too large for her thin face fall instantly upon us. She stands as we reach the steps of the dais.

"Welcome, travelers. I am Themora, the Head Priestess at the Altar of Water. What brings you to Hydros's ancient temple?" Her voice is silken and lyrical, even hypnotic in tone.

"Head Priestess," River begins, bowing subtly. "We have traveled far from Gaia's Keep, seeking refuge, and hoping you will train the Lastborn."

Themora's eyes shift to me, scanning me from top to bottom. Her interest in me piques. She remains silent as she glances back at River, eyeing him as well. Her thin lips curl slightly at River. "It's not often that a Gaian Forsaken graces our presence. If it's true that you're the prophesied Lastborn, then you're the only Myrean Forsaken to step foot in Hydros's temple. Can you prove that you're what he says you are?"

My stomach drops. I hadn't ever been asked to display my powers. They normally only come to life when I'm in danger. The one recent exception being that time with Nani in the Gaian Temple where she helped me call to them. Can I summon the magic again?

All eyes fix on me, and I look around the giant room, resisting the urge to shrink away. I'm used to being unseen, but with all these eyes, I feel more vulnerable than ever. Still, I nod to the head priestess. If she wants to see my celestial powers, then I must try and prove myself.

"Step forward," Themora demands. "Show us your celestial magic, Lastborn."

I cast one last glance at River. He tilts his head, urging me to go on. My steps feel heavy as I approach the dais, nearly stumbling on the first stair. I look up at Themora, then then at the men and women behind her. They all have similar features. Pale blue skin, silvery blonde hair, and ears pointier than mine. Their clothing varies; women in sheer gossamer dresses like Themora's, in shades of blue. Guards wear loincloths and metal armors. I assume the men in bare loincloths are priests, their arms bound in armbands, necks adorned with large, shelled necklaces. Their bodies are strong and muscular, yet tall and lean.

I shake off my thoughts, and take a deep breath, recalling what Nani told me about summoning my powers. I close my eyes, holding out my palms before me. Steadying my breath, I focus on my core and think of the stars. The memory of how they comforted me on lonely nights, offering solace when people never did. The stars have always been there for me, more so than people ever were. Their magnificence, sparkling like glitter in the sky.

Warmth floods me with the memory. Gasps fill the room as I open my eyes—a galaxy swirls in my palms. Themora's face shifts as she descends the stairs. It's as if she's in awe.

"Great heavens above," she whispers, her dark blue eyes locked onto the stars in my hands. "I never thought I'd see the day."

I raise my palms upward to the ceiling and release the stars. They sparkle overhead, with the glittering chandeliers, while gasps and awes echo through the room. I bite the inside of my lip as I watch them gleam above before fading into nothing. When I look at River, he stares at me in wonder, and for a moment, I think he'll come closer, but it's Themora's voice that pulls me back.

"The Starlight Princess has graced us with her presence." Themora bows her head in approval, and before I know it, all the Hydros Forsaken follow, bowing to me as if I really *were* royalty.

"The Starlight Princess?" I scoff under my breath. No one's called me that. I don't understand it. I'm no princess. I'm barely grasping that I'm part of an ancient prophecy.

Themora gazes through long pale lashes. "We will grant you solace here at the Altar of Water. You may stay and learn for as long as you desire."

Warm tears spill out of my eyes. Refuge. It's all I'd ever desired. And we're finally granted it. "Thank you," I whisper barely audible as River steps to my side.

"Holtian will train you." Themora says, turning back toward the dais. "He is Hydros's heir. We've protected Hydros's bloodline for thousands of years and it'd be an honor for us if you'd allow him to be your guide and trainer here at the temple." She sits on her throne chair, her expression fierce. This is their condition. River's hand slides possessively around my waist.

"I want to stay close to Mya—as her... protector." River's voice hardens.

Themora doesn't flinch at the request. She simply waves her hand with quiet authority. "Very well. Holtian!" Her voice echoes through the cavern. "Please make yourselves comfortable and if you should require anything, do not hesitate to let us know."

A tall and lithe man about my age enters the room. There isn't an ounce of fat on his muscular body. He has silvery-white hair, shaved on both sides of his head but braided at the top, cascading down to the middle of his back. Small golden rings adorn the braids. Leather bands wrap his upper arms and wrists. Beaded necklaces rest on his sculpted chest. My breath hitches at his pale blue skin and dark gray eyes. River stiffens beside me, as the man approaches us.

"Holtian, this is Myalis Lucernas and River Dune," Themora introduces us. "Myalis is the Starlight Princess. You're to show them around the temple and train the Myrean heir while they stay with us."

Holtian's steel gaze meets mine as he strides over and extends a hand. "It'll be my pleasure," he purrs. I place my hand in his and he brings it to his lips, gently pressing his mouth on the back of my hand. "Come, I'll give you a tour of our sacred home."

Holtian keeps hold of my hand leading me toward a door beside the throne room. River grumbles behind as we leave, stepping into a series of hallways.

"It's nice to meet you." I say awkwardly. My small talk could really use some work. I've never been great with strangers. I watch Holtian closely as he leads us, sharing the temple's history.

"It's an honor to meet you as well," he replies. "We never believed we'd see a Myrean Forsaken."

"I only recently discovered who I am," I admit, cheeks flushing as I watch him. "So, is it true that you're the heir of Hydros?"

He chuckles, flashing bright teeth and incisors sharper than most. "I am. In the days before the reign of darkness, I'd be king of the Oasis Peninsula. The Altar of Water is the most sacred place here. Hydros himself lived here when he graced us with his presence on the mortal plane. It was his castle. We have done all we can to preserve it for whenever he decides to return."

What a delusional thought. The Elementals will never return, but who am I to dash his hopes? It's no wonder the temple feels more like a castle than a place of worship. The sandstone halls glitter with shiny items, chandeliers, and torches. It's vibrant and warm, despite being placed in an underwater cavern. "It really is beautiful."

"It is. For thousands of years, we've thrived here. We've learned how to cultivate food. We've a farm on the far side where we breed animals. Because this is a sacred place, our population isn't anywhere near as large as Volantis, but we have our own thriving community here."

Holtian guides us down a series of hallways before we arrive at one where doors line opposite of each other. "That sounds incredible," I admit, disbelief coloring my tone.

"I'll show you tomorrow," Holtian grins. "For now, these are your rooms. You've had a long and arduous journey, I'm sure you'd like rest. I'll have a meal brought to you." Holtian opens the deep blue wooden door, revealing a beautiful, airy room. "This one's yours, princess."

Princess. The nickname off his tongue sends a curl to my toes but I shrug it off as we enter the space. It's a much larger room than I thought it'd be. In the center, there's a four-poster bed with crisp white linens and gauzy fabric hanging from the posts. A stained-glass window paints one of the walls in shades of blue, depicting the ocean. Above, a pearl chandelier flickers with soft light—magic, I think. Opposite the bed, there's a mosaic-tiled fireplace with a cozy couch in front of it. Another door sits on the same wall as the fireplace.

I look around, stunned by the luxury. Disbelief floods me. I'm staying here, and I'm safe. "There's a bathing room through that door there," Holtian explains, nodding toward the door I noticed. "Feel free to pick any clothing from the wardrobe over here," he adds, gesturing to a large piece of wood furniture taking up a lot of the wall space.

I nod, awed by the space that'll be mine. "Thank you, Holtian. This is wonderful."

He smiles brilliantly. "You're welcome, princess. And please, call me Holt," he winks and my cheeks turn pink. He turns his attention to River, who is all but steaming. "You'll be right next door." Holt heads to the door, beckoning River to follow.

River lingers in my room, placing my rucksack on the ground by the door before following the Hydros's heir. Quietly, I tread toward the door and peek into the hallway to see the two men entering the room right next to mine. Holt doesn't stay long with River. Just long enough to show him the room before he leaves. As Holt passes my room, he gives me another smile, and nods before turning back.

He flusters me. I feel stupid just watching him walk away. All of his lean muscles are on full display in that tiny shard of clothing he wears.

"You're gawking." River growls, leaning against his doorway, arms crossed. I meet his gaze.

I grit my teeth. "No, I'm not." I step inside to close the door behind me. River's hand catches it as he pushes the door in. Once he's in my room, he slams it shut behind him.

"Yes, you were." River is instantly behind me. I feel his massive presence, and turning to face him, I clench my fists along my sides.

"What's wrong with you?" I bark, incredulous. "So, now I apparently can't look at any other men, aside from you?"

River is silent. His jaw tenses, nostrils flare. Silence falls. I hold his gaze, reading his expression until a thought strikes.

"Are you... jealous?" I tease, and a smirk stretches across my face.

River shrugs, avoiding looking me in the eye. "Why would I be jealous?"

"You are, aren't you? Huh," I scoff. "I never thought you'd be so insecure."

River's blue eyes electrify, a tick in his jaw follows. "So? What if I am?"

"You were the one who called me your *companion,* River." I snap. "If you really wanted to stake some sort of claim on me, maybe you should've said so back in the throne room."

River hisses, "we've not talked about that. How the fuck am I supposed to introduce you to a bunch of strangers? Especially without knowing where their loyalties lie."

I shrugged off my bow and quiver, dropping them by my rucksack. He really wants to get into this right now? Fine. "We haven't talked about our relationship, River, because you betray me over and over again, twisting my emotions around in circles. Even the seareniss warned me about you. About trusting you. So, honestly, I don't know what to think about *us*."

He stumbles back as if I'd slapped him. His face twists, my words landing hard. The air shifts. My skin buzzes as River comes dangerously close to me. I hold my breath, unsure what he's about to unleash.

"*Us*." River's voice is so low, I barely hear the word. I brace myself for whatever's coming next.

Chapter 23

Myalis

My eyes drift toward the door, it's my only exit from the room. River catches it and, in a flash, pushes me against the wall. "*Us*, Myalis?" His hot breath hits my face, and I shudder as he cages me. "You're right. What *us* is there? Everything I've done, has been for *you*."

He points a finger, and I shake my head, not understanding a word.

"Yes," he says. "I have traveled with you across the goddamned continent trying to find someplace where we can be safe, where *you* would be safe. I have saved you from harm, whether it's General Grimsbane or the Larkfury or the Dark King himself. I've told you over and over that I care about you and want to be with you and yet, you still push me away. You still don't *trust* me."

"River... I—"

"No," he cuts me off. "I don't want to hear it." River pushes off me storming out the door, slamming it behind him. The sound startles me and the breath I'd been holding in rushes out. Guilt floods through me as his words sink in.

River's right. He has done nothing but protect me since I met him. He's been with me through all of it, even when I pushed him away.

I don't know how long I stand against that wall before sliding down and wrapping my arms around my knees. My mind races. When did everything get so complicated? One minute, I'm safe in Sunhollow, minding my own business. Safe from the Dark King, living a quiet peaceful life, albeit temporary. The next, I'm traipsing across Elemi with a Gaian Forsaken to discover that I'm a long-lost prophecy. And now? Now what am I doing?

A knock stirs me from my stupor. My breath hitches as I stagger to the door. I open it, and a priestess is standing there, holding a tray. She's pretty and young, even younger than me. Her pale blonde hair cascades down her back, and she has ocean-blue eyes. A nervous smile crosses her lips.

"Master Holtian requested food be sent to your room," she explains.

"Right, thank you." I reach out and accept the tray from her, but she stays in place. Her large eyes stare in wonder. Awkwardly, I smile at her as she clasps her hands.

"Master Holtian also said to tell you that you'll start training with him first thing in the morning."

"Ah," I nod. "Thank you again." She bows and then walks down the hallway, her silk dress flowing in her wake. I turn closing the door behind me, setting the tray of food on the round table next to the couch. I remove the lid to reveal a plate of assorted cheese, dried meats, warm rolls, and a sumptuous looking red fruit.

It doesn't take me long to dive into the food. It's delicious and filling, and I moan in delight as I finish everything off the plate. I decide to check out the bathing room that Holt mentioned. Exhaustion crashes over me, and I'm emotionally drained from my fight with River. I want to clean up and rest, especially if I'm training with Holt tomorrow.

I freeze when I enter the bathing room, its beauty halting me. Iridescent fish scale tiles cover every space. To my right, a large mirror hangs above the basin of clear water resting on a driftwood table. In the center stands a glass enclosure with a silver contraption hanging from the ceiling. Curiously I study it, puzzled by the lack of a tub.

I step inside the glass enclosure. It's like a tiny room with transparent walls and an entryway. I gaze up at the silver fixture above, spotted with tiny holes. A drain sits near my feet. I stand, baffled. All I want to do is bathe—what's this glass room's purpose?

"It's a shower." I jump at the voice behind me. Holt stands in the doorway, with a crooked smile and arms crossed over his taut chest.

"You startled me," I sigh. "I didn't hear you come in."

"Apologies, princess." He strides to the shower joining me. "I didn't mean to frighten you. I just wanted to see how you were adjusting."

How am I adjusting? This all feels incredible, and I'm grateful to have a comfortable place to rest my head tonight. "It's great, but you're right—I have no clue what this is." My face flushes red.

Holt chuckles, light-hearted and warm. My stomach flutters hearing him laugh. "I thought of that after I left you. Pretty much everyone in the temple can wield water.

As a Hydros Forsaken, working a shower is an easy feat. Here, step out for a moment."

I do as he asks. He flicks his wrist, pointing at the shower, swirling his hand. Water pours from the silver contraption—a heavy stream, like rain. I gape stepping closer to let the water trickle over my hand. I grin.

"What a fantastical creation," I breathe. "A rainstorm inside."

Holt's silver eyes squint with amusement, his smile revealing a hint of teeth. "If you want, I can run the shower for you. I promise, I won't peek." He chuckles, and I find myself blushing, again. Holt's dangerously pleasing to look at. Perhaps too much. I want to *shower*, but not with him in here.

"Thanks, but I don't think I know you well enough for that." I tease before my smile fades. Looks like no bath tonight. Disappointment fills me. Holt's expression falls.

"I can have a wash tub brought in instead." He suggests and I look up instantly. His features are strong with silver eyes like icicles, with blue flecks through them.

"Can you do that? It's not too much trouble?" It sounds like a lot of work to bring in a whole basin.

Holt nods. "I get whatever I want—I am the heir of Hydros after all. Although Themora is the head priestess, I am a prince. I shall see it done. Anything else you need for tonight?" Holt's gaze lingers, and I shiver.

I shake my head. "No. Thank you. See you in the morning for training?"

A smile spreads on Holt's face. "Of course. See you then."

Holt winks, leaving me alone, heading toward the bedroom door. His loincloth leaves little to the imagination. It reveals every muscle of his body. I watch his back muscles twitching as he disappears. A breath rushes from me as I return to the bedroom and sit on the couch. Bath or no bath, I close my eyes.

It's been such a long day. It's hard to believe how far we traveled before facing the trial. It all happened today. The strain catches up, as my body sags on the couch. My thoughts drift back to River. I sigh, fighting sleep.

A knock wakes me. I didn't realize I fell asleep sitting up and I didn't know for how long. I go to the door and open it. Two priests stand there, carrying a round wooden tub and large pitchers of water. They bow, and I let them in.

Silently, they set up the tub in the bathing room under the shower. They pour hot water into it. Before long, two more men arrive with more pitchers, following suit. When the tub fills, they bow and leave. I gawk but am impressed.

Relieved, I undress, starting with my boots, then my tunic and finally my leggings. I look around and notice a couple of bottles nestled on the wooden shelves. I pluck one off and pop open the cork to smell it. Orchids. I pour a little into the tub and sink into the warm water.

It seeps into my sleepy, aching body, bringing me instant bliss. I hiss softly as I settle, eyes closing. I dunk my head to wet my hair into the water for a few seconds, then surface for air. Reaching for the orchid oil, I pour some into my palm and use it to wash my hair and body.

I don't stay in the tub for long. Just enough to wash myself, because I'm too tired to linger. My eyelids are heavy, and my mind feels too exhausted. I amble to the wardrobe to look for sleepwear. When I open the door, I gasp seeing the clothes. Everything is thin, silky, or sheer. Soft colors, mostly in shades of pastel blue or purple. Some fabrics sparkle. Others shimmer. The clothing is mildly revealing and not something I've worn before. The pieces look sensual and seductive, and I'm already blushing just looking at some of them. I'm so accustomed to tunics and leggings; leather, wool, and heavy boots, that I never thought of myself in these fine, delicate pieces.

I find a small silver satin dress with thin straps and pluck it out from the wardrobe. The fabric is silky-soft but looks revealing. It will do for sleep. Quickly, I pull it over my head. I glance in the bathroom mirror, barely recognizing myself. My legs are fully exposed as the dress falls mid-thigh. My arms are bare, and the neckline plunges between my breasts. Grateful no one will see me like this, I head to bed quickly.

The bed is luxurious with the warmest bedding I've ever felt. I tuck in and fall asleep instantly.

Surrounded by darkness, I'm alone. Only the sound of my heavy breathing echoes around. I'm running, but go nowhere. Panic consumes me. I don't know where I am or what's happening. The dark terrifies me.

I run, my bare feet splashing the darkness beneath me. It's like running on water. I look down and realize I'm still wearing the silver nightgown dress from earlier. I clutch my chest, trying to cover myself.

"Hello?" *I call, my eyes searching. I sense a presence but see nothing, feeling trapped.* "Hello!"

A figure appears—a silhouette I don't recognize. The being is tall and lean, almost unnaturally. An onyx crown with sharp points adorns his head, and he's dressed in all black robes. My chest heaves as I try to back away, but it only comes closer. I find myself frozen, unable to move.

"Myalis," *his voice coos, a sensual caress across my bare skin, sending goosebumps down my spine. I stand stiff as he reveals himself, and I gasp in horror. Although I've never seen him in person, I know who he is.*

The Dark King.

I shiver, his presence is icy, like he brought winter itself. A chill settles as his piercing blue eyes stare down at me. The palest shade of blue I'd ever seen. His other features remain shadowed. Cloaked in darkness, he reveals only what he wills. His glowing eyes skim my body, and I feel naked and exposed.

"Why am I here?" *I demand.*

"You summoned me," *his cold voice wraps around me.* "Tell me, Starling, why am *I* here?"

I growl. "I did no such thing. I didn't summon you. You... you're haunting my dreams."

A chuckle rumbles from his throat.

"Your power grows, Myalis. You're somewhere powerful; I can sense it. Where are you, my Starling?" *He reaches a pale hand out toward my face, and I flinch. His long fingers hover just before touching my cheek.*

I shake my head. "Get out of my mind."

"Where are you?" *He asks, voice harsher. His crown glints in the dark. His eyes captivate me, searching my soul. He seeks the truth inside me. I feel pulled, my body not my own.*

I shut my eyes, shake my head fiercely. "Get out of my head!" *I yell, thrusting my hands forward to push him away. A blinding light erupts, enveloping me.*

I sit up, gasping in horror, sweat beading on my brow. My chest heaves as I realize that I'm in my bed, at the water temple. I toss the bedding off and swing my legs over, feet hitting the cool sandstone floor. I take a deep breath, stand and move toward the door, leaving my room behind. I go to the door next to mine, lift my hand to knock, then hesitate.

My heart races as I wait in the dim, torch-lit, silent, hallway. I don't know the time, only that it's deep into the night. I blink, but the Dark King's face appears beneath my eyelids. I gasp and snap my eyes open. The memory of his presence in my dream leaves me on edge. Goosebumps rise along my neck. I ball my fist and pound the door. Nothing. I knock again, frantically, hurting my knuckles.

The door flies open; River stands there, disheveled. My breath catches at the sight. He's shirtless, pants hanging low on his hips, muscles carving a sharp V. I gulp as I study him. His scowl softens when he sees it's me.

"Mya?" His sleep-heavy eyes roam over me, heat soon igniting in his gaze. "What's wrong?" He shakes his head, trying to wake up.

I storm into his room right past him. He shuts the door and follows. The room smells of wrathhog smoke and alcohol. I stop by the couch similar to the one in my room. The room is identical to mine with only a slight differentiation in décor. My gaze finds the floor and stays there. I pause, trembling.

"What happened? Are you okay?" River's hand circles my biceps. His calloused thumb gently rubs against my skin, eliciting a shock of pleasure down to my core. I push the thoughts aside as I rest my hands on his chest. His skin is warm, muscles firm, grounding me. I need his presence to convince me I'm truly awake. His chest tenses under my lingering touch.

"I..." I stutter, shaking my head. "The Dark King... I... I saw him. In my dream... He was in my head. I... He wanted to know where I was."

"Shit," River hisses.

"I need you, River." I finally look up at him and admit it. "You're right. Everything you've done has been for me and I've done nothing but hurt you in return. I'm sorry. I'm not a good person. I'm selfish and stubborn, but right now, I need you. Please..." My eyes shut close, tears threatening to fall. I'm not even sure what I'm begging him for. "Please tell me that you're real and that you're here and not a dream."

River pulls me into his body, wrapping his arms around me tightly. I press my head against his chest. "I'm here, Mya."

I listen to his heartbeat and my breath calms. River's fingers slide up my neck and through my hair as he holds me close. My skin heats up, burning with pleasure.

"Please forgive me," I whisper. "I need you. You're right." I repeat my words.

River kisses the top of my head. "You're forgiven, Mya. You're right as well. I..." He pauses and takes a breath, his body relaxes. "I was jealous. I'm sorry too."

I look up at River, and his stormy blue eyes meet mine. I'm not used to seeing him like this, disheveled from being woken unexpectedly. His dark hair cascades around his face, accentuating his jaw. I reach up and slowly run my fingers through his hair. He usually keeps it tied back, but now it falls loose, soft, and silky beneath my touch.

My finger slides down on his face, tracing his jawline. It's rough because of his dark scruff. River's entire body stills as he lets me touch him. I don't know what I'm doing. My mind goes blank, but my hands explore him like it's the first time I'm really touching him. Maybe it truly is. Since I'd met River, we were always running, in fear for our lives. The couple of times we'd been intimate... they passed in a blink of an eye. Now, we finally found refuge.

Honestly, I feel safe in River's arms. Safe here at the temple. Despite the fear of my nightmare, I know I'm safe.

"River," his name is a whisper across my lips, like a prayer. My entire body heats up, the air surrounding us charging. River's gaze intensifies and my breath staggers.

I don't know who grabbed whose head, but our lips collide, and I'm swept in a whirlwind of desire. His mouth devours mine, his tongue demanding entrance, and I allow it. River's hands roam across my bare skin, eliciting heat in my core.

"This fucking dress." River groans against my mouth sending shivers down my spine. His fingers dip into the string, and with a swift move, he slides it off my shoulder. His other hand grips my ass, and I moan. Guiding me with his body, River staggers me to the bed, never releasing my mouth. When the back of my legs hit the bed frame, I gasp and fall backward onto it.

I look up at River as he stands over me, a possessive look upon his face, forcing his body between my legs. He towers over me, his gaze scouring my sprawled form. Heat flushes across my cheeks, and I bite my bottom lip staring at his muscled body. River is a god among men. Carved with delicacy and hard work, by the Elementals themselves. Seeing him takes my breath away. My breathing stops as my eyes glance over every goddamned muscle. His eyes glow, as if summoning his lightning power.

He's never done that before and when I try to prop up using my elbows, a mischievous grin sprawls across his face. He pushes me back down. "Uh uh, *princess*." He uses the nickname Holt gave me.

I sigh, "I'm not a princess. Why are people calling me that?"

River runs his fingertips along my exposed thighs, skimming under the thin piece of fabric that barely covers me.

"Because you are. You're the only Myrea Forsaken to exist, by right, that makes you her heir, a princess."

I feel flustered as River teases my thighs with his gentle strokes. Need builds and I shake my head in disbelief; my dark hair whipping around my face.

"It's true." River kneels between my legs and begins leaving a trail of kisses from my knee toward my inner thigh. Heat rushes to my core. Wetness pools between my legs. "Voras is the heir of Tazra and our King, but that's because Tazra forced that order upon Elemi. If each territory had royal courts, Holtian would be king of the Oasis Peninsula, if he really is the heir of Hydros. And if Myrea had a territory that still existed within our world, you would be its queen."

I barely focus on his words as his lips moved closer to my center. He pauses for a moment, gazing up at me. "Now, allow me to worship you, my queen."

In a quick move, River grasps my undergarment—a silky, thin piece of fabric—and pulls them down my legs. He drags his tongue through my core, and I can't contain the moan that leaves my mouth. My head falls back as the sensation of his tongue overwhelms me.

River inserts a finger in me, and lazily strokes it in and out. My body heats and my back arches. The wetness grows between my legs. He sucks my clit between his lips, and I gasp from the delicious pleasure. My breath quickens as River speeds up and inserts a second finger inside. I gasp from the sensation. The wave of bliss building higher within me.

Then he pulls out. A discontented groan leaves me as River stands and shoves his pants off, revealing his entire glorious body to me. My eyes widen as I gaze at his length—thick and erect. It's not like he hasn't been inside me before but really seeing him makes my mouth water. I watch him, anxiously, waiting for his presence.

He joins me on the bed and spreads my legs wide as he settles between them. His large hands tease my thighs before he grasps my hips and lines his cock up to my entrance. In a slow, agonizing thrust, he inserts himself, forcing a breath out of me. I grab his forearms and close my eyes, focusing on the pleasure of River stretching my insides.

His skin buzzes, as if the electricity within him desperately wants to run rampant around us. Through gritted teeth, River thrusts harder into me. His grip on my hips hardens with the pace.

"You feel so good, Mya," he rasps. "So, fucking wet. This fucking dress." I can't help but smile. He likes what I picked to wear to bed.

"And you're a fucking masterpiece, River," I reply, breathless. He leans down, claiming my mouth. The kiss is soul consuming. My head spins—dizzy as the pleasure inside me builds higher. Without pulling his mouth away from mine, River strokes my clit with his thumb and the dam within me bursts. I moan against River's mouth as my body convulses beneath him. River allows himself to come after me and for a moment the world stills around us. Our breaths mingle as we come down from the high of pleasure. My racing heart slows back to a steady rhythm. River pulls out and rolls over next to me.

He brings his face to my neck and rubs his nose on it, lovingly. I run my fingers through his hair, the gesture comforting us both. My nightmare... or, I guess, my vision, scared me. I don't know what to call the interaction I had with the Dark King. But the connection scared me more than I really care to admit. I don't want to think about it.

I want to enjoy this. The feel of River against my body. The glow from my orgasm. The bed. Everything. He drags an arm across me and pulls me closer to him. A quiet snore sounds, and I can't help but smile. Rest. We are finally able to get some real rest.

Chapter 24

Voras

I snap out of the daze and face the throne room once more, filled with my formally dressed subjects. We are celebrating Nythera—the start of our Autumn and the lengthening nights here in Night Spire. With Autumn's arrival, night's darkness bleeds further into day, something I, as the King of Darkness and heir to Tazra, relish. The people of the Netherfields embrace the approaching darkness and honor me as their king.

During Nythera, we hold the Ball of Forthcoming, where my people bring me offerings of Autumn and Winter. In return, I provide them with food, drink, and entertainment for the night. The event is dazzling—my dark, gothic castle is transformed with gilded, golden adornments. Attendees don autumnal, dark hues. Lords in suited attire and Ladies in elegant gowns. I wear the Crown of Onyx, created by Tazra herself, with black and silver robes symbolizing moonlight and darkness. The tradition spans centuries, though I rarely participate in the song and dance of the evening.

Tonight however, something unexpected happens. Without warning, my vision blacks out, and I'm pulled into darkness. It's unprecedented, and while I control darkness, my curiosity is uneasy. A distant "hello" beckons, and I follow. Approaching, I'm shocked to find my beloved Starlight Princess calling from the shadows. She looks irresistible in a tiny silver garment, revealing much and leaving little to the imagination. My mouth waters.

Though I'm not fond of surprises, this one pleases me. My curiosity deepens. Somehow, she's summoned me into her dreamscape. I will need to study how this is possible. One moment in my ballroom, next in the dark realm she shaped. I should be alarmed, yet I remain calm, captivated by her beauty.

How I long to have her beside me tonight at the Ball of Forthcoming. I yearn for the day she's mine, and we reign together, bringing peace to Elemi. I cannot yet reveal her to my people. I do not wish to evoke fear in my subjects, especially with a celestial being back. No one really understands what a celestial is, and many don't even know of the Elemental Myrea. They could rise against her, especially amid whispers of the Lastborn prophecy circulating secretly in my court. A plan is in motion, and I must stick to it.

She's alarmed to see me. Of course she is.

"Why am I here?" she asks, fear seething off her sun-kissed skin.

Fuck if I know. "It is you who summoned me," I say, calmly. "Tell me, my little Starling, why am *I* here?"

"I did no such thing," she barks like a rabid dog. The ferocity in her trembling voice is adorable. "I didn't summon you. You... you haunt my dreams."

"Your power is growing, Myalis," I observe. Only someone extremely gifted with magic can do something like this. I ponder how she manages to do this. "You're somewhere deeply rooted in magic; I can sense it. Tell me, where are you, my Starling?"

I reach out to touch her, curious if contact will bring her to me through a portal or if it will break the connection. I hesitate. What if it brings me to her? I don't know where she is, but from the state of her dress, I have an idea. She's somewhere in the Oasis Peninsula. My guess, probably at the Altar of Water. A sacred temple I'm unable to penetrate with my powers. Damn guardians slithering in the haunting waters around it... and damn Hydros for using his magic to solidify the sacred place, barring Dark Kings from entry unless granted permission. But what if I'm wrong and she's not there? If I touch her and portal to wherever she is, would she hurt me? Would I be ambushed?

"Get out of my head." She shakes her head, her chestnut waves cascading over her shoulders. Again, I can't help but admire her figure. She's malnourished, mostly skin and bones. Yet subtle curves show through her tiny silver dress. With proper nutrition, it can be easily remedied. When she's mine, she'll be strong and fit. I'll nurture her mind and soul. She'll want for nothing. Tazra above, I long to keep her in my castle, tending to her. I've waited long enough.

"Where are you?" I demand sharply. I arch a brow, intrigued by this powerful connection to the dreamscape. I want her to concede, to answer me. But before she answers, she shouts and pushes me away. Instantly, I return to consciousness, seated on my throne again, with music and laughter filling the space.

My chest heaves as I look around and reacquaint myself to my surrounding. I force a neutral expression. I cannot show my Lords and Ladies any sign of weakness.

Especially not that my princess summoned me into her mindscape. That could reveal me as vulnerable.

"Your Majesty?" a low voice interrupts. I turn to see General Grimsbane, recently recovered from Myalis's attack and standing guard nearby. He looks better, though his failure still grates on me.

"Yes?" I snap sharply.

"Are you alright?"

Fucking busybody.

"Yes." He hesitates, pondering. It's maddening. "What is it, General?"

"It's just that, you seemed to have left us for a moment. You were whispering, albeit unintelligible." My eyes widen briefly before I mask it with neutrality. General Grimsbane revealed more than he intended. "I just want to confirm you're alright."

I hiss through clenched teeth, inhaling deeply. "Just lost in thoughts, I suppose," I lie smoothly. No need to have him or anyone else worry. I'm already unsettled enough.

Most of the people in my territory haven't heard of the Lastborn prophecy, but I have. A nasty, vile lie that's shaken many Dark Kings before me. For the past eleven years, I've hidden the return of a Myrean Forsaken, a celestial, into our world. Now that Myalis moves, word about her will spread. I must maintain my composure. I don't want my people thinking that the Lastborn prophecy will come true and that my reign in threatened. That's why I urgently want Myalis here, to show Elemi our unity. I'll do whatever it takes to maintain peace.

I shift my focus back to the dance. I snap my fingers, and a servant brings me a chalice of blood-red wine. Dry and strong, it helps clear my head. Ulnisi is sitting on the floor on my left, chained. My seer. I remember when she was gifted to me on a night just like this. It brings a smile on my face. She's compliant and loyal. And while it may seem cruel, her chains are for her protection—from others, even sometimes herself.

Tonight, she's silent, which is somewhat unsettling. These events usually awaken her visions. Sometimes, the crowd tosses coins at her, coaxing a vision about their fortune from her. Though I allow it, I remember their faces well. Then if those people ever ask a favor of me, I flat out deny them. Despite how unreasonable it may seem of me.

I am King of Elemi. Ruler of all people and Forsaken in this land. And while I feel that I am a just ruler, I know there are many that oppose me. Uprisings spark here and there, and I quell them easily. Despite murdering my brothers for my crown, my two sisters still live, they're closely monitored. I spared their lives because Arabella lacks magic, and Iselda stated she'd not murder for a throne she did not desire. I took her words as truth. Both my sisters reside here in the castle at Night Spire. Easier to watch over and protect them.

They are among the many beautiful ladies dancing with handsome bachelors tonight. I watch my eldest sister, Iselda—two years elder than me—dance perfectly to the drums, her sapphire gown sparkling. Her dark black hair is styled in simple braids cascading down her back. She wears a bright smile that warms me tonight. More than once, she has requested me to seek a marriage match for her. I've postponed the decision, but perhaps it's time to grant her some happiness.

I spot Arabella slipping off the dance floor with a tall man. They whisper sweet nothings to each other, and heat in my blood begins to rise. That man should know better than to take advantage of a princess of the crown. Arabella has always been the more spirited of my two sisters. She stirred mischief, and once I became King, I realized how much of a handful my father had with her.

Her bluish-black hair is swept up in jeweled coifs matching her silver gown.

She and the man sip wine, drinking heartedly as her laughter echoes through the room. When the man meets my eye, I shoot him a deadly glare and his entire frame tenses. It's Sir Davian Krill, son of the wealthy Lord Crimson Krill, a prominent merchant in the Netherfields. I make a mental note of him as I rise from my throne. Just as I pull myself up, Ulnisi gasps. I turn to her, sensing she's receiving a vision.

Her blind eyes roll back, and she enters a catatonic state, her lips moving. Her whispers are barely comprehensible. "Change is coming. A new prince will rise. Ashes and fire, green with desire."

She halts, her sharp features softening to her usual calm. Her breath evens and she gazes toward the crowd, though she's sightless.

"Well?" I raise a brow. "What does it mean?" I expect her to elaborate, but she gives me a blank stare. Her plump pink lips and eyebrows crease.

"My King?" she asks. I get irritated all over again. She knows better than to play dumb with me.

"Don't act coy, Ulnisi." I seethe through gritted teeth. "Your vision. What does it mean?" She looks my way, and her expression changes. She's genuinely confused. I let out an exasperated sigh and step toward her. The music stops and all eyes fall on me. I'd never heard a room go so silent, so quickly.

Feeling my presence, Ulnisi lifts her face up toward me. "Please, Your Majesty. I mean no disrespect, but I don't understand what you're speaking of."

I yank her collar's chain, forcing her to her feet. Tonight, Ulnisi wears a pale shimmering fabric serving as a shift dress. I want to strike her. Yet with eyes upon us, I restrain myself. Especially not over a vision. My eyes scan the throne room, and I lift a finger in the direction of the musicians. Music resumes instantly, and the people go back to celebrating. While they're distracted, I pull her closer by her chains, and whisper in her ear.

"You just spouted out a vision and I demand for you to tell me what it means." My voice is low and stern, but I've regained my calm.

When Ulnisi's face twists into horror at my words, it dawns upon me that she doesn't remember it. This hasn't ever happened before. I bite my lip, nostrils flaring in frustration. If she can't remember, then what in the great hells below does that mean?

Chapter 25

River

The next morning, I wake to find Myalis gone. For a moment, I wonder if it was just a fever dream as I shake my head and yawn. Unnatural light filters through the small stained-glass window. I roll on my stomach and realize my cock is hard as a fucking rock. Shifting to adjust, I catch a whiff of orchids in my bed. The scent pulls me back to last night. Mya. I hadn't been dreaming after all.

She came to me in the middle of the night. After our argument, I'd come back here and stewed for gods know how long. When one of the priestesses brought food, I asked her to for some alcohol. Something strong. Luckily, I had some wrathhog left to drown my frustrations.

After the incident at the Sweet Apple Tavern and Inn, I gave up smoking and drinking. I'm trying to be better for her—trying to deserve her—but who the hell am I kidding? I'll *never* deserve her. Not in a million turns around the sun. She's the Starlight Princess, the Lastborn, a chosen prophecy. And me? Who the fuck am I? Just a Gaian Forsaken, hellbent on revenge.

Once the masses find out about her, everyone will want her. Males and females alike. Every Forsaken man will want to breed her for her power. Hells, they'd probably deem her the new Myrea, a goddess among us. Eventually, she'll leave me in the dust. I know this. I'm just a small phase in what will be a grand life for her. Especially once we end the Dark King's reign. Then hers will begin. And the way she was ogling Holtian last night, it wouldn't surprise me if she picks him to rule beside her. A king fit for a queen.

I groan, rolling over again. My body aches from the journey. Everything about it has been taxing and exhausting. I don't want to leave this bed, but I want to find Mya. I vaguely remember Head Priestess Themora saying Holtian would train her. Maybe that's where she's gone.

But my heart aches that I didn't get to enjoy her as I woke. I won't see the pale blue light from the stain glass color her sun-kissed skin, or her brunette hair cascading around her sleeping face in waves I'd run my fingers through. I won't claim her pouting lip in sleep and wake her with sensual kisses. I sigh heavily at the thought of what could've been, lying alone in my bed—naked and fucking hard.

There's a knock on the door. I force myself up and pull on the pants laying on the floor by the bed. "Coming," I call, trying to hide my boner, my voice is raspy from sleep.

When I open the door, a priestess stands there holding a tray. "Breakfast, sir." Her voice is timid, her eyes cast downward as her pale blue cheeks pinken. She's a young Hydros Forsaken, likely new to the priesthood. She wears shimmering blue silk robes and bangles. Her pretty blonde hair, the color of pale sand, cascades down her back. Her large, ocean-blue eyes avoid mine.

I reach for the tray. "Thank you." I nod and turn back into my room, but pause, and look back at her. "Do you know where Myalis is?" The question slips out before I can think twice.

"She is training with Master Holtian in the shallows." Her voice is hesitant, almost like she's sharing a secret she shouldn't.

I clear my throat. "And where are the shallows? I'd like to meet them after I eat."

The young woman hesitates. "It's at the back of the temple. I can send someone to escort you once you're finished."

"That would be great, thank you." I say. I close the door, trying not to let the jealousy eat me alive as I sit and eat the food provided. I stew but remind myself she chose me last night. Not Holtian. Then again, if she knew where he slept, perhaps she would've run to him. Frustration builds as I eat faster than necessary, eager to wash and get dressed.

Within half an hour, I'm led to "the shallows"—a training area behind the palace, where priests and priestesses hone their Forsaken powers. We're outside of the temple in a vast cavern. A round pool, a little more than six inches deep, lies before us. *The shallows.* Clever. The air is warm, despite the bioluminescence gleaming around the darkness and an odd magic meant to mimic sunlight. Torches circle the pool, casting light in the surrounding area.

In the center stand Holtian and Mya, their bodies close as if sharing secrets. My blood boils. Has everything between Mya and me last night been a fluke? Was she playing me for a fool? I swallow my rage and step into the water.

Both Holtian and Mya turn toward me.

"River." Mya smiles, and I stop dead in my tracks. She seems happy to see me, but it could all be an act. I quirk a brow and stare at Holtian, who looks less pleased to see me. He shrugs and crosses his arms.

"Holt was just showing me ways to relax and summon my magic," Mya says.

"Is that so?" My voice stays neutral. "Feels like that's something I could've showed you."

Holtian scoffs. "But you didn't. I'm surprised you did nothing to train Myalis during your journey."

My fists clench, jaw tightening. "That's because I was busy trying to keep her alive, but what would you know of that, locked away in this little cave your whole life." Neutrality turns to disdain.

Holtian's lips curl into a crooked smile that unnerves me. "I am a prince of my people," he says. "It's for my safety and theirs that I stay here. But you're right, River, I haven't left my 'little cave.' But just because I haven't left it, doesn't mean I don't know how to survive or fight."

"Is that a challenge?" I seethe. Holtian chuckles, the sound grating on my nerves.

"River—" Mya steps forward, but Holtian blocks her with an outstretched arm.

"Let's," Holtian confirms. "I'd love a good challenge, especially against a Gaian Forsaken. There's no grand greenery for you to summon here, no dirt to command at your will. The first to submit, wins."

I grin. He's cocky enough to underestimate me. He doesn't know my gifts and I'm not about to clue him in. "Sure. Let's do it." I step into the water, closing in on Holtian and Mya, until we stand in the center together.

Mya shakes her head, disapproving. "River, come on. Please don't do this."

Does she think I can't beat him?

"It's fine." I reassure her. "It's all in good fun, isn't it?" I glance at Holtian.

"Indeed," he says. "Go stand on the outskirts, Mya. This'll be a good lesson for you."

"He's right, Mya. Good for you to see how Forsaken battle." I give her a tight smile. She wants to protest; her plump, pink lips purse and her hands go to her hips. That's when I notice what she's wearing. Gods above this Oasis Peninsula attire is sensual and even scandalous. A pale blue dress with a deep V that goes right between her breasts and thigh slits almost to her hips. A gold chain belt adorns her waist. The fabric's thin and silky and all I want to do is rip it off her. I don't want anyone else to see her looking so delectable.

I take a steadying breath, shrug off the distraction, and turn my attention back to Holtian.

"Fine," Mya relents. "But I don't want either of you to hurt each other. One wrong move and it stops."

We both nod in agreement. Hesitantly, she walks out of the center of the shallows and moves to the outskirts. Now, it's just Holtian and me. I look at her one last time, her disapproving eyes linger on me. It's like she's trying to warn me, but I look away and focus on my opponent.

I yank off my tunic and toss it aside. Holtian and I stand, facing each other, silently studying. Then we move into defensive stances and circle, waiting for an opening. Holtian is cocky—he'll want to strike first. I'll wait him out. He already underestimates me; I won't give him the advantage.

Holtian's maybe my age, or a little younger maybe twenty-five, give or take. I'm not sure. But what I have over him is years of travel and battle experience. Through my travels, I've faced a lot of nasty creatures of Elemi. Not just that, but I've also dealt with trained foes sent by the Dark King himself. Holtian's muscular, no fat on him. His many beaded and shelled necklaces, though, will throw off his balance. He wears no armor—only the loincloth. He'd be shredded against a real foe.

"Come on, Gaian," he teases. "Show me what you've got. Aside from dance skills." I can't help but smile.

"Ladies first." I reply coolly. His smile fades. With a yell, he lifts his hands and pulls streams of water from the pool. Holtian shoots toward me. I tuck my body and roll away. The sandy shallows slow me a bit, but I'm back on my feet. I sweep his legs out from under him using mine. His body splashes into the water, but he pulls water over him, like a protective shield and stands again, unfazed.

We circle again. "Good thought," I coax, "but you'll have to do better than that." As expected, he's rash and impatient. He charges at me with his body and wraps his arms around me. My feet slide few inches backward, but I retaliate and wrap my arms around him, throwing him into the water. On all fours, he raises his hand, commanding the water around us. He throws it at me, this time however, in the form of a wave.

I brace for impact crossing my arms in front of my face, but it knocks me down. An endless torrent crashes over me. Holtian's waves bash over my head, the force strong and unyielding. I hold my breath, desperate for air. He keeps pounding, pulling more water from the cave, each wave stronger than the last.

"What's wrong, Gaian? Can't escape the riptide?" His voice laughs, muffled beneath the waves. He's trying to be funny, but it's time to show him what I'm made of. I bring my hands up commanding the sand beneath our feet. The granules rise out of the water. Holtian's brows arch in curiosity. I start pelting him with sand, catching him off-guard. His water attack ceases. He staggers back momentarily before regaining his footing and forming water whips in his hands. The first whip strikes my skin, the pain stinging like a real whip. I grunt through my teeth as another one hits my arm.

Welts bloom on my skin. Holtian glares at me with a wicked grin. Though my skin stings, I'll not bow to this arrogant prick. Now, I let my inner fire burn. Using my fingers, I pull water from the pool toward the cavern ceiling. Holtian pauses, confused. His silver eyes track my movements as I start forming clouds above. Energy thrums through me; my gaze locks on him.

"What the—" he whispers.

With a pull of a hand, I command lightning to shoot down from the clouds above, striking the water at our feet and electrocuting Holtian. He drops instantly. A satisfactory grin crosses my face.

"Holt!" Mya screeches from outside the shallows as she charges in. Our eyes meet, the fury in hers is undeniable. "River, what the fuck?"

I cross my arms as she kneels next to Holtian, pulling his head from the water.

"He'll be fine," I shrug. "Unfortunately."

"This isn't funny. I don't think he's breathing." Mya's hands touch his pulse points, and my jealousy flares again.

"Alright, alright." I storm over and kneel beside him. I place my ear against his chest. His heart *is* beating. I slap his face. Holtian's eyes snap open, gasping sharply for air.

He inhales deeply and sits up, but when his eyes meet mine, he scurries away as fast as he can. "The fuck was that? How did you do that?"

"I may be a Gaian Forsaken, but I'm an Elemental wielder first," I say with a grin. "The 'greenery and dirt' is just a secondary skill." I smirk wider. "A lesson for you, heir of Hydros: never underestimate your opponents. It might get you killed."

"*River*," Mya seethes, shooting me death glare with her golden eyes.

"It's fine." Holtian says, managing to stand on shaky legs and extending a hand. I eye it, suspiciously.

"I appreciate the duel, and the lesson." His face is sincere.

Shit. Is he really being the bigger person? I take his hand, and we shake, calling a truce.

"Perhaps we can train Myalis together," Holtian suggests. "Seems it would be better for her to have two Forsaken Elementals to learn from, not just one. Yeah?"

I have to give him credit. Holtian has a boyish charm that draws you in. He is charismatic, and I can tell that he'd make a fine leader if given the chance. Though he still has a lot to learn. Just like Mya has a lot to learn about her magic before she's able to fulfill the prophecy and end the Dark King.

Perhaps once he's defeated, the different Elemental territories can establish their own rules, with their own leaders—as it should have originally been. That's the ultimate goal. At least, that's the Elemi I hope for. Truce and peace.

"Sure." I say, turning back and leaving the shallows. I'll let Holtian have his fun for today and "train" Mya however he sees fit. I already knocked him on his ass and embarrassed him in front of her. No need to prove how much better I am. I can feel Mya's gaze lingering on my backside as I head back into the temple. If she wants me, she can come find me.

Instead, I plan to explore the temple—mostly curious about their library. What knowledge might it hold for me? Maybe I'll find something new from their texts and documents. As they're familiar with Myrea, they must also be aware of the Lastborn prophecy. Do they have any records on it? Or information about the Dark King and how to defeat him? One thing's for sure: before we leave this place, I'll find out everything I can.

Chapter 26

Myalis

A few weeks have passed since we arrived at the Altar of Water, and training has been going well. River and Holt have been teaching me hand-to-hand combat. My magic is still hard to call upon and wield. It's frustrating. I don't understand what's wrong. So, for now, the focus has been on physical combat. River tries to keep my spirits up, reminding me it's good to work on self-defense.

We spar and train from morning until late afternoon. By the time we finish, I'm exhausted with sweat soaking my skin. My time here has made me stronger and built my stamina, which I'm grateful for. I need this to improve myself, hoping it will help me when I finally wield my magic.

Working with my celestial powers has been challenge. Training with a Gaian and Hydros Forsaken doesn't make it easier. They understand their own powers, but mine only produce fleeting stars in the sky or a mini-light show in my palm—when it decides to work at all. River and I think back to each time I was attacked. It seems my powers kick in only when my life is in danger. Fear evokes them. Emotions are uncontrollable, and in the past, it's drained me to the point of blacking out, like during the Larkfury attack.

To avoid that, we've been experimenting with different ways to wield my power. No one truly understands how celestial magic works. I am the only Myrean Forsaken known to exist. Knowledge of my powers and what they can do is minimal, if not absent, from history. We decided we wouldn't give up. We'd keep trying to find ways to use them safely.

After our sessions, River disappears into the library to search for answers. What exactly he's looking for, I'm not sure. So far, his time there has turned up nothing useful about my abilities. I try not to let the disappointment show. At night, when River and I aren't too tired, we spend our time wrapped up in each other's arms. My feelings for him have deepened, I'm falling in love with him. Yet a little seed of doubt lingers in the back of my mind that I can't seem to shake. Our conversations focus more on training and what comes next than on us or our past. We still haven't discussed the prophecy much either. In some ways, although we're growing closer, there's still a long road ahead.

Then there's Holt. He's charming, funny, and laid-back—striking and playful. When I'm with him, my stomach flips. His magnetism draws me in. He's easy to like—fun, flirtatious, relaxed. Sometimes, I feel guilty flirting with Holt, even if it's just playful. River's possessive, and when he sees us together, his jealousy flares. For some reason though, I enjoy antagonizing him.

I don't know why I'm like this. I wish I weren't. My feelings for these men are complicated. With Holt, it's amusing and distracting. With River, it's yearning and a crackling passion. Nothing between us is easy. It never has been. Since day one with River, it's been tough. My emotional lines blur, and I find myself caught between them both.

A splash of water across the face snaps me out of my haze. I turn sharply toward Holt. Mischief sparkles in his silver eyes.

"You're distracted today," he says, approaching. I stand in the shallows, water up to my ankles, and take a breath. The water is warm, the cave air humid. I'm thankful for the silk blue dress with thin straps exposing my arms—I feel cooler. The dress has two thigh-high slits allowing freedom of movement. The fabric clings to my curves. I've grown to like the Hydros people's fashion. It's beautiful and sensual and makes me feel more like a woman than a fugitive, living in holes in the ground.

"Where's that head of yours?" Holt stands before me. My eyes dart to the dark blue loincloth hanging dangerously low on his hips. Slowly, they drift upward and my heart flutters at the sight of every muscle on his pale, blue-hued body. Multiple beaded and shelled necklaces adorn his neck, resting gently at varying heights on his pectoral muscles. When my gaze catches his slender face, my breath hitches. He runs a hand through his silver braids.

"I don't know," I lie. "But you're right. I guess I'm not mentally with it today."

The temple has been my sanctuary. I feel healthier than I've ever been before and I think I'm getting some fat on my bones. It's been incredible soaking in Hydros's culture. The feasts, the clothing and the music have been alluring all my senses. Yet, I still fear what awaits outside these caves. I know we can't stay here forever, but I'd love to.

The persistent threat of King Voras looms over me, stoking my anxiety. He hasn't highjacked my dream since the first night I was here, and we've not heard anything about him either. The first night's dreamscape still puzzles me. I don't understand how Voras and I collided into it, but I don't want it to happen again.

The Dark King will keep hunting me, whether I stay put or run. We still don't fully understand his motive. I know once River and I leave, we'll be on the run again. I'm not ready for that yet.

"Want to spar it out?" Holt quirks a silver brow, one side of his lip curled upwards.

"Sure," I say.

"Get in your stance."

I shake out my arms and legs, planting my feet in the water. Barefoot, I can move easier within the soft, sandy bottom of the shallows. Once settled, I assume my defensive stance and Holt stands opposite.

"Let's go," he charges at me. Holt's effortless in water, it being his wielding ability. I'm, however, sluggish.

Holt lunges for my waist, but I spin away, avoiding his grip. From behind, I reach for his neck. He ducks and sweeps my legs out from under me. My back splashes into the shallows, my face briefly submerged.

I sit up, but he's on me, mimicking my move, and locking me in a choke hold from behind. I'm stuck in an awkward position, sitting in the water.

"What's your move, Myalis?" Holt whispers, playful in my ear. "How do you get out of this?"

Using all my strength, I grab his arms and force him to flip over me. It's awkward and far from graceful, but it works. The move distracts Holt long enough for me to grab a dueling stick from a rack on the edge of the shallows. I sprint back toward him and swipe his legs out from under him with the stick.

"Hey," he complains, "I thought this was hand-to-hand. If you wanted to play dirty, you should've just asked."

Holtian then summons water around me, swirling it into a whirlpool. I grip the dueling stick to anchor myself, but the spinning of the water weakens my footing in the sand. Soon, I'm caught in the vortex.

I cough hard, choking on the water as the whirlpool spins relentlessly. I search for an escape, trying to orient myself. I plant my hands into the sand beneath me, struggling to steady myself. I focus, forcing my knees, closing my eyes, and gritting my teeth. My mind holds firm—and suddenly, everything stops.

The water is still. My breath comes in heaves as I soak in the calm. When I open my eyes, Holtian stands before me. His thick brows knitted.

"How'd you do that?" he asks offering a hand.

"Do what?"

"Stop my water attack?"

I take his hand and rise, hesitating. "I'm not sure." A confusing daze settles in my mind. The cave is eerily silent. Not even the sound of water dripping from stalagmites or the waterfalls in the distance breaks the quiet.

Holt and I stand, gazing at each other. An odd sensation passes between us, and for a moment, I'm held captive by the Hydros heir. He lifts his hand to my cheek, gently tilting my face as if inspecting something. His stare is deep and intense— his touch sensual, caring. I wonder what Holt is trying to discover within me.

"What the *fuck* is going on here?"

I snap back to the present, seeing River seething before us. My face flushes at the sight.

"River... I... we..." Words elude me. What the fuck is happening again?

"I'm just looking at Myalis." Holt says dreamily, awe-struck.

"Were you? It looks as if you're about to devour her," River retorts.

My eyes drift between both men as the air thickens with tension. I know it's River's powers, his jealousy's getting the best of him. His body stiffens, fists clenched at his sides.

"River," I call, breaking him from his stare. His deep blue eyes blaze like a turbulent storm as he gazes back at me.

"Myalis," he replies curtly.

"It's innocent. We were just sparring and something weird happened, that's all." I'm not afraid of River, but his jealousy has begun to suffocate me. I have strong feelings for him—I know that. I just wish he believed me.

"What do you want, anyway?" Holt asks, frowning.

River approaches me, glaring at Holt, who then takes a step back. He towers over my frame, looking down his nose at me. "We're leaving tomorrow," he says.

I gasp. "What?"

"I read about a shaman who lives on the cliffs near Volantis. Themora thinks she might help with your celestial powers."

Holt exhales behind me. "Vivicus."

"Yes," River confirms. "We need someone who can help you wield your power without triggering your emotions. The sooner, the better. We leave tomorrow morning."

"Are you sure this is right?" I snap. "What's the hurry? We're safe here. I've been training."

River shakes his head and turns away.

"Once we leave, we're back on the run! Back to exhaustion and watching our back." Desperation seeps out into my voice.

Frustrated, River flings an arm up as he heads toward the temple, stopping at the edge of the shallows. "If you wish to explore your sexual desires with *him*," he pauses jerking his chin at Holt, "tonight is your last chance."

River walks off. I stand there, speechless. Shocked. Where did that come from? Does River really not trust me? Does he really think that Holt and I are involved? Suddenly all the flirtation over the past few weeks hits me.

My heart pounds in my chest and nausea rises as realization sinks in. We're leaving. Continuing on this dangerous journey, and I'm not ready. I don't want to leave. I know River's right. To master my powers, we need someone who can help. I draw strength from the stars, and being in this cavern for so long away from the night sky that fuels my powers, it weakens me.

Holt sighs and places his hand on my shoulder. "I guess we'd better prepare for your departure." Sadness laces his voice, and I feel it too.

"Yeah," I murmur, shoulders sinking as I walk out the shallows.

"You know," Holt calls after me, "you don't have to go if you don't want to." Surprised, I turn to him.

"You can stay here, with me. I'll protect you."

I huff. "Your people are loyal to King Voras. He'll stop at nothing to find me." I explain. "Eventually, the King will come for me, Holt. Nothing will stop him. He's been sending his knights for me for eleven years. I won't risk you or your people falling under his wrath. Especially if he suspects you're hiding something he wants."

Desperately, Holt grabs my hands and pulls me close. "We can hand-fast. Become husband and wife. It's not much, but you could be a daughter of Hydros. A princess of my people, as I am a prince."

A small smile creeps my lips as I consider his desperate plea. He's not wrong. We could have a good life, a happy life. But for how long? "That does sound wonderful," I admit.

"Then let's do it." He tightens his grip. "I know we haven't known each other that long, and I know you care about River. I wouldn't restrict you from taking him as a lover if you desired. We're not as traditional as Gaians seem to be. And should the King ever grace us with his presence, we would tell him that you aren't a threat to him or his rule. That you wish to live in peace."

Thoughts race through my mind at a speed I can't keep up with. Perhaps it would work. Maybe it would be okay.

"Please?" Holt's silver gaze pleads as he kisses my knuckles gently. "I like you, Myalis. There's something growing here. I'd be honored to explore that with you."

My heart pounds, and I don't know what to say. I cup the side of his face, rubbing my thumb along his smooth jaw like he did to me seconds ago. I shake my head, conflicted. Desperation fills his expression before he hungrily kisses me, enveloping me in a passionate embrace. Never to let go.

Chapter 27

River

Dawn quickly arrives, and I stand alone in the throne room where Mya and I first entered weeks ago. Now, I'm waiting for her so we can leave this place—most likely for good. A small crowd has gathered to see us off: the head priestess, Themora, among them. She's provided me a map and plenty of provisions for the road ahead.

During our time here, the Hydros priests tended to our horses, Buttercup and Ash, and the steeds are ready to travel again. All I need is my partner. We stand in silence, waiting. I find myself shifting on my feet, clearing my throat. The expansive room is quiet, except for the noise of waterfalls pouring into pools at the back.

Minutes crawl by, and I find it hard to swallow. My throat tightens. I gave Mya permission to bed Holtian.

What the fuck was I thinking? What kind of an idiot am I? Is that what she's doing right now? Are they enjoying each other's embrace? Was Holtian tasting what I crave for the rest of eternity, and never wish to let go of? Were they sharing passionate kisses and the feel of each other's body while I stand here waiting like a fucking fool? Gaia above, how I want to smoke wrathhog and sink into oblivion in an opium den.

Nerves unravel and sweat beads on my brow. This damn humid heat. The throne room feels like a sauna. How long should I wait? Mya is coming with me, right? If not, it's over. The prophecy dies.

I shrug, impatient. She can't just walk away from destiny and refuse to learn her celestial powers, can she? I'm not so sure anymore. Maybe she'll choose to live in peace with the Hydros prince for the rest of her life. And that's her right. Gaia above, these thoughts overwhelm me, swelling in nausea.

I clutch the Gaian pendant hanging around my neck, praying silently. Please let Mya come through that door in the next ten minutes. We need to travel hard and fast if we want to reach the Bay of Stars in a couple days. There's no true rush, but I don't know what we'll encounter on our journey, and I don't want to draw any unwanted attention.

The King had been tracking us before. Does he know we're here? Ever since Mya told me they had connected mentally, I worry it would happen again once we leave the security of the temple. Voras can easily track us if he's able to penetrate Mya's mind.

Ten minutes pass. Then twenty. A half hour. I let out a loud sigh. "Where is your prince?" I ask sharply. Themora arches a pale brow and beckons another priestess, murmuring in her ear. The younger priestess then rushes off into the hall, disappearing.

"I'm unsure. Keeni will look for him," Themora's voice is calm, as if nothing were amiss. She sits patiently on the ancient throne, her silk dress cut low to her navel. Beaded embroidery forms wild lilies across the fabric.

Maybe I'm missing something. The longer I stand here, the dumber I feel. Images of Holtian and Mya swirl through my mind, making my stomach churn.

I swallow, lost in thought. Did the way I act yesterday, push Mya away? Did I overstep? My jealousy seemed to take on a life of its own. It made me crazy and reckless. My heart races. Fuck. Perhaps I let it get the best of me. Footsteps echo from the hallway, pulling me from my thoughts. My shoulders relax a little when Mya enters, her chestnut hair tied in fishtail braids. She's dressed for riding—a pale blue tunic with black pants and matching boots. Her pack is slung over her shoulders, along with her bow and quiver. When her gold-laced eyes meet mine, my heart skips a beat.

Holtian follows close behind, and it takes all my self-control to not rip him apart. The man looks like his usual peacock-self. Barely dressed, revealing all his lean muscles.

Mya pauses before crossing the room. Holtian stands before her, leaning down to whisper something in her ear. I can't hear it, but Mya nods and manages a weak smile. They split, Holtian stepping onto the dais to join Themora while Mya comes to my side.

Themora rises from the throne and gestures for Holtian to take her seat. She descends the steps leading down the dais and pauses in front of us. "Having you both here has been a pleasure," she says with a smile. "We all wish you well on your journey to Volantis. Should you wish to return to the Altar of Water, we'd be more than happy to host you again."

We nod our respect before a guard escorts us out of the glittering throne room, with waterfalls cascading down, and into the entryway. He opens the door, and begins weaving his magic, shaping a tunnel through the water to the surface. Mya and I take a deep breath, steeling ourselves as we start our ascent.

We walk in silence through the swirling water tunnel under the Dread Lagoon. We steal nervous glances at one another, unsure what to say after yesterday. The image of her wrapped around another man makes me physically sick. I know I can't keep her to myself though— we aren't hand-fasted. We aren't husband and wife. At least, not yet. Who am I to tell her who she can or can't sleep with? She deserves happiness, whatever shape it takes. Still, the more I dwell on it, the angrier I get.

I'm a storm of anger and confusion. Angry at the blatant flirting between Mya and Holtian. Confused, because she was always with me at night, in my arms. So, what the fuck was really going on? Is she just playing me for a fool?

When we emerge from the lake, Buttercup and Ash are waiting for us. They look strong, well-fed, and rested, and I load my rucksack on Buttercup as Mya does on Ash's side. We mount with practiced speed, setting out into the forests surrounding the Dread Lagoon. The mountains we originally traveled through were now in the opposite direction.

The sun sits low in the morning sky, but the air's already uncomfortably warm. It takes what seems like forever for my eyes to readjust to the sunlight, after staying so long beneath the surface. I wonder if Mya feels the same.

Hours pass with no words between us. The awkwardness of yesterday evening lingers. I cast a side glance at her and notice she seems lethargic. Her full lips are tilted downward, as are her eyes. What's going through her mind? Ugh, it's eats away at me.

"Are you alright?" I ask, trying to keep my emotions in check.

Finally, Mya lifts her eyes to me for the first time since leaving the Altar of Water. "I'm fine."

Well, I know that's a bullshit answer. I sigh. "Do you hate me for making you leave the temple?" The silence is unsettling. Leaves rustle as a breeze stirs overhead, and our horses' hooves clop along the dirt path.

"No," she says eventually. "I don't hate you, River."

Sweet relief washes over me. When Mya doesn't say anything else I arch a brow at her, trying to read her face as to what's bothering her. "Do you miss Holtian?"

Her face tightens in a frown. "What?"

She's really going to make me say it. "Holtian? I'm assuming you had a pleasant night with him. Are you missing him? Wishing you could've stayed there with him?" I halt Buttercup, fixing all my attention on her. I try to keep my face neutral, but I can feel my frustration showing. Mya stops Ash, her honeyed eyes boring into mine.

"I like Holt. He's fun, charming, and being with him is relaxing."

I huff and shift in my saddle. After a beat, a knowing grin sprawls across Mya's face.

"Are you jealous, River?" She slides off her gray-speckled mare, approaching me.

"I... uh." I stammer, again like a fool.

"Is that what's in your head? Are you imagining all the ways Holt took me?" Mya stands next to Buttercup, tracing her hand on my thigh. My heart drums against my ribs, my throat tight. She tilts her head, those large doe eyes with long lashes batting up at me.

Trying to keep my composure, I scoff. "Well? You mean to say you didn't?" I swing my leg over Buttercup and stand in front of her. My stance is domineering as I cross my arms against my chest. Mya's eyes skim my body, and it sends all the blood right to my dick. She's hungry for something and for a moment I wonder if Holtian, Prince of the Hydros Forsaken, could not satisfy her enough? Or has she become greedy? Maybe she's just playing me.

"He offered me a quiet life." Mya murmurs, voice dropping low and sensual. "Told me I could stay, he'd protect me. He brought me to his room and whispered all the things he wants to do with me."

A scowl darkens my face, but when her feather-light touch grazes my arm, I freeze. Mya's gaze never leaves mine as she takes a step closer. Her chin barely reaches my chest as she tilts her head up.

"But," she pauses. "The more we talked about what the future would look like, the more my heart ached that it wasn't with you."

My brows shoot up in surprise.

"Holt is attractive, magnetic, fun. And I enjoyed his company and the idea of the life he could've offered. But in the end, he's not you, River. The temple, him, while it was a beautiful distraction, just doesn't feel like home. We talked it all through, parted amicably, and he said I'm always welcome should I ever change my mind."

My arms drop, my heart thudding faster. I stare at her, bewildered. Is she picking me? Did she really choose me?

"You've crawled under my skin, River," Mya continues. "You've planted yourself deep inside my heart. While I enjoyed the thought of Holtian, I know I could never love him the way I love you."

Fuck. Of all the things she could say, this wasn't what I expected. Heat thrums beneath my skin. My dick twitches in my pants. I'm planted so firm in my spot that I'm unable to move.

"You love me?" My voice is so small and insecure, it's embarrassing. Mya smiles and closes the tiny gap between our bodies. She places both her hands on my chest, sprawling her fingers. Shivers travel up my spine.

"I do, River," she chuckles. "As crazy as that might sound, I love you."

My breath hitches before I grab the back of her neck and crash my lips onto hers. Fuck, they feel good against mine. My other hand grasps the small of her back and pulls her flush against my body—it's rough and dominant. A little gasp leaves her lips as my cock hardens against her. Having Myalis in my arms feels so right. I never want to let her go. She opens her mouth and slips her tongue into mine and I swear I almost come undone at that moment.

Our hands grow frantic as I push Mya against the closest tree, our lips never leaving each other's. It's a frenzy as she pulls my shirt up, brushing her hands up my chest, her fingers outlining my tattoos. The feel of her hands against my bare skin sets my soul on fire. I kiss down her neck, lightly nipping at her skin as I go.

I grab the bottom of Mya's tunic and rip it over her head, tossing it to the side, revealing her supple breasts. I bring my lips down to one of her erect nipples to take it into my mouth and start sucking on it. One of Mya's hands pulls at the loose strands of my hair. I undo the strings of her pants and pull those down her thighs.

There, against the tree, Myalis stands before me— needy, wanting, with a lustful gaze in her eyes. I admire her body. My eyes skim down her sensuous form. The subtle curve of her breasts accentuates her hourglass shape. The weeks of nourishment and training have filled her in, and she looks healthy and strong. My power thrums through me, and my cock strains against my pants.

Mya's sparkling eyes dart to my crotch, she's panting in need. A feral growl stems from my throat as I rush at her and push my mouth against hers in a bruising kiss. With one hand wrapping around her, keeping her against me, I use the other to stroke her clit. There's already wetness between her legs, and I can't contain myself from the fervent need within.

Her hands tangle with my pant strings and when she touches my dick, my entire body shudders. I pull her pants down and rip her boots off before throwing the pants to the side as well. I hoist her up, and she wraps her legs around my body. Mya brings the tip of my cock to her wet entrance in teasing strokes. I groan.

"Gaia above, *princess*..." I breathe with eyes shut closed. I enjoy the feel of her stroking my length. It feels so fucking good.

Mya brings her lips to my ear. "Fuck me, River. Give me what only you can."

Without further hesitation, I thrust into her, unforgiving and hard. A moan echoes through the dense forest, sending birds flying from the trees. Fully within her,

I use my strength and the tree as leverage to pull out and thrust in again. My grip on her tightens. Her nails scratch my muscled back—the sensation's overwhelming. Anywhere I can place my lips on her, I do. Tasting her isn't enough. Fucking her isn't enough. Gaia above, I want our souls conjoined. I never want to leave this space. I wish my cock could permanently stay between her legs.

I quicken the pace, going faster, in and out of her tight core. *Fuck*, why do I fit inside her so perfectly? My powers are going haywire from within. My body is short-circuiting and it's something I've never encountered with another woman before. I grit my teeth and my arms shake. My knees weaken from the control and the angle against the tree.

I give in and fall onto them, bringing Mya onto my lap. Her hands press against my chest. I pause and stare at her. Our foreheads meet causing our breaths to mingle. I'm holding a fucking goddess. I shudder before her. My queen. Those fuck-me eyes were captivating, causing my cock to twitch inside her.

"River."

Her husky voice stirs me from my haze. I wrap my arms tight around her, pressing our bodies together. Slowly, I rock my hips as she rolls hers. I'm so deep inside her, my spine tingles. Closing my eyes, I let out an exhilarating breath before kissing down her neck. Her little gasps spark my soul to life.

Mya wraps her arms around my neck. With this angle, her breasts are perfectly aligned with my mouth, and I can't help but lick her nipple with my tongue before pulling it into my mouth and sucking on it, hard. I bring my left arm from behind her to knead her other breast. Mya's head drops back, and her full lips open in an "o" while I pump inside her at an agonizingly slow pace.

It's the hottest, grittiest sex I've ever had. I don't want it to stop. It's like a fever dream. I'm lost in the sensations. My brain flashes with images of all that I want to do to her. My lips pop from her nipple and I move to the other one, gently sucking on it. While doing so, I bring my hand between us and use my fingers to circle her clit.

Her core tightens around me, and I groan. "Fuck." My teeth grit instinctively. "You feel like you were made for me, princess. I never want to leave you."

Mya comes undone by my words, cursing. She spasms in my arms and I feel her wave of pleasure flood my dick. I follow right behind her, unable to control myself any longer. Our chests heave against one another's, our hot breath mingling as we stay still, holding each other.

Sweat slicks our skin, but I don't care. I don't want to let Mya go. I don't care we're naked in the wild, leaning against a fucking tree. I want to remember this moment in time forever.

"I love you." Mya sighs as she brings her gaze to mine. Her honeyed eyes glitter with stars and my lips curl.

"My love for you is grander than the stars, Mya. It's infinite," I admit. I don't even know how Mya got so far under my skin, but she has. What started as a personal vendetta mission has now become so much more. I would do anything to protect her. To keep her from the clutches of the Dark King. We have to find a way to destroy him. *I* have to find a way to keep him away from Mya forever.

Chapter 28

Myalis

We've been riding for days following the map River received from Themora. According to it, we're close to Volantis, where the shaman Vivicus is said to reside. According to River, Vivicus, lives on the cliffs, high above the Bay of Stars. She's believed to draw power from the stars themselves, and I can't help but wonder if perhaps she too is a celestial. Maybe I'm not the only Myrean Forsaken after all. But we won't know until we meet her.

Since leaving the Altar of Water, my powers have subtly stirred again. I never realized what dimming my magic was like, until the stars were gone. I hate to admit it, but I missed the stars. I need their presence. I hadn't grasped how much being outside truly affected me. Now that I know I'm a celestial, and after having spent time away from the outside world, I see that my powers call to nature. I can't hide away from them, or who I am, despite how much I might want to.

I shake my head, thinking back on our time at the Altar of Water. I almost agreed to stay with Holtian in their sacred underwater cave. The life he offered me would've been incredible—peace and harmony for the rest of my days. It was tempting. Yet, I knew deep down I didn't belong there. My heart belongs to River. I don't know when I gave it to him—it just happened. A smile spreads across my lips.

"What are you thinking about over there?" I look up to meet River's gaze. The sun dips low in the sky, reds fading into purple and blues as night creeps over the horizon.

I shrug, trying not to give River too big of an ego boost. "You." I say casually.

He perks a dark brow and smirks. "Is that so?"

I scan the vast grassy field surrounding us and take a deep breath, soaking it all in. "Yes."

I gently pat Ash's neck. These horses have saved our feet, and I'm forever grateful. I think back to the start of our journey and how we traveled on foot. Even though my butt aches from hours in the saddle, I'd take this pain over the deep, aching soreness from walking for days straight.

Night approaches faster than we expected. River pulls the map from one of Buttercup's side saddles and scans it quickly. I stop Ash to watch him. He glances up at the landscape, thoughtful.

"We should stop for the night," he says. Out here, we're exposed to anything, and anyone that could find us. It unsettles me, especially since we haven't encountered the Dark Knights or Voras himself. I'm relieved, but I know it won't last. We'll run into Voras eventually. When we do, I need to be ready to defeat him. My stomach twists at the thought. If it comes to a battle with him, I won't survive. I'm neither strong, nor prepared enough.

"This way." River says, pulling me from my thoughts. He nods to the right. "If I'm reading the map right, that rolling hill leads to the cliffs above the Bay of Stars. Vivicus lives there." He sighs, weariness showing. "It doesn't seem to be too far. *Perhaps* we can make it there by nightfall."

I remember River saying it'd only take us a couple days to get here, but it's taken a lot longer than anticipated. Our pace has slowed, since we don't seem to be in immediate danger. I don't mind the slow trek, but the longer we travel, the more anxious I grow.

"Come on." River orders, galloping ahead on Buttercup. I follow, hoping he's right. If we ride hard, maybe we'll have a bed to sleep in. Is that too optimistic? I miss the bed at the Altar of Water. The temple was a luxury I hated leaving. But maybe if I learn more about my powers from Vivicus, we could return. Or find someplace quiet, hidden where King Voras's wrath won't reach us.

"Another far-fetched dream." I mutter, wind whipping through my loose waves. Ash keeps up with Buttercup as I follow River's lead. Soon, the hills turn rocky, and we climb an incline. The land stretches away between us, with an adjoining cliff across. A bizarre, complex landscape.

Mountains, I recognize. Cliffs, too. No waterfalls below—it's just more land. Are we climbing a mountain? A plateau? I'm confused but say nothing. River's following the map, and I only hope it's accurate.

The air thins, and I start panting from the exertion of riding Ash uphill. When the path evens out, it opens into a flat grassy knoll. River slows, and I do too. The sight before me steals my breath away and I'm all too glad that we didn't stop to make camp. A dark violet sky sprawls overhead, scattered with thousands of glittering, diamond-like stars.

"Gaia above." I whisper, dismounting. My legs wobble but hold as I breathe in the crisp night air. The pull of the nightscape tugs at me. Warm air brushes my skin; a mild breeze caresses my body.

"At last, you arrive," an unfamiliar voice says. My eyes fall upon a small woman approaching. Her large, bright violet eyes glow in the dark, looking wide and catlike on her round face.

"Are you Vivicus?" River dismounts and steps protectively beside me.

"That's Madame Vivicus to you," she chuckles, then looks back to me. "So, you are the Myrean Forsaken that's been prophesied."

"You've heard of me?" I ask.

"Rumors spread like the wildfires of the Scarlet Lands, especially when they involve an extinct Forsaken line that most don't even know about."

Madame Vivicus stands before me, petite compared to my height. I only notice it when her thick dreadlocks shift. A large, intricate tattoo centered on her forehead—an eye surrounded by swirling designs—mostly hidden by her umber skin and the night's shadow.

"Are you a… celestial?" I ask, watching as Madame Vivicus circles me like a shark stalking its prey. Her long peppered black dreadlocks cascade down her back, some adorned with metal and wooden beads. She wears a loose blouse and layers of flowing skirts that swish with each step. Dozens of metal earrings line both ears, and a variety of necklaces chink softly as they dangle from her neck.

She shakes her head, the beads in her hair clinking together. "No, dearie. Just a humble shaman. But I'm well-versed in chakras and herbal remedies."

My shoulders slump. I haven't realized how high my hopes were until they came crashing down. She isn't a celestial—not a Myrean Forsaken. Which means I truly am the only one. *Extinct.* That's what she called the Myrean line.

"What is it you desire of me, Myrean?" She stops circling and stands firm before me, hands on her wide hips, thick pierced brow quirked.

"We've traveled for your—"

Madame Vivicus raises a hand up toward River's mouth without even looking at him. He immediately stops.

"I know what *you* want, Gaian. Your body vibrates with it. 'Tis *her* who must speak her desires."

Silence falls over us. Only my heartbeat fills my ears. I glance up at the enchanting stars, steady my breathing. "I wish to learn them... my magic."

"Hmm." Vivicus murmurs, eyeing me inquisitively. "Your powers are blocked... hindered." Her large, plump lips tug to the side. She gently squeezes my arm. "I think I can help you."

I sigh in relief and hear River do the same. "Thank you," I say. Vivicus turns and beckons us to follow her. She leads us to a small wooden cabin, surrounded by an expansive garden with dozens of sprouting plants from herbs, scenting the warm air with beautiful fragrances.

"I don't have much room. There's a barn over there." She points toward the wooden building to the side of thick woods. "In the barn is a loft space where you can sleep. It's not much, but it's private. Though, you'll share space with the animals below." Her milky voice chuckles.

"You can keep your horses in there as well. There's room," she continues as she leads us to the front door and waves us inside. "Come. I was expecting you. There's warm stew brewing over the fire. Once you eat, you can rest. I feel

your weariness. Tomorrow we can start working on your...
abilities." Her violet eyes meet mine, and something
mischievous glints in them as she flashes me a toothy grin.

Food and rest sound amazing. It's all I could ask
for. That, and safety. I glance at River, who's been quiet,
but seems trusting of Madame Vivicus. As we approach the
door, he gives me a subtle nod. Together, we step into the
shaman's den.

Chapter 29

Myalis

Grass tickles my cheeks as I lay on the ground on a warm spring day. A bright blue sky hangs overhead with puffy white clouds floating above me. My eyes fixate on the sky as Mama and Papa lay next to me.

"That one looks like a flower." *I grin.*

Mama raises her hand upward, a finger pointing at a fluffy cloud above. "That one looks like a cat."

"All I see are big white puffs." *Papa laughs, making both Mama and me giggle. Papa never had much of an imagination. He works tirelessly as the village butcher, and I help him whenever I can. Mama never really approves of me sneaking off and following him to the tiny village center into his small shop.*

It was a perfect spring day and instead of slaving away, Mama and Papa decided that we should take a picnic into the fields behind our house and enjoy the rare sunshine in Dustfall. Being that we lived a small village on the most southern-east tip of the Netherfields, we were fortunate to occasionally get some warmer weather.

A disturbance in the ground halts our picnic. I feel the cool breeze first, causing me to sit upright. The sky that was a vibrant blue is now morphing into unnatural shades of gray and black. My parents sit up as we stare at one another. Papa's hazel eyes burn with concern as the three of us stand.

Tendrils of darkness began racing from the trees surrounding the meadow we were lying in. "Run!" Papa commands. We take off into the woods. Hand in hand, the three of us run, dodging tree limbs and roots. The once lively trees deaden before our eyes. The varying hues of green and florals turn black—into ash.

"Faster!" Papa barks as he squeezes my hand tighter. The three of us run in tandem, hands clasped. Sweat falls from my forehead. My panting pounds through my ears. Suddenly, Mama's hand is ripped from my grasp. Dark tendrils grab at her ankles pulling her into the abyss. I scream, watching her face twist in horror. Her large brown eyes are wide with fear. Her

hands and fingers claw into the dirt to keep herself from the darkness.

"Go, go!" Papa drags me. I almost trip, wanting to stop and go back for her.

"Mama!" I cry out.

"She's gone, Myalis! Keep moving!" Papa's grip falters, as he too gets ripped from my grasp.

"No!" I scream as warm tears fall down my reddened cheeks.

"Keep running!" Are the last words I hear before the abyss devours him. My heart rips from my chest, aching and numb. The distraction causes me to trip on a tree root. Dark tendrils take hold of my body constricting around my throat. I can't breathe, can't think as my vision blackens around the edges.

"You belong to me." The Dark King's piercing ice-colored eyes flash before me, and I scream. My body thrashes, slicked with sweat. My heart races, my breath quickening.

"Myalis!" A voice calls to me. My body shakes violently. "Wake up, Mya." The deep timbre is urgent and panicked, and my eyes flare open. River's there, his face

worried. His eyes are stormy—clouded with concern. His lips pressed in a tight frown.

"It was a dream, Mya. You were dreaming." His voice is soothing, as he runs his fingers up and down my arms. My chest heaves in and out. Taking in my surroundings, it takes me a moment to remember where I am. Madame Vivicus's barn. We made it to the shaman and her home just above the cliffs of Volantis over the Bay of Stars.

River and I made a comfortable spot in the loft space of her wooden barn housing two cows and a surly goat with us. We also brought Buttercup and Ash into the vacant stalls. The animals are quiet now as I glance around, realizing that it's still night.

I sigh, standing up. River follows my lead.

"Thanks for waking me." I haven't had that nightmare in such a long time now.

"What were you dreaming of?" River gazes at me concerned, trying to pull me into an embrace. I clutch my arms around myself and take a step back, shuddering with the memories of the past.

"The day my parents were killed. It's haunted me for so many years," I admit. I make my way down the rickety ladder leading from the loft to the bottom floor. River follows as I make my way out the barn out into the night air. Stars glitter brightly above, and an instant relief washes over me. I trek toward the edge of the cliff, with River quick on my heels.

"I'm sure it's terrifying to relive." His sympathetic voice calls out. River knows how it feels to lose one's parents. Although, he was much younger than I was, the absence of one's parents is like a void. One that doesn't ever seem to fill, no matter how much time passes.

"Do you ever have nightmares of losing yours?" I glance over my shoulder. Half-heartedly, he gestures, deep into the memory. He runs his fingers through his dark tousled hair swept loose around his face.

"I was so young. It's only flashes. I never saw their deaths, so, while it was traumatizing, it's nothing like your experience." River keeps walking with me and when we reach the edge of the grassy cliffs, I gasp looking below.

A glittering city sprawls below us in the canyon, its lights shimmering in the darkness. It's too dark to make out the details, except for one large, glittering palace nestled within the cliffs opposite us. But what truly takes my breath away is the bay. Now, I understand its name as I stare in awe.

The bay curves like a giant crescent moon, the stars reflecting off the vast ocean before us. The dark water glitters, mirroring the sky itself. It is surreal—magical. Here, in this exact moment, I feel closer to Myrea than ever before.

"Incredible," I breathe. What a wondrous place. Such a beautiful view. How has this shaman kept this land all to herself?

As I take it all in, my mind goes back to dinner. The conversation was sparse—just pleasantries. Madame Vivicus said that we'd talk *business* tomorrow. Instead, the three of us sat in her small house and savored the delicious vegetable stew she offered us.

The house, built of wood and stone, is modest with three rooms. The large main room serves as a kitchen, where she cooks and brews medicinal and herbal remedies. There's a small round table to seat four people. In the massive stone hearth sits an iron tripod holding a large cauldron. Baskets of vegetables rest around the hearth. A twine wire strung across the hearth holds a variety of herbs drying in the warm air. There's a little counter for meal prep, with a cupboard above storing mugs and plates. Next to it, a wooden basin sits beneath a water pump—for washing dishes, utensils, and maybe laundry.

Opposite the room is her workbench, as she calls it. I can't tell everything she has there, but dozens of jars filled with flowers, herbs, and tools crowd it, maybe for preparing the remedies. Shelves line the wooden wall above. Some jars hold unsightly creatures that I'd rather not look at.

A door to the right of the hearth leads to Madame Vivicus's bedroom and bathing room. River and I did not want to be nosy, so we stayed at the wooden table in the kitchen, graciously accepting the food and drink she provided. Madame Vivicus also baked a beautiful loaf of bread that tasted simply divine with the soup.

After a quick dinner, she led us to the barn, carrying a few blankets. "There's plenty of hay up there for makeshift beds. Lay a blanket on the hay and use the others as coverings. I'm sorry I can't offer you better accommodation, but this place," she gazed at the barn, "will do, and it's more private. I assumed you kids would want that."

Vivicus gave River and me a knowing look, and I blush.

"We're grateful for your kindness and hospitality," River said, reaching out to accept the blankets from our host.

She nodded, handing them over before turning back to her house. We stepped into the barn, taking note of the animals inside, and then brought Buttercup and Ash in so they'd feed and rest. Once the horses settled, River and I climbed to the loft.

It was more spacious than I had expected. River instantly set to work shucking the hay into a pile making a bed of it. I put my rucksack down to assist him. I don't know how he still had energy. My entire being was weary as I worked to make a bed out of hay and began laying the blankets. Once we settled, it didn't take us long to stretch on the bed, lie down, and fall asleep.

Now, large, muscled arms wrap around me as my focus falls back to the ocean before us, reflecting the glittering stars in the middle of the night. River brings his face close to mine, resting his chin on my shoulder as I stare, his grip around me grounding.

"I feel like since the first night we met, we've not had a moment like this." His voice brushes softly against the tip of my ear.

"Like what?" I breathe, turning my head slightly, our lips inches apart.

His grip tightens around me as he pulls me closer into him, my back pressed against his strong chest.

"Quiet," he murmurs with a sigh. "Peaceful."

And it's true. We are surrounded by tranquility up here on the cliffs. For a moment, I dream that we could stay frozen in time like this. River brushes my hair away from my face, then leans in, pressing his soft lips on mine. The kiss is gentle, barely a caress, but it ignites warmth through me.

When his lips part from mine, his gaze returns to the ocean. Yet all I see is him. Desire for his lips makes my mouth water. Even in darkness, with the night sky as our light, his strong features are silhouetted, eyes glistening.

"What are you thinking?" I ask, desperate to know his thoughts.

He shakes his head subtly, snapping out of a reverie. "Of you," he admits. "Of us. What will become of us. Our future. Everything." His breath trembles as our eyes meet. In that moment, nothing else matters. We're in this together, until the end.

My heart races as his expression morphs into something else. Lust. Yearning. Desire. My breath quickens as I turn toward him. His expression's hungry as he slams me against his body. River's lips crash down on mine in a bruising and all-consuming kiss. I open my mouth for him and his tongue slides in, skillfully caressing my own. I moan against his mouth as my fingers tangle into his silken hair.

Together, River and I fall to our knees, and his hands begin stripping my clothes. Swiftly, fervently, I reciprocate. It's like our skin needs to touch. We're alight with desire for each other. With the barrier of clothes gone, River lays me down on the grass as his lips trail down my neck, down between my breasts, his hands gingerly tracing the curves of my body. I shudder beneath his touch. Every time his lips touch my heated skin, a spark of electricity flits through me.

Down my body he kisses, and I desperately want to hold him. I don't even know where, I just want my hands on him—I grab his wavy hair. Using his hands, he pushes my legs apart and his mouth meets my wet center. I hiss through my teeth at the sensation of his mouth sucking me, my body convulsing beneath him. River groans as his tongue slips inside of me, and I moan in return, my eyes taking in the night sky, as the feeling of ecstasy crawls up my spine. My hips rise from the grass beneath me. River uses his arm as leverage to push me down on the ground.

As River continues to work me with his mouth, he applies pressure with his thumb on my clit. My body seizes in pleasure. Gaia above, he is good at this.

"Yes!" I cry out and I want to fuck his mouth harder. I lift my hips up with each assault of his tongue. River wraps his arms under my ass and pulls me tight against his face.

"What do you need, princess?" He breathes between licks and sucks. My chest heaves as I cry out. My climax rising within me, my heated skin chilling with goosebumps in the breezy summer night.

"All of you, in me, right now." My voice is a command. River pauses his motions and gazes up at me from between my legs. A dark brow quirks, amused as he licked his lips.

"As you wish, my love." River slowly crawls over my body and as he does, I wrap a hand around his hardened dick, stroking him. A guttural moan escapes from his throat as he brings his face to mine. "Cruel, wicked, princess," River hisses, teasing as he grabs my mouth with his teeth. The taste of my arousal still on him.

Bringing his hands up, River cups my cheeks before running those strong hands over my hair. My gaze shifts back on him; a side smirk sprawling on his mouth. When he brings his lips back to mine, the kiss is gentle, sweet—his lips warm. His body feels like a furnace. He sinks his hard, throbbing cock into me, and I release a gasp. It was soft, meant just for his ears. Panting, gasping, breathless, and desperate for more of him. It's a plea for him to fill me further.

My eyes slam shut when River pulls out of me slowly, only to thrust back harder. "You take me so good, Mya. Fuck."

His one hand kneads my breast as the other supports his weight above me. I wrap my legs around his waist and River's pace quickens. My vision is lost in the stars above as my climax shatters through me.

Chapter 30

Myalis

*T*hud.

Thud.

Thud.

I startle awake to the pounding noise, momentarily forgetting where I am before the memories of last night rush back. I stretch out on the makeshift straw bed in Madame Vivicus's barn loft. Bits of straw poke through the blankets, agitating my bare skin. River isn't lying beside me, and as I sit up rubbing my eyes, I wonder where he disappeared to.

Thud.

Time eludes me. How long have I slept? I shuffle off the bed and find my clothes neatly folded by my bag. A smile creeps across my face recalling how River and I ditched our clothes last night under the breathtaking stars.

Quickly grabbing them and putting them on, I climb down the ladder passing Buttercup and Ash, as well as Vivicus's barn animals.

I'm grateful for the fresh air as I step into the late morning sun. Though I've grown used to the barn scent, I appreciate the smell of the damp morning grass, blooming flowers, and herbs surrounding Vivicus's home. The sun crests low over the ocean, blinding me with its brightness. It's a picturesque sight. I've never seen water so crystal-blue and clear. But the sweltering heat of eternal summer already presses. I roll up my tunic sleeves, eyes catching River, shirtless and chopping wood by Vivicus's dwelling.

Thud.

My mouth waters watching him. Sweat glistens off his rippling back muscles as he swings the ax up and down. I stand frozen, gawking, admiring the man before me.

"He is quite a handsome being, isn't he?" Madame Vivicus drawls next to me. I jump at her sudden appearance. In the morning sun, her dark skin glistens, dewy and radiant, despite her age. She holds a medium woven basket at her hip as we both watch River.

"He is," I admit, the flush of embarrassment streaking across my face.

"You two are important," Vivicus states. I crease my brow in confusion, dragging my gaze from River to her.

"How do you know?"

She flashes a toothy smile and points to the eye tattoo in the center of her forehead. "I sense things. You both share a deep connection. Your paths are intertwined, but it won't be easy."

We stand silently as I glance back at River, continuing his chore. He pauses, wipes sweat from his forehead with his arm, and takes a breath. Gaia above, he glistens like a god. My heart stutters. A chuckle beside me rings through my ears.

"Shall we begin your training?" Vivicus asks, drawing my attention from River. I'm uncertain what to expect, but hope training with her will help me finally understand and control my celestial powers.

"Yes." I nod. Vivicus beckons me to follow, and I do. She heads toward her house, and I pause, casting one last glance at River. I don't expect him to return my gaze, but our eyes lock. His lip curls in a boyish grin that ignites a fire in my core. My breath hitches as he winks. Gaia above, he's intoxicating. His black hair is pulled in a bun atop his head, some strands loose from his chore of chopping wood.

His blue eyes sparkle like the sky above, stark against the dark facial hair adorning his face.

Quickly, I turn and follow Vivicus inside. She sets the basket of herbs and vegetables on the table, ambling over to her workspace to pull jars onto it. Efficiently, she selects a variety of items from the jars and begins crushing them in a mortar. I take a seat and watch as she brews tea, then pours me a cup.

"Thank you." I say, nodding as I take a sip. It's earthy with an odd aftertaste I can't place.

She nods, the beads on her dreadlocks clicking. "Now, Celestial Forsaken... what do you know about the forgotten Myrea?"

I shrug, taking another sip of the tea. "Not much. I only really know what River told me. She was—or I guess is—a forgotten Elemental. Her powers are extinct from this world... at least, they were until I came along. He says I'm part of some prophecy to save the world from the Dark King. I don't know if I'll live up to River's expectations. I don't feel like any kind of prophecy."

Saying it aloud makes me realize how lost I am. Madame Vivicus's face remains impassive as she observes me. Silently, she sits beside me.

"Do you know why Myrea was considered the peacekeeper of the Elementals?" She raises a brow. My eyes lift to her violet ones. I hesitate before shaking my head. A toothy grin sprawls across her face. "'Tis 'cause Myrea, as a celestial being, had the abilities of all the Elementals."

My brows furrow in confusion. "What?" The shock freezes me inside. My hands tremble.

"Myrea, the Goddess of Order, could wield any power necessary to maintain the peace between the Elementals. You could say that she was the ultimate being. Tell me, Myalis, while you say you have trouble communing with your celestial gifts, have any others made themselves known?"

My heart thuds as I sift through memories of wielding magic, whether accidentally or on purpose. I've avoided using them, but the few times they surfaced, I never quite understood how to label them. My mind drifts back to when River and I first started our journey and were chased by the Dark Knights. I remembered screaming and unleashing a strange power.

"Potentially." I admit sheepishly. "I don't know whose power it was."

"What happened?" Madame Vivicus leans in, eager.

I sigh, recalling that day in the clearing. "I screamed, and it seemed to deafen or melt the minds of those chasing us. We don't know what happened to them. We didn't stick around to find out." I don't know how else to explain. The entire incident bizarre and unbelievable, but it did happen. Thinking it over, I feel like it's a power that shouldn't exist at all.

"Darkness." Vivicus replies simply.

Air leaves my lungs, and it feels like I've been punched in the stomach. "No," I object.

Madame Vivicus nods in return. "Indeed, dearie. Any powers tied to the mind connect to Tazra and her abilities. Tell me, where do you originally hail from?"

"Dustfall."

She nods in understanding. "A region in the Netherfields. Were your parents Forsaken as well?"

"No," I reply numbly.

"But that doesn't mean the bloodline isn't part of your heritage," she explains. "You come from the land where darkness reigns, which could explain why Tazra's powers influence you more than Myrea's. By working through your chakras, I can help you find your true celestial connection. That's where our training shall begin." Vivicus rises from her chair and moves to her workbench, gathering various jars and herbs.

"Wait," I abruptly stand. "I don't understand… what are chakras? How will that help me?"

Without looking up, Vivicus continues her task. "Chakras are energy centers in the body. When your body is unbalanced, the energies don't work in tandem. As a celestial and a peacekeeper, it's vital that your chakras stay balanced so you can wield efficiently. I'll observe all seven of your chakras and see which ones we need to work through. Once we get to the root of the unbalanced chakra, you should be able to connect to Myrea, and your celestial powers will shine."

My head spins with confusion. I don't understand a word of it. I stand frozen, watching her work. She speaks no further, and I don't know how to respond to this spirited woman. The sound of the front door opening pulls my attention. River steps inside, sweat dripping from his brow.

"Mind if I grab some water?" he asks, unaware of the tension between Madame Vivicus and me. She waves approval while grabbing another jar. River's eyes meet mine, a brow raised. "What's she doing?"

"I don't know," I admit. "But apparently, I have blocked chakras. And, Myrea had the abilities of all the Elementals, so she thinks if I am able to unblock my chakras, I might wield them all."

River's surprise flickers across his face, before he regains composure. Calmly, he grabs a glass from one of her shelves and fills it at the sink. "That's news to me," he says. "I wish I'd realized it sooner. The powers you showed before never made sense. Holtian could've tried to show you water wielding."

I think back to the training ring and how I stopped Holt's whirlpool attack. He asked me how I did it, and I didn't know. Now, I wonder if I wielded water without realizing it. I shrug as confusion and frustration knots in my chest. Maybe we should've stayed at the Altar of Water longer. I wish that we'd have thought it through.

Eventually I'll have to return and learn true water wielding from Holt. For now, my thoughts are a tangled mess. This shaman isn't giving me any clarity, instead, I'm more confused. What have I gotten myself into?

I sit back down at the table and cradle my head in my hands, staring into the teacup. The sight steadies me. With a sigh, I finish the rest of the cup in one go.

The clatter of wooden bowls clanking draws my gaze back to her workstation. It seems she's making a paste of some sort. I groan, hoping it isn't something that I'll have to eat. Whatever it is, it's a lot. She mixes a large batch and proceeds to scoop the muddy-colored goop into a bowl.

When that's done, she starts filling a sack with other items—flat black stones and items I can't exactly make out. Suddenly, she turns to me, her long dreads swinging over her shoulders.

"Come with me," is all she says before heading out. River and I share a glance. I scoot myself up from the chair and follow her outside. River gives me a look of encouragement before he heads to continue whatever chore Madame Vivicus assigned him.

The petite woman is quick on her feet as she heads into the woods. "Where are we going?" I call after her, lengthening my stride until I finally catch up to her. She doesn't falter; she isn't winded by the pace.

"There is a small hot spring through here. I use it to help with my chakras."

"What are you planning to do?"

Vivicus grins wide, showing all her teeth. "I told you; I'm going to view your chakras. With the energy of the hot spring and the concoction I made, I should be able to sense your aura. It'll give me insight into your celestial being."

What the fuck does that mean? I keep my thoughts to myself as we tread through the forest around her home. I don't know how far we've walked. I don't even know where we are or how we'll find our way back. At this point, all I can do is trust Madame Vivicus. After all, she's the entire reason we came this far, hoping she can help me uncover my magic. While I have my doubts about the chakras she's mentioning, what the hell do I really know about it? About anything, in fact. What do I have to lose by trying it her way? Nothing.

The sound of trickling water draws my attention, and we enter a small clearing, surrounded by ancient, enchanted-looking trees. The hot spring sits in the center, and next to it is a makeshift table likely crafted by Madame Vivicus.

She places her burlap sack on the table, then starts unpacking the ingredients. Carefully, she takes flat black stones and places them in the water, resting them on shallow rocks just beneath the crystal-clear surface. Vivicus mutters to herself, words I can't make out. I just watch, my curiosity piqued.

She continues until all the rocks are steaming in the water, and I stay silent. Then she turns to me, her violet eyes almost glowing. "Undress," she commands simply.

I freeze, staring at her. When I don't move, she repeats. "Undress, Myrea Forsaken. Fully."

"You want me to get naked?" I ask, caught off-guard.

Vivicus chuckles, the sound unsettling. "Did I stutter?"

I huff out a breath but then nod. My face flushes with embarrassment but I pull my boots off and start to remove my leggings and tunic. I stand bare before the shaman. My body flushes as she looks me once over. She trots to the table where the large bowl with the goop rests. Grabbing the bowl of paste, she returns to me.

She dips her hand into the mixture, then begins to slather it on my skin. It's cold and sticky, but it smells floral with a tinge of something bitter I can't place. "What's this mud for?"

"Shh," she hisses, refusing to explain further. She works briskly, smearing the paste down my arms and legs, then covering my face and neck. Then, giving me a knowing look of where else she needs to put it, she waits for my consent. My breath hitches, embarrassment creeping all over my skin. My throat dries as I give a subtle nod. Vivicus works quickly as she spread the paste on my chest, my breasts, skimming down my stomach and then along my back and rear. Yes, I'm fully mortified.

"Get into the water," Vivicus instructs once she finishes. I oblige and head toward the pool of water. I dip a bare foot into the hot spring and immediately pull out from the scalding heat.

"Fuck," I yelp. It's boiling—like I'm about to be cooked alive.

"You'll be fine," Vivicus assures, as though she can read my mind. I shoot her a wary look, wondering how many times she's done this to herself, or even others. Gritting my teeth, I put my foot in again. My skin instantly reddens, but I proceed placing my other foot in as well. I give myself a moment to adjust before I wade fully in the water. The steam opens up my pores and sinuses. Damn, it's the hottest fucking water I've ever endured.

I bite my lip to avoid crying out. Eyes squeezed shut, I breathe through the pain as I submerge to my neck. Once acclimated, I watch Madame Vivicus throwing in a variety of leaves and flowers and oils into the hot spring. She chants, soft at first then louder. Vivicus shakes a rattle that dangles from her belt. Only now do I notice how many strange talismans hang from her hip.

She motions me closer, then steps into the spring herself, dipping her fingers into a red substance and painting strange markings on my face and forehead. Vivicus chants in an old language that I don't understand.

"Now, float within the springs." The instruction barely registers. Again, I obey and allow myself to float in the hot water. The poultice makes my skin tingle. My eyes slip closed, as my surroundings melt away. Calm washes over me as Madame Vivicus hums, her chanting rising and falling in the air.

I drift off—where, I'm not sure. It's a peaceful, warm, cozy, and safe. Woods surround me. The scent of the earth comforts me. Strong hands slide over my skin, embrace and caress me. A lustful touch makes my breath hitch. The smell of River's skin fills my senses. Behind closed lids, flashes of red, yellow, and white lights dance before me.

Suddenly, I'm submerged in the water. My long hair tickles my face as the gentle current beneath the surface sweeps it with the current. I hold my breath, lungs still. There's no pain or panic, and I don't feel like I'm drowning. I'm simply existing. My mind is at peace as other lights begin to dance. Green and blue stars swirl in my vision, but I can't make out any meaning. What am I supposed to see? What is Madame Vivicus looking for?

The calm fades as anxiety overcomes me. I'm still submerged. Grays and blacks swirl around me; it feels cold now. A pulsing glow beats at the storm's center in my mind. No shapes, no figures, no memories; it's just darkness. It's scary and isolating. I hyperventilate. Water fills my mouth and nose as I involuntarily inhale. I writhe, unable to move, unable to break free. It's a pull I can't escape. When a pair of ice blue eyes bore into mine, I scream into the water.

All of a sudden, I feel hands on me, yanking me up. I gasp, and quickly drag out of my stupor. Madame Vivicus's spindly fingers wrap around my forearms. I blink away the water and poultice, her face coming into focus.

My chest heaves, my breath ragged. I feel vulnerable and raw, as the shaman examines me.

"Welcome back," she says with a smile. Breathless, I look around as the hot spring and ancient trees return to view. The forest is eerily silent. The aroma of oils and dried flowers from the spring wafts through the air.

"What happened?" I ask, as she leads me out of the water and hands me a thick cloth to dry off.

"I saw your chakras. Come, get dressed. I'll explain on our way back."

It's a weird feeling. I don't want to leave the hot springs now. It's calling to me, luring me in. I ignore it as I scrub off the paste from my body with the cloth before getting dressed. Madame Vivicus already packed up her things and was heading back the way we came. I follow, waiting for answers, wondering what—if anything—she saw. The silence stretches between us until I grow impatient and nearly bark, "well?"

"As expected, your chakras are blocked. More than one, in fact," she answers. "Your Root, Third-Eye, and Crown chakras are the primary blocks. The Root chakra is at the base of your spine. It represents grounding, stability, and basic needs. We must support and unblock your Root chakra, it's vital to unlocking the rest."

She points to the tattoo on her forehead. "The Third-Eye chakra is associated with perception, insight, and intuition. Unblocking it will help guide and balance your power when you wield it. The last blocked chakra is called the Crown chakra. It's the seventh and highest chakra in the body. It's associated with spiritual awareness, enlightenment and will connect you to the divine. Only when this chakra is unlocked, will you be able to connect with Myrea. It'll take some time, but if we focus one by one, we should be able to unravel them and bring you balance."

She keeps her eyes ahead as she speaks, and it might all have been gibberish. I'm not sure what I have to do to unblock these chakras or what it will entail, but I grow anxious as I think about it. What if I can't connect with Myrea because she no longer exists? If I unblock it, will anyone be there to answer my celestial call? It seems like a lot of work. Work I'm hesitant to dive into. The dive into the hot spring was fine until I almost drowned in it. How many times will I have to feel that before a specific chakra unblocks itself? I sigh behind her. "So, what does it mean? What do I have to do?"

Vivicus stops in her tracks, and turns her head toward me. She smiles warmly and places a hand on my shoulder. "Lots of meditation, self-improvement, herbal exercises. You'll be fine. We'll work through everything together." Then she moves on, leaving me standing in the woods, confused and hoping that somehow, someday, it'll all work out.

Chapter 31

Myalis

For weeks, I meditated for hours on end, participated in acupuncture, soaked in the hot springs and covered in various pastes and oils that Madame Vivicus concocted. I learned tai chi, breathing exercises, and anything and everything the shaman told me to do to help unblock my chakras. At first, I felt stupid— like it wasn't helping, but as I continued to do what she told me, somehow, I felt lighter, my mind clearer and calmer than before.

When I wasn't following Madame Vivicus's regime, I trained with River, keeping my body fit and practicing Elemental powers. He tried teaching me some Gaian magic. The progress was minimal, but it was progress, nonetheless. I tried not to get frustrated, reminding myself that learning my powers would take time. It wouldn't happen overnight like I initially hoped. River told me it took him several years to master his abilities. I shrug, just wanting to learn faster.

I want to understand what they are—how they work. I want to protect myself and stop running from Voras. The Dark King lingers at the back of my mind. Often, I wonder when he'll turn his head again, because when he does, I need to be ready.

I know I can't defeat him in my current state, but I must keep training and working. Most days I'm exhausted; my body sore from whatever Vivicus's methods demand, or by hours of physical training with River. Tonight, I plan to meditate on the cliff, staring up at the glittering stars reflecting off the clear bay water below.

I take slow breaths. In through my nose, out through my mouth. My legs crossed beneath me. I'm wearing nothing but a lightweight linen shift. A light breeze soothes my skin. I place my hands on my knees, palms up toward the sky, and close my eyes.

I try envisioning the colors of my chakras and feel them within me. According to Vivicus, I've managed to balance my Root Chakra. However, my Third-Eye and Crown Chakras are still unbalanced, despite trying everything.

As I breathe through my meditative state, a strong hand presses on my shoulder. It startles me out of my thoughts, and open my eyes to see River.

"Hey," he offers me a quiet, weak smile.

"Hey," I reply, smiling back.

"May I join you?" he asks.

I nod. "Sure." He sits beside me and shrugs. I frown. "What's wrong?"

River looks up at the sky and inhales deeply before meeting my gaze. The stars reflect in his eyes as I wait for him to speak. "Madame Vivicus just returned from the city."

She'd left yesterday to restock ingredients and supplies she can't grow up here. At first, I'm excited to hear of her return, but River's face remains heavy.

"And?" I egg him on.

He takes another deep breath. "She told me that the city is filled with Dark Knights. Our time here is running out."

My brows scrunch, and I quickly shift from my peaceful position. "No," I protest. "I still haven't connected to Myrea. I still haven't unblocked all my chakras. I haven't come into my power yet, we can't leave."

"Mya," River's voice is gentle, consoling. "If the Dark Knights are here in Volantis, then it's only a matter of time before they find us. She booked us passage on a cargo ship bound for the Scarlet Lands. It leaves tomorrow night. We'll continue to the Ember Temple where we can seek sanctuary from Voras. Maybe someone there can teach you Prometheus's magic—fire."

My frown deepens. I don't want to flee again. I'm happy here and feel like we only just got settled.

"But—"

"Madame Vivicus assured me that she's given you all the guidance you need." River's expression is sincere, but my stomach churns. Will I be able to do this without her? Without all the crazy herbal remedies and practices? As if sensing my hesitancy, River places his hand upon mine.

"We'll do this together. Nothing has changed, Mya. Only the location will."

My brows knit as I soak in his words. I don't want to leave. I feel connected to the stars here. It literally overlooks the Bay of *Stars*. This is what I want, what

Madame Vivicus has: a small, humble home with a couple animals and crops to tend and an immaculate view of the night sky. Despite the ungodly heat, this feels like forever to me.

I shrink inward, my head spinning. A wave of melancholy sweeps over me. River takes notice, quickly crouching on his knees in front of me, cupping my face in his hands.

"Hey," he murmurs with a weak smile. "What's going on in there?"

I struggle to meet his gaze. "I just don't want to leave," I admit. "This is where I want to be. I feel like this is where I belong." A tear slips down my cheek before I realized it. River wipes it away gently with his thumb, pulling me close into a warm embrace.

"I know, princess," he says, running his fingers through my hair as he holds me. "It's been amazing here. A life I could see for us, too." A sob escape from me at his words. We could've had a life here. If I weren't being hunted. "You know as well as I do that it's no longer safe here. You're right, Mya, being on the run, it's shit. But as long as we're together, we can find happiness in these moments. Until we can have them forever."

I find myself looking into River's stormy eyes. There's so much love there. I press a chaste kiss on his lips. He returns it, then hugs me tighter. "Come on, let's go to bed. We have a lot to do tomorrow before we leave."

"Okay." We rise from our spot on the cliff and head toward the barn. It'll be our final night here. Inside, we climb the ladder up to our loft. River and I undress and settle into each other's arms. It takes only moment before I fall fast asleep.

Dawn comes sooner than expected. Sunshine glints through a hole in the barn's roof, waking me. I groan and roll over into River's bare chest. I feel the comfort of his arms and inhale his masculine scent, a mix of cedar and campfire. A chuckle rumbles from his chest. I gaze up at his face, his sleepy bluish-gray eyes return the stare.

"Good morning, princess," River's deep, raspy voice stirs me deliciously. He kisses the top of my head as I snuggle deeper into his arms, which tighten around me. I feel his morning wood press against me—I flush at the feel.

"Good morning," I whisper back. We lie quietly in each other's arms until I speak again. "I wish we could stay like this forever."

"I know." River yawns, rubbing my back with one knuckle. "But we have to start moving. We need to pack and begin our trek to the bay to catch the boat. It'll take a couple hours to get there."

"Even on horseback?" I raise a brow.

He sighs, rolling onto his back. "They're not coming with us."

I sit up, heart aching at the thought. "What? What do you mean?" Buttercup and Ash have been our travel companions for months now. It feels weird, almost wrong, to leave them behind.

River caresses my arm. "They can't go on a boat. And once we reach the Scarlet Lands, we'll have to find other means of transport. They won't be able to handle the terrain. The landscape there is too harsh for them."

"I see," I reply, recalling my avoidance of the Scarlet Lands, because I knew it was vast and harsh. It isn't a great place for hiding, considering it's mostly desert. I avoided it as much as I could during my years on the run. I have to trust River's judgment. He has traveled through the Scarlet Lands, so he's familiar with it. It makes sense that people who live in the desert terrain would have other animals to help them navigate the land.

"Vivicus agreed to take care of them," River says, pulling me from my thoughts.

I nod, relieved they'll be safe here. I get to my feet, and dress in my leggings and tunic before putting my boots on. River follows suit in silence. I make sure to check all my equipment. River told me that I have to leave my bow and arrows. We don't want to draw suspicion as we travel through Volantis. My heart breaks as I leave them, but I pack my dagger in the small knapsack that I'd carried during my travels.

It felt weird packing up again. First having to leave the Altar of Water and now here. These weeks of respite have healed my soul. It reminds me of the peace I found back in Sunhollow, which seems like a lifetime ago. A much simpler time. But the more I reflect on my time there—the more I realize that I hadn't truly been living. I survived in a hole under a damn tree, barely able to feed myself. It feels ludicrous now. How I had done that for a year was beyond me.

This life isn't much better, but I'm not alone anymore. I've met people. People who seem to be on my side and are rooting for me to succeed. I have River—a companion I never thought I'd have. Yes, my life has changed drastically, but this is only the beginning. I can't forget what lies ahead of me. There's the King to contend with, and I'm not sure how we'd handle him when the time comes. I'm grateful that I haven't seen him in my dreams since that one time in the Altar of Water. I hope it never happens again.

Behind me, River secures his stuff in his rucksack. We make sure that the loft is back in order before descending the ladder down. I pause at Buttercup and Ash's pens, giving them gentle strokes and gratitude for everything they've done for us. They've been good to us, and I'm glad that Madame Vivicus is going to care for them.

Outside the barn, I see Vivicus tending her garden. She looks just as usual, the beads in her dreadlocks clacking, the items on her belt jingling. A woven basket sits beside her as she picks vegetables. A smile creeps across my face as I study her for the last time. She really has been a wonderful mentor for me. I'm going to miss her.

When we approach, she stands flashing a toothy grin. "Come, Myrea Forsaken. I have things to give you for your journey." I glance at River, and he nods at me before I follow Vivicus back into her house.

She walks over to the worktable and gathers a variety of pouches and small jars. The smell of rosemary and mint fill the room as she boils something in her cauldron. I stand next to the shaman silently as she begins handing me items.

"Teas for muscle relaxation and headaches, or pain," she explains, opening pouches to show me the contents. "Medicinal herbs in case you need them. A jar of the meditative mud, should you wish to use it." My arms fill with her offerings. I let out a soft chuckle, prompting her to quirk a brow at me. "Yes?"

"Thank you for everything," I say, emotions welling up in me, but I don't allow myself to crack. Vivicus's shoulders relax, and a genuine smile lights her face.

"I know you don't want to leave," she starts, standing before me. "But you're ready to fly from the nest. You know what you need. Continue your journey, and Myrea will answer your call."

A beat of silence falls between us before she starts packing her herbs and ointments again. She then hands me a large ration of food. I place them all in my bag and bid her one final goodbye.

Vivicus follows me outside and addresses River with a command. "You keep her safe, Gaian. Our world depends on it."

River smirks. "With my life," is all he says. We begin our journey into the city below. I glance back once more at the life I've cherished here. Vivicus waves, and I do too in return, turning before the tears begin to flow.

Sensing my sorrow, River's calloused hand grabs mine and gives it a delicate squeeze. "We'll come back one day and make a life of our own."

It's a hopeful thought. One I'm not sure will ever be a reality.

Chapter 32

Myalis

The journey to Volantis is uneventful, but now, at its cusp, my heart races with anticipation. My feet ache from the walk, yet adrenaline flows through me. Before us is a colossal gate, guarded by Hydros Forsaken—tall, lithe men, armed with spears as tall as themselves, and clad in armor made of opalescent, mother-of-pearl shoulder plates and wrist cuffs—similar to the ones protecting the Altar of Water. Their pale blonde hair, almost white, hang loosely over their shoulders with intricate war braids at the sides of their heads. Even from afar, they seem fierce and powerful.

The traveler flow through the gates into the city of Volantis is sparse, but there are enough. Some push carts filled with crates for trade. Others, look weary from long journeys. The afternoon fades to evening, and the sky's bright blue shift to shades of deep orange. In the distance, the city lights begin to glow.

"Just keep your head down and stay silent," River whispers as we approach. "We should blend in without any issue."

I nod, but my heart races as we get near to the entrance. Will we be allowed in? Can we truly slip inside unnoticed? My stomach flutters as we get closer to the magnificent gates. Once I'm in close vicinity, I take in the sight, and notice it's made of silver, imbued with sparkling blue gems. They are ornate—a design of whimsical waves and starlight above, represented by opals larger than my hand.

The guards stand stoic, their eyes scanning the people walking in and out. Hand in hand, River and I move, passing through. A wave of relief washes over me.

"Thank Gaia," I sigh, as we finally enter inside the perimeter of the enchanted city.

"We'll follow the travelers going in toward the epicenter. From there, we'll make our way to the docks." River says, alert as we walk along the scenic dirt path flanked by rolling hills and cliffs on either side, leading to the heart of the city. I nod in response but keep my own vigilance sharp.

The people walking in the same direction chatter as we hasten our pace, walking past. Thankfully, we're not burdened by a large wagon filled with goods or animals to potentially sell or trade which may slow us down like them. The sooner we get on board the cargo ship, the better.

We left our large weapons with Vivicus to avoid suspicion. But carrying just a dagger, I feel naked and exposed, especially without my bow. It's been my companion during all my travels and to be without it feels... strange. River assures me that when we arrive at Firerock—the port for which we are sailing to—we'll buy new weapons. While I appreciate his words, and although this part of our journey is shorter than what we've already been through, I still feel uneasy.

The closer we get to Volantis, the more civilization comes to view. Wooden houses scatter around us, growing closer together, the further we walk. People look at the road as we pass. Some nod, others smile, and I'm grateful they seem friendly. When we get deeper into the city, my anxiety starts to grow. The crowds become denser. Buildings are pressed closer together. Volantis guards meander the streets in glittering armor, patrolling the city.

My breath quickens as I scan every angle, my eyes sharp for any sign of the Dark Knights. River grasps my hand firmly, squeezing it in reassurance. I glance at the shops lining the now-paved streets and then stop dead in my tracks. River tugs my arm, pulling me.

"Come on, it's not too much further…" His voice trails off, finally following my gaze and he lets out in shock. "Fuck."

I stare at a drawing eerily similar to me. In fact, it's supposed to be me. A *wanted* poster, with my name and description upon it. Offering a grand reward for my delivery to King Voras. My heart races, sweat trickles down my brow, and my breath quickens into hyperventilation.

"Come on," River whispers urgently in my ear, tugging me between two buildings and into a small alleyway. My mind whirls. Thoughts go a mile a minute. It's as if my entire world shifts beneath my feet. My back hits something hard as River's hands press firmly on my shoulders.

"Look at me." His voice a stern command. My eyes flick to his steady gaze as panic consumes me. He breathes slowly and deliberately—trying to calm me. I match his rhythm, gaining control of the panic attack threatening to take over.

"A fucking wanted poster, River," I exhale. "A *reward*. For me. What in the underhells are we going to do? How many of these fucking pictures are plastered all over Volantis? Will we even be able to board the boat without someone recognizing me?"

River's face grows pensive as he takes another breath. "I don't know Mya, but we have to try. We're this close." River lets me go and begins to rummage through his sack. He pulls out his dark green cloak. "Here, put this on. Keep your face covered."

I scoff. "That's not fucking suspicious in this eternal fucking heat. No one is wearing a cloak, River! That'd draw even more attention."

"Then what do you propose?" he snaps. "We don't have many options here, *princess*."

We glare at each other in a silent standoff. I think of other options. We must get to the docks. We have to board whatever vessel Vivicus has secured for us. It's the only way for us to safely leave. I sigh, as no better idea comes up. Relenting, I grab the cloak from River. I don't know how much further the dock is, but the sun is beginning to lower in the sky, and I know we need to get there quickly, since the boat is supposed to leave by nightfall.

I throw on the cloak, tossing the hood over my head. He nods in approval. "It's not much further," he says. "With the sun setting, we should be able to blend in and keep to the shadows without notice."

Hand in hand, River and I continue toward the docks, following signs plastered on buildings that point us in the right direction. I wish we had more time to take in the city's splendor. The glittering sandstone structures sparkle as the sun starts its descent from the crystal-blue sky.

But we don't have time for that. "Wanted posters" are nailed to walls and stalls, while the streets bustle with people in bright-colored clothing. They seem mostly to be customers, buying everything, from fabrics to produce. But I kept a keen eye out for Dark Knights, as does River.

We pass an array of merchant stands—some glittering with jewels, others selling sandals. I keep my head down, listening to the vendors calling out, trying to make one last sale of the day. River and I pass many stalls with brightly colored canopies overhead. Then, the first set of Dark Knights appear. Bile rises into my throat, and I falter.

River holds my hand firmly, pulling me along, never missing a beat. "Keep moving," he says, under hushed breath. I nod and keep my eyes downcast at the path beneath our feet. I pray to Gaia that we avoid their attention as I stare at the sparkling pavement flecked with bits of crushed shells.

"Hey!" a shout rings from nearby. Both River and I freeze, holding our breaths. My stomach churns and I feel nauseous as we turn. The Dark Knights approach us before walking past to a merchant stall. A burly man selling an assortment of knives grabs their attention. I sigh in relief that we aren't caught, and we continue our way.

Entering the marina district, the merchant stalls shift to fresh fish and fishing gear, the smell of sea thick in the air. Taverns line the streets, and sailors pile in and out, laughing and drunk. Nostalgia hits me as I think of Badger and how much I miss The Dirty Fox. Shit, I could use a drink myself.

I take a moment to observe our surroundings since River remains vigilant. I've never seen this part of Elemi, and despite how brief it's going to be, I want to look around during our visit.

The Bay of Stars district, dominated by the bustling port and docks, is far busier than the part of the city we passed through earlier. The bay is the heart of Volantis, nestled between towering cliffs. Hundreds of boats are docked in the massive marina, some ready to depart, others slowly docking. Fishing vessels return after a long day at sea. I'm captivated by the vibrant activity.

I'm pulled from my silence as our boots hit the wooden planks of the dock. River successfully navigated us through it, guiding me as I observed. He says, "the vessel should be right ahead. Vivicus said dock ten."

Approaching dock number ten, we're greeted by a large man standing at the gangway with a paper in his hand. He has peppered black hair and a full beard and mustache. He's not alone either. He stands tall, towering over another man dressed in a nice, tailored outfit in shades of browns. Definitely not a sailor.

"Me list is settled for this voyage," the larger, gruff looking man says. "I can get yer cargo the next trip when I return in the week."

The well-dressed man groans, running a hand through his slick dirty blonde hair. "Fine. But make sure I'm a priority next time. I cannot hold onto this cargo for long." He stalks away, his dark eyes scanning us.

The man with the list turns toward us, his brow raised in curiosity. "Can I help ye, folks?" His baritone voice is rough around the edges and up close I can see the wariness in his gaze. River steps forward, cutting me off from view as if to protect me.

"We've booked passage on your vessel to Firerock. Forgive me, but I assume you're the captain?" River's demeanor is calm.

The man chuckles. "Ye be right there, sonny. Name's Captain Gillian Waternoose." He extends a beefy, calloused hand toward River. He confidently shakes it.

"Names?"

At the captain's request, River hesitates. I too, take a step back. Do we dare say our real names? With wanted posters plastered around the city bearing my name and face, we'd be discovered instantly. I bite lips and stand silently, waiting for River's response.

"Should be under the names Dunigan. This is my wife," he says cautiously.

Captain Waternoose raises his brows, scanning the document in his hand. "Dunigan... Dunigan..." he murmurs, reviewing his paper. The longer it takes, the more anxious I turn. My stomach coils in knots. I discreetly squeeze River's arm. Is this going to work, or are we going to be caught before we can even whisper a prayer?

"Ah, here we are." Relief washes over me. "Reynaldo and Maraleese Dunigan."

I bite my lips to stifle a laugh at the names Vivicus gave us while feeling grateful they're on the manifest. "Now, if I could just see yer papers."

Again, my stomach drops. Papers? Do we even have fucking papers? I glance nervously at River, seeing a slight tick in his jaw.

"Of course." River reaches into his bag and pulls out small pieces of paper, handing them to the captain. I silently pray we're able to board this vessel. My gaze flicks to a small group of Dark Knights meandering through the dock markets. My heart races.

"Lower yer hood, ma'am," his voice commands, but my eyes stay on the Dark Knights. "Ma'am?" The command is louder. I finally focus on the captain, his dark, brown eyes fixed on me.

"Your hood, darling," River attempts to soothe my nerves, but all I feel is panic. Slowly, with trembling fingers, I hold the cloak's wool, and remove the hood, revealing my face. Captain Waternoose's brow crinkles as he studies me. Tense silence hangs thick in the salty air as he looks back down at the papers.

"Yer all set," he announces, returning the documents to River. "You'll be in cabin H, below deck. Ain't nothin' special, but we'll get ya where ya need to go. We set sail in an hour. Get settled. First Mate Berjin can answer any questions ya have 'til we depart."

River nods at the captain. "Thank you, sir." He grabs my hand, and together we walk up the gangway and onto the boat.

Chapter 33

River

Once aboard the boat, I let out a deep sigh. Gaia above, that was more stressful than I ever thought. I'm grateful that Vivicus provided me everything we needed, but forged documents are always iffy, especially with how quickly she had to get them once she realized how many of Voras's cronies roamed through the city.

The boat itself is nice for a medium-sized cargo vessel. Truthfully, I wasn't sure what to expect when Vivicus booked us passage, but this is better than what I imagined. The deck is bustling with Waternoose's crew, loading cargo boxes, or inspecting parts of the ship. A younger gentleman shouts orders from the starboard side. I assume that's First Mate Berjin. Deciding that I don't want to bother the crew, I hold Mya's hand tightly and lead her toward the stairwell descending into the hull.

Mya follows silently behind me as we walk down the narrow, wooden hallway with doors lining either side. Above each door are letters, which I assume are the cabin labels. As we get closer to the middle of the hall, I spot the door marked with the letter "H."

"This should be us," I say, turning to Mya; her eyes wide open as she looks at me. She's been unusually quiet and nervous during our trek through Volantis, and then even more when she saw her wanted poster. How can I blame her? It's a sobering reminder that she's still being hunted by Voras and his Dark Knights.

All I want to do is protect her. If I can take her away from all this, I would. I'd just steal her away and do what I can to keep her safe. But she's part of a destiny bigger than this. The prophecy still lingers in the back of my mind, while trying to give her space to learn her powers. Now, we're closer than ever to ending the Dark King's reign. With Mya by my side, we can do this. We can change Elemi for the better. No more bitter and unnecessary violence. A peaceful future where Mya and I can live a happy life. I see all the possibilities when I stare into Mya's large eyes. My heart jumps at the thought.

I open the door to our cabin, revealing a small room. More like a closet. Mya and I barely fit inside. I can't help the chuckle that escapes from my throat as I pull Mya in and close the door behind us. Her whole body sinks as she leans against the wall, sliding down to the floor.

"Shit." I step over her and kneel beside her. "Are you okay?" I cup her face, forcing her to meet my gaze. Those large, golden-flecked eyes look weary.

She nods silently. Her long dark waves fall around her shoulders. "Yes. Just glad we made it. The adrenaline's finally crashing, and I feel exhausted." I run my thumb along her cheek.

"It's been a long day, but we can rest now. Once we depart, there's no going back, only forward." I look around the small space and spot our beds; two hammocks hanging within an alcove built into the wall, one on top of the other. A small ladder is attached so a person can climb into the top one. I instantly make the decision to take the top hammock, since I don't mind climbing up. Moreover, it reminds me of my treehouse.

Carefully, I help Mya take her boots off, unlacing them. Her breathing is calm and steady as I slide the boots off her feet. I unbutton the cloak I gave her and peel it off her shoulders. She gasps softly at my touch. My eyes meet hers and for a moment, everything else melts away. I can't resist the urge to straddle her and place my fingers under her chin, rubbing her plump lips with my thumb.

Mya runs her hand through the loose strands of my hair. I take a deep breath closing my eyes, savoring the tingling sensation along the back of my neck. My cock twitches as her fingers caress me. My heart thuds faster, and I pull Mya's face to mine, crashing our lips together. Her warm lips part a little as I thrust my tongue between them. As much as I want Mya in any and every way possible, I know she needs rest. I don't want to take advantage of this small, closed space. At least, not immediately. Maybe, once she gets some sleep.

I force myself to pull away, helping her to her feet. A small moan escapes Mya's lips as I slide her bag's strap off her shoulder. "Lay down, rest. We'll be departing soon. You're safe. I'll see if I can find us some food in the galley." I guide Mya to the hammock, making her sit.

"Thanks," She gives a weak smile before lying down in the hammock awkwardly, shuffling to find comfort in the thick canvas tarp. As I study the cramped closet that'll be our quarters for the next few days, I notice a half-sized wooden door opposite the hammocks. Opening it, I find a small latrine and a bucket on a minuscule table with water for washing. I frown, but notice that the water looks clean.

The captain was right. It isn't much, but we'll take it. At least, it's not permanent. Just a few days crossing from the Bay of Stars through the Firerock Pass, then onto the capital of the Scarlet Lands, the City of Embers, where Prometheus's temple resides.

I hang our travel sacks on hooks attached to the wall before leaving the room in search of the galley. I'm nervous leaving Mya, but I trust that Vivicus sent us on a trustworthy vessel. I won't be long. I go down the hallway, back the way we came, and onto the bustling deck. Sailors dressed in sea-worn tunics and knickers strew about. Some carry small crates, while others pull various ropes. Berjin shouts last minute orders into the darkening night sky. His First Mate coat looks pristine compared to the clothes of the rest of the crew. Captain Waternoose meanders the deck, double checking the work. The gangplank has been pulled up and the sails are being unfurled as we're about to depart.

I call out to the captain. Whiskey barrel-colored eyes, wrinkled with age glare back, but they soften when he sees me. "Aye, Reynaldo," he replies, walking toward me. "Find yer room, alright?"

I nod. "We did, thank you. Forgive me for the disruption in your tasks, but I was hoping you'd point me toward the galley."

"Course." Captain Waternoose nods in the opposite direction of where we stand. "Take those double doors beneath the quarterdeck. It leads to the galley. Though, Jorjie may not be pleased with ya peepin' about after dinner hours." The old man chuckles. I thank him and continue to cross the deck.

"Get ready to raise anchor!" Captain Waternoose yells behind me. The crew echoes the cry as I head to the wooden double doors he mentioned. Behind it is a hallway encased in pine wood, just like the one in our room. At the end of the hall is a large open room filled with long tables and benches. The room is dark, a deep-maroon color, and dimly lit lanterns hang above. Despite being a larger space, it seems small and cramped in the dark. The smell of stale fish wafts through the air accompanied by banging sounds from behind a swinging door on the other side.

Assuming that's the kitchen, I walk down to the swinging door and enter. "Ya missed dinner, laddie. Ain't got no spares ta hand out tonight. Ya can grab a stale loaf a bread if there's any."

An old man stands at a dump sink rinsing a pot as big as his chest. He's almost bald, except for a crown of gray hair around the sides. His cream linen shirt is covered in dark stains, as is his burgundy apron tied around his waist. The man wears dark trousers and sturdy boots. I can tell he's probably been doing this most of his life and I can't hold back a smirk as I approach him.

"Sorry we missed dinner. We're humble passengers that just boarded. Can you let me know the schedule so we don't miss mealtimes."

Jorjie stops and turns to look at me. His eyes rake over me for a moment before they relax. "Aye, forgive me. We don' get regular passengers too often, an' the crew can be wily ones, thinkin' I don' know who come an' eats. Welcome sonnie, name's Jorjie. Been cookin' on this shithole for the past thirty years, but a labor of love, it is. Ya said ya needed some eats?" Jorjie turns off the running water in the sink, wiping his soapy hands on his apron as he approaches me.

"Please," I request. "For me and my wife." I love that word, especially when it describes Mya. If only I can make it a reality, but we have a mission and only when it's over we can talk about what our future holds. I snap out my thoughts and extend a hand to the old man. "It's nice to meet you, Jorjie."

His rough, calloused hand takes mine in a firm shake. "Wife, you say? Eh, better keep an eye on her then. These men might try to proposition her."

A raucous laugh that escapes from my throat. "I'll keep that in mind. Although, they'll have to deal with me first." I'd never let anyone touch Mya if it's the last thing I do. Jorjie chuckles before turning his attention to the stocked pantry to our left.

"Well, I's got a loaf a bread that ya can have, a couple apples that're on the way out, but still good, and a small wedge of honey cheese that ain't enough to cook with, but ya can 'ave it if ya want for your wife?" He raises a thick, gray brow, awaiting my response.

"That sounds great, we appreciate it," I say. Watching him gather the food, I continue to look around. "Please tell me, when are the mealtimes?"

Jorjie grabs the items and begins to wrap them in a clean cloth. He then goes into a makeshift icebox and pulls out a small bottle of corked water and hands it to me, along with the food. "Meals are at six, noon and seven. I provide a small cart service of munchin's around three in the afternoon as well."

With a polite nod, I thank him and take my leave.

Chapter 34

River

Gently, I sway in the hammock as the waves rock the ship. Even though exhausted, I sleep lightly with one eye open, heeding Jorjie's advice about the crew. I must've, however, fallen into a deeper sleep than I realize because I wake up to the sound of vomiting. Rubbing my bleary eyes, I turn toward the bathroom door and see Mya on the ground, face buried in the latrine. *Shit*.

I sit up, climb down the ladder, and rush to her side, pulling her hair back as another wave of bile rises in her throat. "Are you alright?" I ask, rubbing her back as her body convulses.

"I think I'm not fond of riding boats," she speaks, catching her breath. It dawns on me she probably hasn't ever been on a ship before, and a small laugh escapes me.

Hearing it, she gives me a weak elbow to the gut. "Not funny."

"Sorry, princess. I didn't think about seasickness. It should've occurred to me as a possibility. I might have prepared better." But I feel like a helpless idiot as the woman I love purges the little food, I managed to get her to eat. Quickly, I grab the half-empty bottle of water. Uncorking it, I extend it to her. She eyes it warily before grabbing it and taking a small swig.

She settles on the floor, and rests her head against the wall. Handing me the bottle back, she closes her eyes. The ship sways under a strong swell, knocking me into the wall. I thrust an arm out to catch myself to avoid falling on her. "Ugh," she groans at the movement.

"I highly doubt Jorjie's in the kitchen right now, but first thing in the morning, I'll see if he has any ginger root for you to gnaw on for the rest of the journey. Maybe some of the tea Vivicus gave you will help? I can grab some hot water in the morning." Mya nods without looking at me.

I bite my lip, searching for a way to temporarily ease her seasickness, but with our limited supplies, there isn't much I can offer. Lost in thought, I feel gentle fingers brushing the side of my face. Her touch is cold as a thumb strokes the beard along my jaw. My eyes snap to hers, barely open and weary, but her plush, rosy lips are curved into a small grin.

"Of all the challenges we've faced during our journey here, I didn't think a boat ride would be the worst."

It's a joke. She's making a joke.

I stare at her, momentarily baffled, then scoff. "Yeah, the Larkfury was a piece of cake compared to this."

Laughter fills the small space. Hers and mine, and it's like music to my ears. A balm to the stress in the moment. As it fades, silence settles around us except for the sound of the ocean outside. I pray to Hydros to keep the seas calm and that Mya won't get sick again.

"Do you think you're well enough to get up and lie in the hammock?" I ask.

When she gives a weak nod, I shift out the door offering her my hand and help her up. Mya stumbles to her hammock and sits down. As she settles, my eyes fixate at her thighs. She's wearing a long linen shirt that falls mid-thigh. All I want to do is worship her in every way possible. Though our current circumstances make indulgence difficult, I've already thought of all the ways I can ravish Mya here.

Once she lies down on the hammock, I sit by her head and gently stroke her loose locks with my fingers. "If you feel like you're going to be sick again or need anything, just let me know, okay?"

"Thanks, River," her voice is barely a whisper as her heavy eyes droop, and her breathing steadies out. Instantly, she falls back asleep. Leaning my back against the wall, I sit by Mya, hoping she'll be alright.

Mya is sick throughout the entire journey. Clearly, she's not made for the sea. Anything I feed her even broth or the "seasick" tea Jorjie prepares, comes back up. Nothing settles her stomach. One day, I even brought her on deck, in hopes that fresh air or the sight of the stars would help. It didn't. Guilt swims through my chest every time she gets sick. I watch Mya's color fade more and more with the each passing day. She's getting weaker, and once we reach the Scarlet Lands, the grueling climate and terrain will challenge us even more before we get to the City of Embers.

Thankful that we're only half a day away from our destination, I start thinking about our plans after deboarding. Mya needs to recover and gain her strength for the trek to the temple. We'll have to find an inn by the port to dock and take a night to rest. It'll be the best choice. Perhaps the Captain or Berjin will have recommendations for a place we can stay once we touch land. It's all I can hope for as we wait for our journey to end in the coming hours.

At dusk, we dock in Firerock, the only accessible trade port by ocean in the entire Scarlet Lands. The rest of the coastline is steep with cliffs impossible to scale. Firerock is a large town. It's probably the most habitable place in Prometheus's region, aside from the City of Embers where the Ember Temple stands. The city lies a little over a day's journey through desert and sand dunes, but I'll worry about that once Mya's well enough. For now, I thank Captain Waternoose as we disembark and focus on finding us a place to sleep for the night.

The market stalls by the docks still buzz with activity. It's been a few years since I've been through the Scarlet Lands, but during my travels here, I've never ventured this far south. I take in all the colors and smells of spices as I hold onto Mya by her waist, supporting her weak muscles.

"I feel like an idiot," she murmurs under her breath, taking in the city around us. "It's really beautiful here. I wish we could roam the stalls."

It's true, the desert at dusk is a sight to behold. In the distance, the once bright yellow sunlight fades into deep orange, pinks, and purples. Stars begin to sparkle overhead. As we move deeper into the port, the market thins out.

"We need to find lodging for the night," I explain, passing deep red adobe buildings that mark the heart of the town. Flags and banners hang from the walls, displaying a lone flame, the symbol of Prometheus. Soon, I spot a large tavern, with the words "Fire Whiskey" inscribed above its door, and directly across the muddy road is an inn: Slumbering Embers. I breathe a sigh of relief and enter with Mya.

Inside, warmth spreads with a large stone hearth in the center. Chairs and couches upholstered with cowhides sit before it, and a woven patterned rug covers the wood floor. "Evening," calls a petite woman with dark skin and tightly braided black hair. She stands behind a desk cluttered with papers and books. I turn my attention to her and approach.

"Good evening," I reply. "We're hoping you have a room available for the next two nights?" Myalis elbows me lightly, and I already know why. She thinks she'll be fine after one night, but I know better. I want her to get at least two nights of rest and uninterrupted sleep and nourishment before continuing to the City of Embers.

The woman flips through her books, trailing a lean finger along the writing. Beaded bangles jingle on her wrist. "I do," she says at last, her burned hazel eyes meeting mine as she gives me a small smile and reaches beneath her desk. She pulls out a key and hands it to me. "Up the stairs, room six. Forty coppers for two nights. We have a tiny kitchen—I can send up a plate of food if you'd like?"

It's pricey, but I have coin and don't want to look for something else, especially when this place seems quaint and out of the way. "Yes, thank you. That'd be wonderful." I raise a brow at her, cuing to ask her name.

"Angelique," she says, nodding. "Just sign here and you can go on up. I'll send a tray in a few minutes." I take the quill she sets on the book and sign in our pseudo names, Reynaldo and Maraleese Dunigan. Satisfied, Angelique nods as Mya and I climb the stairs adjacent to her desk. There are eight rooms on this floor and at the end

of the wooded hall, another set of stairs leads up to a third
floor. When we approach room six, I put the key into the
hole and turn it, clicking it into place.

Opening the door, Mya and I step into a fairly
spacious room. There's a smaller version of the stone
hearth fireplace from downstairs, the wood logs already
burning, and keeping the place warm and cozy. On the
opposite side of the fireplace, is a medium-sized wooden
bed with intricately-patterned blankets and fluffy pillows.

"Thank Gaia above." Mya gasps making her way to
bed. Taking a seat, she lets out a long breath, her shoulders
sinking. I close the door behind us and shrug our bags off
my shoulders. While Myalis relaxes, I survey the rest of the
room, noticing a small wardrobe between two windows and
a door on the right side of the hearth. I click it open and see
what it is—a bathroom with a toilet, sink and even a deep
soaking tub. I blink twice. No wonder the room was
expensive, but a private bathroom? Truly a rarity among
inns throughout Elemi.

A knock jolts my attention. Mya stiffens, and I
approach the door. "Who is it?"

"Food from the kitchens, sir," comes a young voice.
I open it just a bit and see an average-sized boy, no older
than twelve. He has dark skin and large caramel-colored

eyes. He's wearing a deep blue linen tunic and trousers, and a cream-colored apron is tied around his waist. He holds a tray with a domed plate and a corked glass bottle. I open the door wider reaching out for the tray and thank the boy, handing him a coin. His eyes light up as I close the door.

I bring the tray of food immediately over to Mya, since she's the one who desperately needs it. "You eat first. I'll bathe and then prepare one for you afterward."

She hesitates, but nods. "Thank you."

Smiling at her, I turn and get myself ready for a much-needed bath.

Chapter 35

Myalis

I wake up the next morning feeling a million times better. My headache's gone, I don't feel nauseous or weak, and miraculously, I've been able to keep my food down. Last night's bath was a luxury, the best thing I've experienced in what seems like forever. I *slept*. Boy, did I sleep as if I'd never slept in my life. The bed was so comfortable, once my head hit the pillow, I was out. Not even River's buff body could stir or distract me.

It feels like pure bliss, and I don't want to leave the bed at all. Gazing out the window as the sun comes up, I simply enjoy the quiet peace of this room.

I exhale and turn to look at River. He's still asleep beside me—his dark lashes brushing the top of his cheeks. It's one of those moments I never want to forget. The peace in his handsome, rugged face is breathtaking. Loose strands of black hair frame around his angular face, his breath steady and calm. I can't stop the smile spreading across my face.

There's no denying it anymore. I'm truly in love with this man. My heart beats for him, and I don't exactly know when it happened. Maybe when we were at the Altar of Water. But what I do know is that I've softened during my time with River. I think back to when it was just me, hiding out by myself, with no friends or acquaintances to talk to, and now—now, I have a steady presence by my side. Someone who believes in me, encourages me, and takes care of me. I haven't had that since my parents left.

Reaching out, I cup my hand around River's muscular neck and gently rub my thumb on the growing beard along his chin. He smiles, his eyes still closed. Slowly, his deep, ocean-blue eyes open, taking me in.

"Morning, princess," his sleepy voice is raspy, deep, sending a chill down my spine.

"Morning."

"How'd you sleep?" He wraps his hand around my wrist bringing it to his lips, kissing my hand.

"Fantastic," I sigh, grinning. His other arm snakes around my body, dragging me flush against his. A small gasp escapes at the feel of his taut muscles and an erection, that sends butterflies loose in my stomach.

River's lips find my ear as his other hand travels to the back of my head. He threads his fingers in my hair. "And how are you feeling?" his voice a caress against my skin. The warmth radiates from him sending shivers down my spine.

"Much better." I tease, smiling against his lips. "I had a very good caregiver."

"Did you, now?" he raises a brow, amused.

I nod. "Uh huh." It's barely a whisper as my mouth lingers close to his. River's grip tightens, his other hand slowly roaming down my back before his strong fingers grasp my butt. My core tightens, the sensation tingling, and all I want are those fingers between my thighs.

With my lips parted, I wait for River to initiate the kiss. Our noses touch, and his breath is warm against my lip. I dart my tongue out, just the tip, to brush against his mouth. A groan escapes River as he crashes his lips onto mine, our mouths desperate as ever to claim each other's. River's touch becomes frantic as he pulls me as tight as he can. I grab his hair, the kiss deepening with every passing second.

He snakes his hand between us, stroking my center, and I moan. It's a balm to the fiery need that's built in just seconds.

"Gaia above," River breathes as his fingers gently stroked between my thighs. "Already so wet for me, princess?"

I scoff, but what can I say? It's fucking true. After recovering from being sick for days, my body's yearning for his touch.

"Don't ask stupid questions when you already know the answers." I pant out between kisses. Using his other hand, River travels up beneath my linen night shirt tracing his long fingers up to my breasts. He teases my nipple while his other land lazily strokes my clit. It's a delicious kind of torture. My body arches from the pleasure.

"Come on, princess, sing for me." The command makes my senses spark. In a blink, he rips the night shirt off my body and dips his head into my breast, sucking my nipple with his tongue, causing hard flutters to coarse through my center and tighten around his fingers. River's assaults grow faster, and he presses the pad of his thumb firmly against my clit. I cry out, ecstasy releasing from within me. The shockwaves flow through me as River laps at my other nipple, and then chuckles, "that's my good princess."

"Fuck, River." I whisper, now feeling tired all over again. Even though I've bathed and eaten and slept, I guess it wasn't enough for me to completely recover from the seasickness. River plants a series of kisses up my breast, then on my neck before kissing along my jaw to my lips.

"I know. I've missed you too, but I don't want to wear you out. Let's get you more food and rest and maybe tonight we can pick up where this left off."

I groan, unsatisfied, because I desperately want more. I want to feel River's cock thrusting into me like there's no tomorrow. I want our souls to intertwine, to connect and be one. River's laugh is a tease because he knows what he does to me.

"Fine," I bite out as I roll my eyes. There's a gentle knock on the door and both River and I sit up in alarm.

River gets up from the bed and rolls his pants up his bare body. "Who is it?" He approaches the door and waits for an answer.

"Food from the kitchen, sir." River turns back to me with a raised brow as if to say 'right on cue' before opening the door to the same young boy from last night.

Sweat trickles down my neck as I stand in the middle of the market, the sun blazing down on our head. River's been haggling with a textile merchant for over half an hour, trying to get us desert-appropriate clothing. My frustration—in particularly the last ten minutes—has built significantly, as the heat gnaws at my patience.

This isn't like the heat in the Oasis Peninsula. At least there, there's an occasional breeze to help. Here? There's no fucking breeze. Nothing but oppressive, still, heat. Since we arrived later in the evening last night, we hadn't experienced the true heat of the day. We're now, here in the market, in daytime, and it's making me itchy.

My clothes are made for the climate of Gaia's Keep, the land of eternal spring, not for this hellscape. Of course we need lighter garments, but this merchant is stubborn. This market runs on haggling, but when do we give up? River is persistent and, in my opinion, not unreasonable.

My brows furrow as I glance back at the blinding sun. Gaia above, why is it so damn bright? Frustrated, I take my braid and tie it in a knot at the base of my neck, hoping that will help ease the heat burning my skin. I cross my arms glaring at the middle-aged merchant with deep bronze skin and neatly-combed, thick, peppered hair.

"No, no, this is quality material... I can only accept four bronze coins for the two, no lower," the merchant repeats, his accent thick and unfamiliar.

River stays composed. "I have two bronze coins which is more than fair for these."

The clothes in question are cream-colored, long-sleeved tunics with a matching set of flowing linen pants and head coverings. To me, the garments aren't anything exceptional. They aren't the bright-colored hues of the Oasis Peninsula, which I can understand the expense given how rare those dyes are. No, here in the Scarlet Lands, people wear warm tones: cream, yellow, orange, rust, and brown hues. I know these dyes aren't as exotic or difficult to obtain as pinks, teals, and purples. Mama used to talk to me about fabric colors and dyes all the time. Even if I wasn't passionate about them, I do remember the conversations.

"Sir," the merchant interrupts River, "this fabric is made of the softest, purest linen here in Firerock. The plant is harvested from the local cliffs, finely woven. See, it's so soft to the touch—"

My patience snaps. I draw the knife from my boot and slam it into the wood of the man's stall, nearly missing his hand. River looks at me, and the man's large black eyes meet mine. I turn to River, "clearly, this man doesn't want our business. Let's just fucking go to another stall. Maybe they'll be more reasonable."

River is startled for a beat, then chuckles and nods at the man, "well, thank you for your time, sir." We begin to walk away before the man calls out, ready to accept the bargain.

Chapter 36

Myalis

On the back of a frieshamel, a horse-like creature with two large humps, River and I slowly trot through the Burning Elms desert toward the City of Embers. The creatures we're riding are bizarre, but they're large and steady beasts, calm in nature. They have thick tawny fur—in shades of brown and black— shorn close to their skin. River explains that the humps on their backs are where they store water internally so they can travel the sandy dunes without stopping for days. I guess that's why these creatures are capable to survive and even thrive in the desert.

Seated in an oddly shaped saddle between the two humps, my rucksack hangs off the side of the frieshamel, Sheena. I study her as she strides through the hilled dunes and prickly patches of dead-thorned elm trees and cactus. It's fascinating.

She's an older one for her breed, with small round black eyes, and outrageously long, thick lashes probably to help her with the brightness of the sun.

River rides ahead on his own frieshamel, a younger male named Canyon. Supposedly, he is Sheena's offspring. We managed to get the creatures from the market after the debacle with the textile merchant, then set out to the journey before dawn today. The merchant who sold the creatures to us, told us it's a little less than a day's ride on a frieshamel, if all goes well.

But other creatures lurk these parts of the Burning Elms, too. The most terrifying of them is the jebbucha, which River warned me about. That's why he's riding in front of me, to keep an eye out for any sign of them. The gigantic snake-like creatures are apparently hard to spot and can come out of nowhere. A jebbucha can come directly up from beneath the sand; they are burrowers, and we wouldn't have time to react, since they spring up quickly. The frieshamels are built for endurance, not speed, and so if a jebbucha were to attack us from below, it's likely we'd lose our ride or even our lives.

Quietly we tread through the terrain. The sand is deep orange, and the landscape is filled with endless dunes and an occasional gust of sand wind. Peaceful and quiet, we're the only people for miles, even when we're riding on the main trade route to the city. The sun's just beginning to rise, painting the sky in stunning shades of pink and orange. The last of the stars disappear, and I sigh as I lose sight of them. A weird feeling of emptiness fills my chest. With the sun rising, the oppressive heat returns.

I pull my head covering higher, draping the scarf over my mouth and nose, bracing for the brightness that'll intensify in about an hour. Once the sun fully emerges, it will blaze without mercy. The deep-colored sand glitters and I squint from the brightness. There isn't a cloud in the sky to offer any type of reprieve from the sun, and I've a weird feeling in my gut that this trip to the temple is going to be more tedious than anticipated.

"Let's take a little break." River says—as I catch up beside him—a few hours later. We halt by a small copse of the prickled elms. Though the dead trees don't cast any shade, it's at least a place for us to allow the frieshamels, and ourselves, to rest for a while. I dismount from Sheena, and ungracefully land on the sand, not realizing how numb my butt and legs really are. I huff in frustration, as I force myself up off the heated sand. River stifles a laugh in the distance.

"Don't say anything." I glare at him through gritted teeth, dusting the orange sand off my cream-colored linen pants.

He shakes his head, desperately holding in his amusement. "Wouldn't dream of it." Rummaging through his rucksack, he pulls out two wrapped packages. "Care for something to eat?"

I nod, accepting one. Unwrapping it reveals a piece of bread and some sort of jerky. I eat while walking in circles, stretching my aching legs.

The sand slips beneath my feet, making me stumble as my shoes' soles have a hard time gripping it. I'm grateful that we're on a flat part of the desert and not one of the hilly dunes we'd been crossing all morning. But the sand is still soft and treacherous to walk on. Stretching my legs, even for a few minutes, feels incredible and helps alleviate the stiffness creeping in. River watches me walk in circles, a smirk tugging at his lips. "Are you alright?"

"Fine. I just hate this heat, and Sheena is hard to ride," I admit. "I feel awkward on her. Nothing seems wrong with the saddle or anything. Just a different animal." River grunts, acknowledging that he understands.

"Hopefully we'll reach there before nightfall," he says, checking a small paper map that he got from the frieshamel merchant. I don't understand how he knows where we're going though, considering there are no fucking landmarks out here. It's just miles of sand as far as the eye can see and the blistering sun.

He gazes at the map under one of the dead trees as he eats. I pause to grab my water canteen, gulping some and then pouring a handful on my forehead. It isn't the coldest of water anymore, but at least it helps cool me down a bit.

I close my eyes as I tilt my face to the sky, taking a deep breath. A light breeze tickles the strands of hair that have escaped my braid. "Ahh," I sigh. "That breeze feels amazing." I hear shuffling behind me. I open my eyes to see River staring off in the distance, eyes wide.

"That's not a normal breeze," he says.

I turn to see what he's looking at and notice dark clouds forming overhead.

"What in the great underhells below..." we both stand still as darkness begins to consume everything around us. My heart pounds, threatening to burst out through my throat as unnatural swirls descend from above. I've seen this before.

"Fuck!" River shouts, grabbing my hand. "We have to run!" The panic in his voice terrifies me.

"Run? We're in the middle of the fucking Burning Elms; we have nowhere to run!" I yell, panic rising. No sooner do the words leave my lips, the world plunges into darkness. So much so that even the sun is eclipsed. All I can feel is the sand beneath my feet and River's firm grasp. He pulls me in any direction he can, trying to get us out of the dark envelopment. I want to keep up, but it's too hard to maneuver in the sand. We halt when a portal suddenly opens directly in front of us.

Dark Knights pour out the portal, surrounding us. Clad in dark hoods covering their faces, each one holds a weapon, like swords and axes. My stomach drops as a figure steps forward. It's the one I've been running from for eleven years. I swallow, but my throat dries, my breath quickening. It's the Dark King.

King Voras is much taller than I anticipated. He's even taller than River, but his body is lean and muscular. He wears all black leather armor and boots, no weapons in sight. No crown either, but I recognize him from my nightmares. Those piercing ice blue eyes are cold and calculating as he looks us over, and smirks, his expression, ominous, terrifying.

"Well, well... it seems our game of hide and seek has officially ended." The King's voice is deep and eerily calm. He moves slowly and deliberately, closer to us. We are severely outnumbered, trapped. "It's been quite a long time, but I'm pleased to finally make your acquaintance."

River steps in front of me, a dagger appearing in his hand before I could even notice. "You can't have her," he declares, his voice strong and unwavering, without a shred of fear permeating off him. Voras's eyes remain on me before narrowing at River.

"River Dune... you have been a thorn in my side far longer than you should have. Although, I guess it's nice to see the man who has been trying to usurp me for all these years." Voras stands directly in front of River now, towering over him. I study his face and realize that the King seems younger than I thought—his features sharp and striking, with an angular nose and prominent cheekbones.

"You can't have her," River repeats, ever my protector. My fingers clutch the back of his shirt, damp with sweat. Suddenly, I realize that neither of us are armored. No leathers or weapons for us to wield, except for our meager daggers and powers. Can River defeat all of these men with just his magic alone? Will I be able to wield anything to help?

With a quick flick of Voras's brow, Dark Knights swarm us attacking River from all sides and separating us. They overpower him, forcing him to his knees as they restrain my arms. I scream and struggle, as River grunts trying to break free. He manages to take down a few knights with his hands and dagger, but I barely had time to react, outmuscled.

All my training and preparation seems useless at this moment. Fury radiates through me as my powers simmer beneath my skin. Thunder rumbles from the sky above, despite the fact that we can't see it in the darkness. River strains to summon his magic. He's trying to do anything to get free from the men holding him down. With clenched teeth, his eyes light up. Lightning crashes around us, electrocuting several knights. Men yell in fear; Voras however stands in place, completely unshaken.

"Control him," The King's words leave his mouth, sharp and commanding. Immediately, one of his knights strikes River with the pommel of his sword into the back of his head and then, punches the side of his face. River groans as blood oozes from his temple and nose.

"No!" Heat radiates inside me as my anger grows. Voras moves within my line of sight, blocking River out. He lifts my chin with his finger, so that my eyes meet his; his touch alarmingly cold sending a shiver down my spine.

"If you wish for him to live, you'll come with me." Voras stays calm, unbothered. Simply matter of fact. It's a statement with no room for argument. My mind whirls, trying to figure out some solution. How can I free myself and River from clutches of the Dark King—the man I've feared since I was thirteen? The man I've been running from for eleven years? He wants me dead, he's hunted me... if I go with him, it'll mean death. "What do you choose, Myalis?"

Voras's long, elegant finger grips my chin gently but it's freezing cold. I tremble at the chill, causing Voras to quirk a dark brow.

As we stare off, my mind quickly turns. Perhaps, I can take Voras down from within. Maybe he'll let me live long enough that once we are one on one, I can kill him and end his tyranny. Is it a suicide mission? Most likely. But if it saves River, at least I'll have my conscience clear.

"Fine," I relent. "I will go with you if you allow River to live."

Voras steps back, releasing his grip. "Very well." He extends his hand toward me, his Dark Knights releasing me.

"No, Mya!" River shouts, "Don't do it!" My eyes dart to River and all I can do is stare at the man I love, realizing this'll probably be the last time I ever see him. My heart sinks as I take Voras's hand.

River's anguished yell fills my ears as power emanates all around us. The sound of hand-to-hand combat and thunder roars in the background as Voras pulls me in his grasp. Lightning shoots down from the sky, taking down two or three knights at a time. Time seems to slow as my heartbeat thrums in my ears.

River's on his feet, having killed knights left and right. He has snatched one of their swords, and he guts and electrocutes them in a frenzy. I try to pull away from Voras's hold, but he is unyielding, and I freeze watching River move like I've never seen him do before. A Knight thrashes in from behind him, slashing his arm, splattering his blood across the sand.

"River!" A horrified scream escapes from my throat as we look into each other's eyes. Spinning, River takes the sword in his hand and slashes the soldier that attacked him. The Knight yells as a large gash across his chest appears. River's determined eyes fall back onto me as he strides toward us, his arm bleeding. Voras extends his free hand toward River, and with a simple flick of his wrist, River's neck snaps. His eyes widen as he falls to his knees.

I flinch, my heart plummeting, eyes flooding with tears. Bile rises in my throat, as I watch River collapse, his life slipping away. His eyes stare blankly at the sky. A guttural screech wrenches from my throat as I'm pitched into a portal of complete, utter darkness.

ELEMENTALS: BOOK 2

Coming Fall 2026

ACKNOWLEDGEMENTS

I can't express how excited I am that The Starlight Princess is actually out in the world. It has been over a three-year process, filled with lots of ups and downs and a lot of life. I did a lot of this alone, but now, have so many to thank for it becoming what it is today. Thank you to my Beta Readers and ARC Readers. Your support and critiques meant the world to me.

Thank you to my wonderful editor, Kriti! Without you, this story absolutely wouldn't be as good as it is. I am so glad that we connected and can't tell you how much I've appreciated your support from the moment we connected!

Thank you to my book formatter, Bolu. All my character artists that brought these characters to life via art. Milo with Stardust Book Services for the stunning cartography/map of Elemi, Laney J for my chapter headers and scene breaks. You all brought this story together in a beautiful, physical way.

Thank you, Meet Cute Marketing, for helping with my marketing and ARC team support.

Lastly, thank you to the readers! Thank you for taking a chance on this story and for reading it, being in the world of Elemi, and hopefully recommending it to others. It really warms this indie author's heart! I can't wait to share the next installment with you!

ABOUT THE AUTHOR

photo credit: Kristen Trent Photography

This is Amanda Cirilli's debut novel. Although she has published a few children's books, she's extremely excited to dive into Romantasy and Contemporary love stories—since they are where her heart is.

Amanda lives in North Georgia with her husband and is a mom to three amazing little boys, and a dog. When she has some spare time, she loves reading, writing, of course, as well as watching true crime documentaries/shows and Netflix, acting in community theater, and watching her favorite sports teams.

FOR MORE INFORMATION VISIT:

https://amandacirilliauthor.com

TikTok: AC.Author4